Shattered Past

Lindsay Buroker

Shattered Past

by Lindsay Buroker

Copyright @ Lindsay Buroker 2016
Cover and Formatting: Deranged Doctor Design

No part of this book may be reproduced, scanned, or distributed in any printed or electronic form without permission. Please do not participate in or encourage piracy of copyrighted materials in violation of the author's rights. Thank you for respecting the hard work of this author.

This is a work of fiction. Names, characters, places, and incidents either are the product of the author's imagination or are used fictitiously, and any resemblance to locales, events, business establishments, or actual persons—living or dead—is entirely coincidental.

Foreword

Shattered Past takes place in my Dragon Blood world, introducing a new heroine and letting a fierce, gruff, and occasionally (often) grumpy side character star in his own adventure. The story references events from the series, but can be picked up even if you haven't read the other stories. Thank you for giving it a try, and thank you also to my beta readers, Sarah Engelke, Cindy Wilkinson, and Rue Silver, for helping me keep Therrik in character while bringing out his heroic and slightly-less-grumpy side. I would also like to thank my editor, Shelley Holloway, and the cover artists at Deranged Doctor Design for their work on this series.

CHAPTER 1

PROFESSOR LILAH ZIRKANDER WALKED DOWN the aisles between the desks, setting exams facedown in front of students who alternated between looking warily at her and gazing longingly at the clock. She stood between them and their summer vacation. Well, they stood between her and an exciting summer project *too*.

"For those of you who need to pad your academic résumés—or need extra coursework to complete your degree—Professor Haytar has informed me that we'll need a couple of assistants for our summer project," Lilah said.

"Are you going out to the field again, Professor?" Natashi, a third-year student, asked. She was one of the few students who had seemed to enjoy the class, taking it because of an interest in the subject matter, rather than because it satisfied a math requirement, without actually requiring much math. As if math was something to shy away from. Hmmph.

"No, the project will take place in the science lab."

Lilah handed out the last exam to the sandal-wearing boy in swimming trunks who had *drawn* his answer to the last essay question. Had it been an anatomically correct drawing, she might have awarded a small amount of credit, but his dragon skeleton looked more like a lizard skeleton, and it included genitalia completely inappropriate to either.

"Most of our government funding was siphoned off for military use this year," Lilah added when Natashi's face fell with disappointment, "so we can't afford any projects that involve travel."

Lilah also found the news disappointing, since she enjoyed her annual escapes from the campus, but a quiet summer without any students to teach would be appealing too. She secretly hoped that nobody took her up on the offer for extra credit. It wasn't that she didn't like the kids, but teaching left her feeling fraught. Research was so much more appealing than dealing with people, especially young people. They were so... *recent*. And mouthy. Who could fathom them and enjoy their company? She much preferred fossils.

"We will be undertaking an intensive cataloging project in the lab. All those fossils that were unearthed in the Sundaran Ice Field last summer are waiting to be studied and labeled for a museum exhibit this fall."

"Dragon fossils?" the student with the propensity for drawing asked, his gaze jerking from the window to Lilah's face for a rare moment of eye contact.

"It's an amazingly complete collection of *Glophopteris rugoniana* specimens."

"Gloph-what?"

The student behind him slapped him on the back. "Plants, you idiot. It was on the test."

"Ferns, to be exact," Lilah said. "Giant ferns from more than three million years ago. Iskandoth used to be quite the tropical haven."

Several sets of shoulders slumped. Lilah admitted that fern fossils didn't pack the museum the way that dragon bones did, but there was so much to learn from studying them. And dragons were frustrating. She had given ten years of her life to trying to identify their ancestors so someone could complete their phylogenetic tree in a manner that made sense. Alas, she had never found the missing link. Plants had proven less of a mystery, thanks to the fact that their fossils were so much more easily found.

Shouts and cheers and the stamping of feet came from the hallway, some lenient professor letting his or her class out early. Typically, Lilah would not be disposed to do the same thing, but when two-dozen hopeful sets of eyes turned in her direction, she sighed and relented—it wasn't as if those distracted brains would process anything else she said today.

"You can come see me after class if you're interested in the summer work or in my paleobotany class in the fall," Lilah said and waved toward the door. "Go. Enjoy your—"

The rest of her words were buried in the slamming of books, rustling of clothing, and overall noise of a mass exodus. Lilah dropped her arm and headed to her desk. Let them enjoy their youth. She planned to enjoy the solitude of a campus largely free of noisy students.

"Professor Zirkander?" Natashi asked. She was the lone student left in the room, and she looked oddly nervous as she clutched her books to her chest and smiled tentatively.

"Yes? Are you interested in the cataloging project?" Lilah liked Natashi more than her other students. She studied hard, earned good marks on her papers, and showed a genuine interest in the field. She also dressed appropriately for a place of learning, eschewing the swimming trunks and sandals fashion that had cropped up of late.

"Maybe, ma'am, but I was also wondering... uhm, you're related to General Zirkander, the pilot, aren't you?"

"He's my cousin," Lilah said warily, having a hunch as to where the conversation was going. She endured such inquiries at least once a month. Multiple times a week after a newspaper article highlighted the actions of Wolf Squadron in driving off some Cofah attack farther up the coast. "I don't know him well," she added, waving vaguely toward the north. The capital where the flier pilots were based was more than two hundred miles up the coast.

"You don't visit him?"

"Why would I do that? I don't need anything from the capital. I don't even have a horse for traveling that far."

"But he's General Zirkander!" Natashi said with the dreamy look that suggested she probably kept a few newspaper clippings of him in her notebook, ones that highlighted his face with hearts drawn around it.

"I can't imagine what we would talk about."

Lilah distinctly remembered Ridge—Ridgewalker, thanks to his parents' fondness for quirky names—teasing her for reading books instead of playing with the other kids at one of those dreaded family get-togethers they had endured as children. He was an only child and had been delighted to run around with age mates, hurling balls like a fool. Lilah, with three older brothers, hadn't been nearly as enamored with the idea of siblings and playmates.

"Oh." Natashi bit her lip. "Well, uhm, just in case, would you be able to get his autograph for me if you happen to see him?"

Lilah forced herself not to roll her eyes. She was thirty-seven now. Entirely too mature for eye rolling. "If you haven't graduated by the time I see him next, I'll keep it in mind." Along with the fifty-odd similar requests she'd had in the last year. At least Natashi didn't pull out a bra and brazenly suggest that Ridge might like to sign it.

A throat cleared in the doorway. A short-haired, clean-shaven man in an army uniform leaned in, looking at the student and then at Lilah.

"Professor Zirkander?" he asked.

"Yes?" Lilah waved the man in, though she couldn't imagine what would have brought him to the science and history college. Classes? There was a small navy outpost a couple of miles outside of town, where soldiers visited to practice sea-based exercises, but they did not usually have the time or interest to enroll. "You're not looking for General Zirkander's signature, too, are you?"

"Uh, no, ma'am. I already have that." He lifted a beige folder as he walked down an aisle toward her desk. He stopped a few paces away, clasped his hands and his folder behind his back, and looked at Natashi. "I can wait, but I need to speak with you in private when you're done, ma'am."

He nodded at Natashi, giving her a slight smile. He wasn't much older than she was, and he was handsome in his tidy, pressed uniform and his polished boots. Natashi would do much better to stare dreamily at him, rather than at pictures of someone who had crossed forty already.

"I'll send you a message about the summer project, Natashi."

Lilah dismissed her student with a nod, curious as to what was in this soldier's folder. She was inclined to think uncharitably of the military, especially since they had been getting so much of what should have been the college's funding of late, but she was sure this youngster hadn't had anything to do with it. Besides, he had a sweet face and reminded her of Lieutenant Bakstonis from the *Time Trek* series. She wondered if her visitor had read the popular books and would understand the reference.

As soon as Natashi disappeared, shutting the door on her way out, the soldier opened the folder. "My name is Lieutenant Sleepy, ma'am. I'm from Tiger Squadron, and I'm here to fly you to the capital."

"Pardon?"

"Sorry, it's a nickname. You can call me Lieutenant Derkonith, if you like. Or Jhav." He smiled and glanced at her neck, where she still wore the promise necklace her late husband had given her. At least, she thought that was where he was looking. Breasts weren't far from necks, after all, and a lot of male gazes got hung up on her chest, no matter how demurely she dressed. At least the young men—students, as well as soldiers—weren't usually impertinent enough to grab, bump, or make assumptions that her chest was available for handling. She'd had to snap at a couple of the distinguished professors over the years and had earned a reputation for being... difficult. As long as they let her keep researching and publishing papers, they could call her whatever they wished.

"My confusion wasn't derived from your name, Lieutenant, but rather from your belief that you're flying me somewhere."

"Oh. Well, that's in the orders, ma'am. I'm to allow you time to pack clothing and to collect whatever tools and equipment you need."

"How generous of you. What happens if I refuse to go with you?" Lilah accepted the paper, so she could see for herself what this was about.

"He said you wouldn't, ma'am, especially on account of your classes being finished today."

"He? General Zirkander?" She bristled at the idea of a cousin she hadn't spoken to in nearly five years making assumptions about her.

"Uhm, King Angulus, ma'am."

She blinked and stared down at the paper, glancing at the

signature on the bottom. General Zirkander's messy scrawl was on there, yes, but King Angulus Masonwood III had also signed the page. Nerves twisted in her belly. What could the king want with her? She'd never met the man or even been in the capital for one of his public speeches.

Reading the entire document might help. She started at the top, mumbling to herself as she skimmed it. "...your presence humbly requested... possible dragon fossils unearthed... top-secret facility... determine if the bones are legitimate, and if so, if they should be removed for study or if demolitions can continue." She gaped up at the pilot. *"Demolitions?"*

"I don't know anything about the facility or the demolitions, ma'am. I'm just here to give you a ride to the capital."

"Is that where the bones were discovered?"

"No, ma'am. But we'll pick up General Zirkander there. Oh, I was told to tell you to pack warmly."

Lilah looked toward the courtyard, which was lined by lavender bushes that had been blooming for weeks already. "Somewhere in the mountains?" she guessed.

The pilot shrugged. "I'm just a lieutenant, ma'am. They don't tell us much. I assume the general will give you more details. But I do know enough to recommend that if you have any weapons, you may want to pack them too."

"Weapons?" That was almost as alarming as the idea of demolitions in an area of scientific importance. Were they going somewhere that wild animals would be a problem? She *did* have a collection of hunting rifles, though she hadn't been out on safari since Taryn had passed away, so she hadn't practiced with them in years. It was rare for rhinos and wildebeests to rampage through the streets of Port Yenrem.

"Do you have any, ma'am? The general said he'd send a bodyguard along, but it might not be a bad idea if you take a pistol or at least a dagger. In case, uhm. Well, I'm not supposed to know this, but I heard the general growl something about Colonel Therrik being in charge of where you're going."

The way the pilot said the name made Lilah think she should be familiar with it. She knew of a few historically significant Therriks, but hadn't run into a modern person with the name.

Was it some other soldier who was mentioned often in the newspapers? If so, she wouldn't know about it, since she much preferred historical texts to current events.

"I'm sure you'll be fine, ma'am. I shouldn't have said anything to alarm you. Besides, the king said he'll give you some orders to take with you, orders that will ensure Therrik is polite to you."

The man had to be forced to be polite to a woman? That didn't sound promising.

"Is this Colonel Therrik not someone known to cooperate with visitors from academia?"

The lieutenant rubbed his jaw, as if in memory of a painful punch. "I think he's more likely to *eat* visitors from academia."

* * *

Colonel Vann Therrik followed the outpost engineer, Captain Bosmont, along a goat trail five miles from the front gates of the Magroth Crystal Mines. The path dipped below the tree line as it skirted Galmok Mountain, where nearly a thousand criminals mined for energy crystals and other artifacts that had been left behind by witches hundreds of years earlier. Vann hated witches, hated artifacts, and hated this assignment. He could have allowed the captain to handle this reconnaissance alone, but a chance to escape the irritations of command was not unwelcome. Maybe they would encounter bears or wolves or something else that he could mercilessly pummel.

"We're almost there, sir." Bosmont glanced warily over his shoulder, the concerned expression almost laughable on such a big man. Bosmont might not be quite as muscled and broad-shouldered as Vann, but with that jaw, he ought to be able to take more than a few punches.

Vann grunted a response. That didn't seem to reassure Bosmont, because he frowned and picked up the pace.

Did he think Vann would club him if he made this hike longer than promised? No, as a general rule, Vann only clubbed other officers in the boxing square and on the wrestling mat. Perfectly acceptable locales for such activities. He flexed his shoulders now, wondering if he could talk a couple of the other officers into an exercise session later. There were capable infantrymen up here with whom he sparred, but he missed the challenge of real combat. It had been months since he'd seen any of that.

"Thanks for coming out here with me, sir," Bosmont added as they rounded a bend, the trail littered with scree that had fallen from the craggy peaks above. It made for treacherous footing, but the weather had finally gotten warm enough to melt most of the snow, so they weren't in too much danger of slipping off the narrow trail and falling to their deaths. Only witches would think a headquarters inside of the middle of the Ice Blades was a good idea. At least they were long-dead witches, the best kind.

"I want to make sure you know everything about the fossils and the new location," Bosmont went on. "My replacement is supposed to be an engineer, but who knows what the army will send out here."

"Some deranged reject," Vann grumbled.

Bosmont was one of the few people stationed here who had a couple of ounces of competence. He'd gotten the undesirable assignment after punching a senior officer. Vann could understand that. He'd met many a senior officer who deserved punching.

"Most likely, sir. I'll hope you get someone good, but mostly I'm just glad to be leaving. Less than two weeks left." Bosmont couldn't hide a goofy smile, the smile of a man whose sentence here was almost up. It had been extended after the dragon attack, since he'd been needed to help rebuild, but he'd finally gotten orders to a warmer climate.

Vann wished *he* would get orders. But this assignment was a punishment for him, as much as it was for those who worked under him, and he hadn't served his time yet.

"It's possible the bones won't matter," Bosmont said, "and that you'll be able to start right in with the digging as soon as the supply ship comes tomorrow with the king's response. He may deem the bones worth sacrificing in order to get easier access to the old Referatu stronghold—and all of the artifacts within."

"If you hadn't mentioned them in your report, we could be

blowing them up right now," Vann said. Who cared if they had found old dragon bones? There were plenty of them already in the museums in the capital.

He turned his head toward the trees, noting that the birdsong had quieted.

"I don't think you're supposed to blow up fossils, sir. Archaeologists get uppity about that."

"There aren't any archaeologists around here, and if the king is smart, he won't send any out. Bones are worthless. Artifacts that can power military machines aren't."

"Yes, sir. We'll see what the—"

Vann gripped Bosmont's shoulder, halting him mid-sentence. He'd heard a faint scraping sound from somewhere ahead. Some animal disturbing rocks? He made a fist, the signal for silence.

Bosmont stopped talking and tilted his ear toward the trail. More scrapes sounded. It didn't sound like an animal. The noise was regular and rhythmic, like someone trying to chisel away stone.

"You leave any men out here?" Vann murmured.

"No, sir. I was waiting for the report from the capital before doing further digging."

Vann slung his rifle off his shoulder and waved for the captain to let him go ahead. The trail wasn't wide, so Bosmont had to step off to let him pass, and as he did, his boots crunched on rocks, and a pebble fell free, skidding down the slope. Vann glared at him and made a second sign, pointing at the earth to tell him to stay put rather than follow. What if the Cofah had sent another incursion team to spy on the outpost or try to steal some artifacts? It had happened in the past, before Vann had been assigned here.

Excitement surged through his body at the thought of facing enemies, *real* enemies. A true threat, not a handful of soldiers challenging him in the gym.

Vann stalked up the trail, his boots silent on the loose rocks. He'd been trained for this. Death Walking, as an early commander had called him. He'd liked the name, thinking it suited him fine. What didn't suit him was sitting at a desk and cataloging artifacts in a remote outpost, a thousand miles from enemy territory.

Whoever was up ahead must not have heard Bosmont kick the rock, because the scrapes continued. When the ground leveled slightly, Vann slipped off the trail so he could approach from an unexpected direction. He glided between the evergreens, stepping lightly, toe first, barely disturbing the pine needles and rocks, despite his size.

The first man came into view, someone with a scraggly beard and even scragglier clothes, a mix of ripped flannel and stained buckskins. He cradled a hunting rifle in his arms and gazed up the very goat trail that Bosmont had been leading Vann down. About fifty meters and a few dozen trees behind the man, a team of men and women in similar clothing hacked at a cliff.

The steam-powered mining equipment that Bosmont's team had brought out earlier in the week stood undisturbed, tarps still covering it and protecting it from rain. Evidently, the would-be miners were more interested in what lay in the earth than in the equipment. Bosmont's dragon bones? Or had the intruders heard that power crystals could be found within the mountain? From his position behind a tree, Vann couldn't tell what they sought, but they had tunneled partway into a cliff, or perhaps Bosmont had started that tunnel before finding the bones.

More scrapes and grunts came from within the dim passage, so Vann couldn't get a reliable thief count. All he knew was that these people were illegally trespassing on ground claimed by the army.

Unfortunately, underneath the days' worth of dirt, they had the blond or brown hair and pale skin typical of Iskandians, so he doubted this was some Cofah invasion team. If it had been, he could have killed the intruders outright. No, these were likely opportunists. Thieves. Vann would be expected to detain them, or to simply scare them away, since this was a first offense. Maybe he would get lucky, and they would put up a fight.

He smiled at the idea and counted the weapons around their illegal campsite. There were several rifles, but none within arm's reach of where the people worked. A few of the thieves wore knives sheathed at their waists, but most of them bore only the tools they were using.

Vann stalked through the trees toward the man who'd been posted as a guard. He was far enough from the others that Vann thought he could subdue him without alerting the camp.

As he approached, the man frowned down the goat trail and took a step forward, his finger curling around the trigger of his rifle. Had Bosmont continued after Vann ordered him to stay put?

With a growl half-formed in the back of his throat, Vann quickened his pace. The man lifted his rifle, pressing the butt into his shoulder. Vann sprang from behind a tree slightly behind his target. The guard started to turn, noticing him with his peripheral vision, but Vann struck first, wrapping one arm around his opponent's neck at the same time as he smothered the man's mouth with the other. From there, he could have easily broken the guard's neck. The temptation flashed through him, along with the sensation of exhilaration and power that he always felt in such situations, but he reminded himself that this was not a Cofah soldier. It was some Iskandian thief. Disappointed that this wasn't a true battle, he smashed the man's face into the nearest tree with enough force to stun him, if not knock him out completely. As the thief slumped to the ground, Vann took his rifle and withdrew the dagger from the man's belt sheath.

He glanced down the trail, spotting Bosmont hiding behind a tree, and almost scoffed. The engineer might look tough, but he'd almost gotten himself killed. Like most soldiers who had not been trained for the elite forces, Bosmont had the stealth of an elephant.

Vann shouldered his newly acquired rifle. He almost hurled the dagger down the mountainside, but it had a nice weight for throwing. He kept it, flipping it a few times as he slipped back into the trees. The scraping sounds had halted, so he chose a route that would keep him hidden instead of approaching down the trail. He shouldn't have smashed the thief's face against the tree. That had made noise. A choke would have been a wiser move, but he'd been impatient. And, as always, not quite able to sublimate that quiet rage that simmered inside of him, that always brought with it the urge to choose the violent option over the more controlled option. That rage had been a far worse demon in his youth, but it still rode him, even in his forties.

Two men with chisels had stopped working and were murmuring to each other. Thumps and bangs and voices came from the tunnel. For the first time, Vann spotted what had caused Bosmont to pause in his plans to build a new mine shaft on this side of the mountain. A huge skull, cracked but still recognizable as such, was embedded in the pale rock cliff, the jaw hovering over the top of the tunnel. A pile of small bones had been extricated and lay on a canvas tarp nearby. Unless Bosmont had removed those bones, the thieves were likely here for the fossils instead of for the power crystals. That was a lesser crime, but Vann couldn't let them get away with it, nonetheless. This was the king's land, and those were his fossils.

From his spot on the slope below the tunnel, Vann could count the thieves inside now. In addition to the two people outside, one more man and two women toiled within. He considered attacking, beating the stuffing out of the two outside the tunnel before their comrades could come out, and then dealing with the three others. But he'd already discerned that these weren't warriors, and he doubted it would take much to scare them away. Scaring them would not be as appealing as doing battle, but he subdued his more violent urges. Still, he approached stealthily, so he could surprise them and they would be less likely to cause trouble. He picked up their two closest rifles, slinging them over his shoulder by the straps before casually making his presence known.

"You're trespassing on the king's land," Vann said, standing so he could keep all of the thieves in sight as he spoke. "Leave now, or I'll shoot you." He didn't bother to hide the note in his voice that implied he wouldn't mind that.

The two men outside whirled toward him—they had been looking in the direction of their lookout and gaped at Vann's appearance. The noises inside the tunnel halted.

"The king's land?" one man with gray in his beard asked, glancing toward a rucksack where his rifle had been propped. "There aren't any signs."

Vann waved the rifle, emphasizing that he had it. "All land in Iskandia is either privately owned or belongs to the king. You wouldn't have the right to scavenge here under any circumstances."

The burly man next to the graying fellow dropped a hand to his waist, to the hilt of a knife resting in a leather scabbard. He flicked the snap that held the blade in, loosening it. A familiar hum of anticipation ran through Vann's body, charging him like electricity. Would these fools attack him? He wore his uniform and had most of their weapons. They would be idiots to pick a fight with him.

"Don't, Brik," the older man warned. "We're not attacking a soldier." The graying man nodded to Vann. "We didn't know we couldn't look here. We'll take our things and leave. Delma, Sanikar, Myla, we're leaving. Come on out."

They didn't know. Sure, they didn't. That was why they had set a guard, because they were so clearly innocent.

"Leave the bones," Vann said.

"Those are ours," the burly fellow said, his face reddening with indignation. "We spent the last week—"

"Ssh." His older comrade stopped him with a hand on his arm.

"Those are the king's bones," Vann said, "and this is his mountain."

In truth, he wouldn't care if someone walked off with some old bones—they weren't nearly as valuable as the crystals deeper inside the mountain—but he was here to guard the secrecy of this outpost and this mountain, and he didn't need treasure hunters telling the world about all of the goodies they had found here.

"I tied up the other man," Bosmont said, walking into view, his own rifle in hand.

"Good," Vann said. "Come tie these men up too. They seem to think they're above the law."

"Delma," the leader said, the name almost sounding like an order.

His buddy—he'd called him Brik—pulled out his knife as something sailed out of the tunnel mouth. Dynamite. Vann had seen enough of the brown cylinders in the armory to recognize a stick immediately. He threw his confiscated knife at it and ran to the side. He trusted his aim, but he didn't know if striking the dynamite would deflect it enough to protect him.

Brik charged straight down the slope at him, his dagger now in hand. Vann could have shot him, but he turned one of his purloined rifles into a staff instead. As the stick of dynamite landed in the rocks, he feinted toward the thief's stomach with the butt, then switched the direction of the attack, sweeping it up to club him under the chin. His opponent flew through the air, landing on his back and never coming close to reaching Vann with the knife.

The stick of dynamite exploded as Brik struck the ground. Dirt and rocks flew, turning into tiny projectiles. The ground shuddered, and smoke clogged the mountainside.

The thieves inside the cave—two women and a man— tried to use the smoke to disappear. They fled down the goat trail in the opposite direction from which Bosmont had come. Though the roar of the explosion hid other sounds, it did not last, and Vann heard and saw pebbles shifting as the people ran. Only Brik, now unconscious, and the older man were left behind—he had stumbled to the ground when the dynamite exploded.

Vann thought about dropping to one knee and shooting the fleeing thieves, but the dynamite had been a distraction, not an attack. Besides, he believed he could catch them and apprehend them, so he ran after them. Out of the corner of his eye, he spotted Bosmont approaching the older thief and assumed that the captain could handle him.

Vann raced through the smoke, his long, powerful legs pumping with the eagerness of a hound chasing its prey. He ran every morning, and he doubted any scruffy thieves could outlast him, but he grinned as he tore after them, elated at the chance to prove it.

Before he'd escaped the range of the smoke, he caught up with the woman in the back. He hooked her leg and tripped her. She gasped and went down. Vann kept after the other two thieves and soon caught them. The woman gave up as soon as she saw his face. The man put up more of a fight, and Vann ended up dodging a pickaxe and smashing another face into a tree. Soon, he was marching all three people back to join their comrades.

"Under the king's law, assaulting an officer in uniform is a crime," he said, pushing them into a pile with the other two thieves. "Perhaps even more so than stealing historically significant relics from the king's land." Vann was tempted to drag them back to the outpost and put them to work, but he couldn't forget that the crystal mines were a top-secret facility. Maybe the thieves already knew about them, but he couldn't take the chance. "I'm going to let you walk away, but not with any of your gear." He waved at the chisels, pickaxes, and dynamite. "Leave everything, and get off this mountain."

The thieves grumbled under their breath, but nobody picked another fight with them.

"If I catch you out here again, I'll shoot you." Vann did not have the authority to do that, and two of the thieves gaped at him in alarm. He gave them his evilest grin and growled, "Only the trees would know."

With that threat delivered, the band of thieves scurried away.

"You looked as if you *like* being assaulted, sir," Bosmont commented as they watched the hasty retreat.

"Of course. Don't you?"

"Not when dynamite is involved."

"Wimp."

Bosmont snorted and walked over to the bones on the canvas tarp. "I hope these fossils were broken when they found them. I'd hate to get blamed for that."

"By whom?" Vann stuck a hand in his pocket and eyed the pile indifferently.

"I don't know. I figured someone at headquarters might send science people out to take a look at them, science people who might say cranky things about us for getting their bones broken. You don't think they'd extend a man's assignment here, do you?" The most profoundly distressed expression crossed the man's face.

"You look like you're about to piss yourself. You didn't have that look on your face when they threw the dynamite, did you?"

"No. Because they threw it at you, not me." Bosmont managed

a quick smile, but the haunted expression in his eyes remained. "But, sir, I've been here a year. *More* than a year, on account of the engineering miracles that were needed after the dragon flattened half the buildings in the outpost. I don't know if you've noticed yet, but there aren't any female soldiers here. It's been a year since I got to... exercise my lower regions."

"Shit, Bosmont. I don't want to hear about your regions." Vann stalked over to the tarp and found some rope, so he could tie the corners together and tote the fossils back to the outpost. "Besides, there are female prisoners. From what I've heard, they're quick to jump in your bed if you invite them."

"The women here are even uglier than the men."

"After a year, does it matter?" Vann missed pretty women as much as the next man, but he'd reached the age where a few months without sex wouldn't kill him. He hadn't expected there to be any opportunities to exercise *regionally* up here when he'd gotten the assignment, and he had to accept that. He'd chosen his fate months earlier. What he really regretted was that there weren't any opportunities for promotion here. His entire chain of command had probably forgotten he existed, and scaring away some scruffy thieves would not change that.

"Well. A little. It might matter less if there was more alcohol around. Are you sure you should disturb those, sir? It's bad enough the thieves already yanked them out of their resting place. I..." Bosmont rubbed the back of his neck and stared dubiously at the tarp. Seven gods, he wasn't afraid of some thousand-year-old bones, was he?

"They'll rest fine wherever we put them."

"You don't think that maybe... ah, never mind, sir." Bosmont stared uneasily around the torn-up side of the mountain, shifting his weight from foot to foot on the loose pebbles. A wind gusted through the trees, knocking branches together, and he jumped.

And to think, Bosmont was one of his *better* officers up here. Vann grunted and hefted the bones over his shoulder. They were heavier than he expected, more like rocks than the lightweight hollow bones of something that had flown. If no "science people," as the captain had eruditely called them, showed up to study them, maybe they would make decent paperweights in the headquarters building.

A broken rib bone slipped out of the tarp and dropped at his feet. Sighing, he picked it up and stuffed it into his pocket. Bosmont's mouth opened in mild horror at this carelessness.

"What, did you want this one?" Vann asked, his humor piqued. "Maybe you can win some of those female prisoners to your bunk by promising to let them touch your special bone."

"That's awful, sir."

"Probably so. There's a reason I'm not married."

"Just one?"

"More like seven or eight. That I can remember. My last lover gave me a list." If Vann could think of General Arelia Chason as a lover. Though married, she had decided he would be an enjoyable alternative to spending nights with her white-haired husband, and he had decided... mostly that he didn't want to deal with the repercussions of rebuffing a senior officer. Besides, he'd figured he could use a higher-ranking ally when the king had been kidnapped the winter before and suspicion had fallen on him. In the end, the relationship hadn't done much to help him, and Arelia had delighted in trying to domesticate him, as she'd called it in a comment he'd overheard her make to another female officer. The one positive of being sent up here was that he'd been able to escape from her without having to worry about career repercussions. The last he'd heard, she was domesticating a handsome major in intel now.

"At least when Zirkander was stationed here, he had his witch to keep his toes warm at night," Bosmont said with a sigh.

A growl escaped Vann's throat before he could stop it and remind himself that he wasn't a dog, no matter that he was carrying bones around.

Bosmont arched an eyebrow as they started up the trail. "Was that for Zirkander or for his female acquaintance, sir?"

"Quit saying his damned name."

"Ah, Zirkander."

Vann glared at the captain. "The bastard was the C.O. here for what, a month? The miners all worship him and ask when he'll be back, and even the soldiers get starry-eyed when they talk about him. Worse, I get miners coming to my office and asking for days off because of some book-reading incentive program he started, one that they keep forgetting I promptly canceled. These people are murderers who are here in lieu of being hanged or shot. They're not scholars we're trying to groom for leadership."

Bosmont looked like he might say something, but he shook his head and took the lead on the trail. Vann narrowed his eyes, wondering if the captain was thinking impolite thoughts about him. Vann knew he wasn't the easiest man to work for. Hells, he'd never thought he would get promoted high enough to have to be in these kinds of leadership positions. Working with people wasn't his strength. *Killing* them, now that was a simple matter. He supposed it was hypocritical of him to condemn people for being murderers when the only difference between him and the criminals working in the mines was the uniform. He acknowledged, privately if not publicly, that if not for his family connections, he might very well have ended up here twenty-odd years ago, as a prisoner instead of an officer. But that had been a long time ago. He had since used his love of fighting for the good of the country, and he intended to continue to do so, even if nobody was out here to see it. Vann would remind himself that he deserved his uniform and his rank while he organized these paperweights for whomever came up to look at them.

Chapter 2

Lilah locked her knees to control the wobbling in her legs as her shoes landed on the runway. Lieutenant Sleepy offered her a hand for support. She stiffened her spine, irritated that she looked like she *needed* the support, even if she did.

It had been her first time in a flier, and she had made the mistake of answering, "Sure," to his question of, "Would you like to see what this girl can do, ma'am?" She hadn't expected that to include flying upside down or doing large loops that forced her stomach into her shoes and then back up into her throat. The whole time, she'd been convinced that the flimsy harness would give out and that she would plummet into the ocean five thousand feet below.

She took a few deep breaths as she looked around. A hangar rose up to one side of her, and a cliff that overlooked the harbor and the capital fell away at the end of the runway. The view would have been magnificent if she hadn't been trying to still the queasiness in her belly.

"Sleepy, what'd you find down south?" came a familiar and cheerful voice, albeit one she hadn't heard in several years.

Lilah firmed up her legs even more, determined not to have her cousin see her wobbling—or to throw up all over his boots. Ridge had grown out of teasing her sometime after he had entered the military academy, but he would still get that amused quirk to his mouth whenever she did something to remind him that she found books and bones more comfortable to be around than people. Throwing up on his boots might qualify.

"She said she's a *paleontologist*, sir," the lieutenant said, pronouncing the word carefully, then whispered over to her, "Did I get it right, ma'am?"

"Yes, do they not teach the sciences at your military academy? It was my understanding that officers had to complete college degrees."

"Sleepy got his degree in napping through class," Ridge said, giving the lieutenant a thump on the back.

"I only napped through the *boring* classes, sir."

Ridge winked at Lilah as if they were good old friends instead of people related only by blood who rarely saw each other and who had nothing in common. It was that same wink and roguish smile that he always gave the photographers for the newspapers. Given that he had more than his share of the family looks, it wasn't surprising that her students clipped out the pictures, though the occupation surely had a little to do with that too. Even though he had probably come from an office instead of a cockpit, he wore his leather flight jacket over his regular army uniform, with pins and medals dangling from the breast. He was the only one in the family who had chosen the military, and Lilah only had a vague notion of what the decorations meant. She only knew the ordering of the ranks because of the multiple readings she had given the *Time Trek* books.

"How are you doing, Lilah?" Ridge stepped forward and gave her a hug before she could decide if that was the appropriate greeting for cousins. She didn't even hug her brothers most of the time, though they usually stank of alcohol and cigar smoke, having taken after their deceased father. At least Ridge didn't smell of either, just the leather of his jacket. He released her with a friendly pat on the shoulder, one less forceful than the thump he had given his lieutenant. "Getting along well these days?"

"Getting along fine, thank you." She knew he was thinking of the deaths of her husband and her father, but it had been five years. She no longer mourned for Taryn daily, though when she put her work away for long enough, she sometimes mourned for what she had thought her life would be, of children she'd thought she might have. "And you? The promotion was recent, wasn't it? Will you accept my congratulations?"

His smile grew wry. "It's recent, yes, and I'm still debating whether I'm accepting congratulations. It's involved even more paperwork than I thought, despite Angulus promising that he would ensure someone helped me with it. It's hard to find paperwork enthusiasts in the military."

"Angulus?"

"Yes, he's our king." Ridge arched his brows. "How long has it been since you read anything printed in this century?"

"Ha ha. My surprise was that you're apparently on a first-name basis with him these days."

"Nah, he uses my last name when he curses at me. Much like my superior officers."

"Do you still have those? Superior officers? I thought general was as high up as you can go."

"Yes, but once you're in a group of people who are all the same rank, those who have had that rank longer have seniority over you and can boss you around. At the last staff meeting, General Chason told me to get her coffee and got crabby when I forgot the cream. Honestly, it's kind of like being a lieutenant again. Except your peers all have gray hair."

Lieutenant Sleepy, who couldn't have been more than twenty-three, wore a bemused expression at this revelation.

Lilah thought Ridge might be old enough to have a few strands of gray peppering his brown hair now, but if so, the cap hid the evidence.

"We're waiting for your bodyguard, and then we'll take off." Ridge withdrew an envelope from an inside pocket of his jacket. "I have the king's signed orders to give to the post commander up there, to ensure he cooperates."

"Yes, I heard he doesn't like academics." She glanced at the young officer at his side.

"So far as I can tell, he doesn't like anyone," Ridge said, "but I'm taking you up there personally. I'll make sure there won't be any problems with hospitality before I leave, and I'm sending someone along that even he won't likely cross. Not many people do." He smiled encouragingly.

Wonderful, this bodyguard sounded even more alarming than the curmudgeonly base commander.

"I do appreciate you coming out to help us. I know the engineer who sent the report on the bones, and I read between the lines of his chicken scratches that he's concerned his mining site is now haunted. Do dead dragons haunt people? I don't know, but if half the men believe that, it might be problematic. Besides, I figured there might be something scientifically significant to the fossils and that they could be pulled out of the rocks and brought back for study. The army will cover your room and board, of course. We don't have scientists of our own, unless you count those boys who make weapons, so I thought of you when this came up. We saw your article on the hypothesis of dragon evolution. I think it's an older one that the papers reproduced recently, right? Since dragons returned to the world? Four of them, anyway."

"Yes, I've shifted to other subjects of late. Did you say we? You and... the army?"

"No, me and Sardelle, my fiancée. She's a historian as well as a healer. She chanced across one of your papers and asked if we were related. I know she'd like to meet you when you're done up there."

"Your... did you say *fiancée*?"

"Even more shocking than the promotion, isn't it?" Ridge smirked at her. "I'm still amazed she puts up with me."

"She's a historian? That doesn't seem like your kind of woman."

"She's *beautiful*," Sleepy said with a wistful sigh.

"Ah, much becomes clear," Lilah said.

Ridge's mouth twisted. "I'd say I'm shocked that you think I'd fall in love with someone on the basis of looks alone, but I can only guess what my reputation is down there in Port Yenrem." He shrugged, then lifted a hand toward a tall female soldier who was walking away from a tram system that carried people up to the butte.

Lilah bit her lip, wishing she had kept the comment to herself. Sarcasm ran in the family, and she remembered that he had the knack for it, too, but it was often charming when it came out of his mouth. Comments tended to be biting when they came out of hers. Her husband, fortunately, had possessed the ability to see through it.

"How about you?" Ridge asked. "Have you met anyone new since..."

"Despite the common saying that paleontologists will date anything, I've been too busy to look." She hadn't had to *look* for the well meaning but rather aged professors who had offered their condolences—and their beds—after Taryn's death, but she wasn't ready to resign herself to a lover who needed a cane.

"Date anything?" Ridge mouthed. Sleepy removed his cap and scratched his head.

Lilah sighed. Her husband had laughed at her paleontology jokes. Of course, since he had been an archaeologist, he had *understood* them. That always helped.

The female soldier that Ridge had waved at headed straight for them. She was a rangy woman with a lean face and a sultry smile that somehow did not seem out of place, even though she carried a rifle, a pistol, a dagger, and a large, bulky duffel bag that would have crushed anything but the sturdiest of mules.

As she approached, Lieutenant Sleepy straightened to his full height—a good four inches shorter than what must have been six feet for the woman. His face grew wistful again, and a goofy and hopeful smile stretched his lips as she drew near. Lilah was beginning to think the lieutenant thought *every* woman was beautiful.

The woman stopped in front of Ridge and gave him a lazy salute. "Afternoon, General." She looked curiously at Lilah. "Afternoon, Professor, is it?" The look took in her chest and hips, perhaps the thick auburn hair that had fallen out of Lilah's braid during the flight. "You don't look like a professor."

Lilah offered an edged smile. She got that a lot, which unfortunately came along with the assumption that she wasn't very bright. Even colleagues who had known her for years and reviewed her papers seemed to think that from time to time.

"Would you like to see my lab tools?" Lilah waved up to the passenger seat of the two-person flier, where the lieutenant had secured her gear, including the tools, her clothes, and a hunting rifle, before they had taken off.

"Are any of them explosive?"

"No."

"Then not really."

"Captain Kaika," Ridge said, "this is my cousin, Lilah Zirkander."

The woman—Captain Kaika—blinked. "There are professors in your family?"

"Just the one," Ridge said dryly. "If it had been possible, I would have assumed she was my father's daughter and I was her father's son. I don't think my mother and her mother husband-swapped though."

Lilah stared at him, having never heard this hypothesis. Her Uncle Moe *was* the only other academic in the family, though she wasn't sure he quite deserved the label, since he was a self-appointed and self-taught treasure hunter who often worked in opposition to the academic world rather than with it. As far as she knew, he wasn't, however, a mindless drunk, which was the career her own father had claimed, before it had claimed him. Her father had been reckless and had raced prototype steam vehicles, so she supposed she could see why Ridge might identify with him.

"No?" Kaika asked, not obviously fazed by the notion of husband swapping. "That would have made for some interesting family history."

"The family is interesting enough as it is," Ridge replied.

"Yes. I've met your mother. Has she sent by any baskets of dragon-shaped bars of soap lately?"

"No, she's moved on to candles."

"Dragon-shaped candles?"

"Yes, but we've decided not to burn them. It disturbs Bhrava Saruth to see the heads melted off."

Kaika grinned. Lilah had no idea who he was talking about.

"Are you both ready to go?" Ridge asked the two women. "It'll be dark in a few hours, so I thought we'd leave right away, get you to the outpost this evening, Lilah."

Her stomach made a rebellious gurgle at the notion of going back up in the air so soon. Dare she hope that Ridge wouldn't feel the need to show off his flier's capabilities to her? Or would she end up in the back seat of Sleepy's craft again?

"Then you can go out to the dig site and check on the bones first thing in the morning, maybe even finish up the same day," Ridge went on. "It's not a place where you'll want to linger. Trust me. I was stationed out there for several weeks last winter. Lucky for you, it's summer up there now. That probably means it gets at *least* ten degrees above freezing during the day."

"I brought a jacket."

"Good, because there's nobody up there to cuddle with if you get cold."

"Therrik's up there," Kaika said with a smirk.

"As I said, there's *nobody* up there to cuddle with if you get cold," Ridge repeated firmly.

Kaika's smirk widened.

"That's the colonel who eats academics, right?" Lilah asked.

"*Eats?*" Kaika asked. "My first inclination would be to say that's unlikely. But you are pretty. He might make an exception."

Lilah found herself flushing as the double meaning of the word unraveled itself in her mind, but she shrugged off the notion once it did. She wasn't worried about rebuffing some army officer, and she admitted to being slightly proud of having caught the double entendre. That wasn't her strong point. More than one sexual joke had passed over her head in her lifetime.

She expected Ridge to catch the insinuation right away and to share Kaika's smirk, but the most horrified expression stamped his face. "Seven gods, Kaika. This is my *cousin*."

"Your cousin doesn't get womanly urges?"

"*No.*"

Kaika shook her head, turning her unwavering smirk toward Lilah. "He gets mortified when his mother talks about sex too. You wouldn't think someone so pretty would be so prudish."

"I am *not* prudish. And you're not supposed to say such things to generals, anyway. It's in the rule book, under respect and decorum." Ridge gripped Kaika's shoulder and spun her toward the hangar entrance. "Go throw your gear in the back of my flier. And leave half of it in a locker, will you? We'll be scraping our belly on trees all the way into the mountains if you bring all of that along. Did you raid the armory on the way up here? You're not taking explosives, are you?"

Kaika let herself be pushed toward the hangar, but that didn't keep her from winking at Lilah as she walked away. It took Lilah a few moments to realize that this Captain Kaika was the bodyguard Ridge had mentioned. Lilah had expected someone burly and humorless. And who needed to shave to keep within army personnel presentation regulations.

"Just ignore her," Ridge said, having recovered some of his composure, though a slightly haunted expression lurked in his eyes. "She's known for her ribald streak, but she's a very competent officer. I picked her because she's a lot less likely to be intimidated by Therrik than most of the men in their unit. But I honestly don't think Therrik will be... I mean, he's an ass, but he's loyal to the king and the uniform. He won't break any regulations. My concern is more about the miners there. They're criminals serving out life sentences, and they're a rough lot. You shouldn't have to go into the mines—my understanding is that the bones were discovered on the outside of the mountain—but if you do, keep Kaika with you."

"This sounds like it's going to be more eventful than most of my digs," Lilah said.

Maybe she should have been more worried by his comments, but she admitted to a modicum of excitement. She loved going out in the field and had always enjoyed the safari expeditions she and her husband had gone on in the wild southeast grasslands of the continent. Despite what she'd told her students, she had been disappointed when there hadn't been funding for a field outing this summer. Perhaps this would make up for it. Even if she had moved on from studying dragons, she admitted that the idea of making a new find was exciting. Maybe she would yet stumble across her missing link.

"I hope not," Ridge said. "If you want to change your mind, I'll understand."

"Not at all. I'm ready to go."

* * *

Vann scowled down at the dragon anatomy book, scowled at the bone-filled tarp spread on the table, then returned his scowl to the picture of the skeleton. The musty tome, with mildew creeping along the edges of the pages, was probably as old as the fossils. He ought to give this task to someone else, but he'd done most of the organizing of artifacts that had been pulled out of the mountain, and he was loath to assign one of his dubiously competent soldiers. Besides, his staff was more skeletal than these bones, so it was hard to spare people. He needed the soldiers down in the mines, guarding the prisoners, prisoners who had grown extra uppity as the weather warmed. Apparently, there were about three months out of the year when a man could walk through the pass and escape this mountain hell, and all of the miners knew about it. There had been seven escape attempts in the last month. So far, none of his people had been killed, but some of the miners had been shot to keep an uprising from forming.

Vann would strangle himself before admitting it, but there were times when he wished he had some of General Zirkander's charisma. His career had never required diplomacy or charm, thank the gods. He'd never had to worry too much about developing anything other than his combat skills until he had been promoted from major to colonel. Before that, he had been placed in charge of small incursion missions staffed by battle-loving soldiers exactly like him. Since then, he'd commanded battalions and now an outpost. The years teaching at the academy had been the worst. He didn't have the patience for lippy upstarts or colleagues who questioned his methods. He'd taught as he'd been taught as a young soldier: by pounding the piss out of men until they learned how not to get hit. It was an effective but unpopular teaching style, and as he'd been told by several other officers, the army had changed since he'd gone through the academy more than twenty years earlier. Coddling seemed an acceptable method of dealing with young soldiers. He shuddered to think of those babes defending the nation.

A knock sounded at the door to the artifact room.

"What?" Vann asked.

"Uhm, sir?" Lieutenant Kraden poked his head around the door. "There's a prisoner here to see you."

"Is it about a damned book?"

"Yes, sir."

"Did you tell him that he's not getting a day off?"

"Yes, sir. He said General Zirkander promised it to him, and he's sure you won't go back on that promise."

Vann growled. "Fine. Send him in."

"Yes, sir."

"You put my team together that's going to guard the dig site from thieves yet, Kraden?"

"Working on it, sir. You didn't want me to take anyone off their regular shift, right?"

"Right, this will be a double shift for whomever you pick. You're a signal soldier. Spin it so it sounds like it's an honor. Defending the king's mountain from craven thieves."

Kraden stared at him. "Spin it, sir? Signal is communications, not journalism. Or, uhm, sensationalism."

"I *know* what it is, but you haven't managed to get that new radio installed, so I'm coming up with other uses for your skills."

The lieutenant flushed. "I'll get it working, sir. It *was* working last week. I don't know what's wrong. Bosmont said it might be cursed."

"*Cursed?*"

"On account of the bones. The radio stopped working the same day his team found them." Kraden bit his lip, his gaze drawn to the tarp on the table. "You're brave to be touching them, sir."

Vann picked up the rib he'd dropped a few times on the trek back, tempted to throw it at the lieutenant. But he'd rather throw it at Bosmont. The captain was in his thirties, far too old to believe in cursed bones. "I don't want excuses, Lieutenant. I want a radio. Right now, our bimonthly supply ship is the only way to communicate with headquarters."

He had been shocked when he'd first arrived up here and found out the remote outpost lacked a way to send timely reports back to the capital. Vann could understand not being able to run wire for a telegraph station into these craggy peaks, but given the preciousness of the energy crystals that came out of the mountain, it seemed ludicrous that the outpost was completely cut off from the outside world. Fortunately, his superiors had agreed with him and had sent the equipment out to construct a radio tower. Unfortunately, they had sent a lieutenant who was six weeks out of the academy to do it. Vann neither knew nor cared why Kraden had received such a dubious first duty station, but wagered it had been a punishment, the same as it had been for him.

"I'll keep working on it, sir," Kraden said.

"Send the miner in." Vann waved the bone. A strange tingle ran down his arm. He paused in the middle of the movement to stare at the fossilized rib. "Now what?" he grumbled.

His fingers buzzed, as if they held a strong magnet or something electric. Frowning, he set the bone on the tarp with the others. The feeling disappeared, but when he rubbed his fingers, the tips felt numb. He had been handling that bone all afternoon. What had changed? It couldn't be magnetic, could it? Somehow reacting to something else in the room? He eyed the shelves full of books, tools, and boxes that had been pulled from the mountain, from what had been witch-infested tunnels three hundred years earlier. His predecessor had told him that precious little in this room was magic, and he'd done the cataloging himself and couldn't remember anything magnetic. Besides, fossils weren't magnetic. Even he knew that.

"Colonel, sir?" The miner who shuffled in held a wool cap to his chest and bobbed his head politely, his demeanor at odds with his rough face, one sporting a broken nose, a scar that curled his lip upward, and a burn mark where it looked like someone had tried to brand him like a steer.

"You're not getting a day off," Vann said. "As I've said multiple times now, that policy is no longer in effect."

"But it took me six months to finish the book. I couldn't have come in any earlier to give a report." The miner's gaze shifted toward the bones as he spoke. Bosmont better not have been spreading his theories of curses and hauntings to these people. "We don't get much reading time, see."

"What book?" Vann asked, though he wasn't sure why. What did he care? He hadn't read many of the classics that were in the prison library. When it came to books, he didn't have much interest in the ones that dealt with matters other than military history.

"Milner's *Timeline of Independence for Iskandoth*."

Vann leaned his back against the table. He *had* read that one. He enjoyed the histories that involved his people kicking those scum-kissing Cofah trespassers out of their country. "Go ahead. Summarize it." Maybe a prisoner who could get through eight hundred pages of history might be trusted to do something other than swinging a pickaxe. Such as going along to guard a dig site...

A few seconds after the man launched into a stumbling but accurate summary, a snap sounded behind Vann. He whirled, automatically dropping into a fighting stance. He spotted the reason for the noise immediately. A fresh crack ran diagonally across one of the windowpanes.

"Is some idiot throwing rocks?" After shooting a glare at the miner—maybe he had come up here under instructions to distract the outpost commander—Vann stalked around the table to the window. It looked out toward the outer wall and a tower rather than into the courtyard. He spotted a soldier at his post on top of the tower, but the man's back was toward Vann, as he faced the valley. Vann didn't see anyone on the ground, but some fool could have thrown the rock and then run around the corner of the building. To what end, he couldn't guess. Throwing rocks wouldn't get anyone out of this hole.

"I... was looking right at that window, sir," the miner said, a quaver to his voice that hadn't been there before. "I didn't see anything hit it. The glass just... snapped."

Had it been extremely cold or extremely hot, Vann might have believed that, but it was neither. He scowled out the window again, then walked back to the table, continuing past it to stand next to the miner. He folded his arms over his chest and glared hard, still suspicious that the man was part of some scheme.

"Continue," he said softly, dangerously. He hoped to make the man nervous enough to babble a confession. Nobody here would make a fool of him, nor would anyone successfully escape while he commanded.

The miner appeared nervous—he kept rubbing an old scar on the back of his hand—but he wasn't glancing at Vann. Instead, he kept eyeing the tarp.

"Are those dragon bones, Colonel? I heard... well, that's what I heard."

"So what if they are?"

"Dragons are magic. And a dragon burial site... they say that strange things happen around one."

Vann snorted. "*Who* says that? I don't believe that anyone here has ever seen one. I doubt there even is such a thing. Dragons were rare, even thousands of years ago, and they were hard to kill. *Are* hard to kill, something I can personally attest to now that there are some back in the world."

"Yes, sir," the miner mumbled, his gaze still locked on the table. "You know, now that I reconsider things, I might just stay at work. There's no bones down in the tunnels, right? Should be safe down there." The man backed away from the table, tripped over nothing, and scurried for the door. A soldier out in the hall escorted him out of the building.

"Guess Kraden gets to put together his team solely from soldiers," Vann said when he was alone again. "Ought to put Bosmont on that team. If he's the one who's been spreading these rumors, he deserves it."

Noticing that he was talking to himself, Vann snapped his mouth shut and walked back to the table. He frowned at the rib bone and frowned harder at the cracked window. Magic, please. He could believe that dragons themselves were magical, but some bones that were probably thousands of years old?

"Why not check?" he muttered, realizing he had a way of doing so.

He jogged into the hallway and down the stairs to where the officers had their quarters. He stepped into the room at the back of the building that belonged to him, it being distinguished only by the plaque on the door that read *Commander*. The bunk was slightly larger than those in the other quarters, but the room was otherwise identical. No perks of command here. Not that he cared about luxuries, especially when he had no one with whom to share the bed.

He dropped to his knees next to it. He had been allowed to bring few personal belongings, leaving most of his things back at the family property near the capital, but he had a few books and some of his favorite weapons, which included a sword locked in a dented and charred box under the bunk. Kasandral, a dragon-slaying sword that was reputed to be thousands of years old, had been in his family since the days when sorcerers had ridden dragons and wars had been fought with magic rather than might. Vann shuddered at the idea of sorcery being rampant in the world, and he was proud to be the heir to a weapon that could defeat witches and dragons.

He pulled out the box and unlatched it. The blade rested inside on velvet that covered a metal lining that was supposed to dull its influence. The sword could sense magic and had a sentience of a sort. It had once guided Vann to a witch who was trying to kill the king, and had allowed him to cut through her magic and slay her. It had also tried to get him to slay a witch and a dragon that had been fighting *for* the king. Controlling it was not easy, but he did not mind the challenge.

Unlike when there were magical beings around, those who had dragon blood flowing through their veins, Kasandral lay quietly in its box, no hint of its power on display. The ancient runes etched into the side of the blade appeared nothing but ornamental, but he had seen them glow before and knew what it meant when they did.

Vann pulled out the sword and jogged back up to the artifact room, not answering the surprised stare he received when Lieutenant Kraden spotted him with it. He walked inside, prepared to wave the blade over the table to wake it up. There was no need. As soon as the bones came into sight, the ancient sword started glowing.

He froze, scowling at it, and then at the bones. It wasn't

glowing as fiercely as it did when an enemy who possessed magic was nearby, but a pale green glow definitely emanated from the runes. An alien tension bunched Vann's shoulders, and an image flowed into his brain, an image that involved him taking the sword and hacking those bones into a thousand pieces.

He gritted his teeth and backed out of the room. Bosmont's "science people" definitely wouldn't have good things to say about him if they arrived to find the rare fossils in such a state. In the hallway, Vann closed the door and locked it, all desire to catalog the bones disappearing. Let the scientists deal with them.

Chapter 3

The mountains were majestic, snow and glaciers gleaming under the sun, and absolutely breathtaking. Even though Lilah was freezing in the back seat of Sleepy's flier, her jacket doing little to stave off the wind that the craft generated, she wouldn't have given up her opportunity to see the world like this for anything. She'd flown in a dirigible a couple of times when she and her husband had traveled, but the plodding conveyance had been nothing like these fliers. Sleepy, following in Ridge's wake, swooped in and out of canyons, glided across ice fields, and dove through valleys carpeted with the most amazingly colorful meadows of wildflowers. Now and then, her stomach protested, but the cold fresh air helped alleviate her queasiness.

The fliers rounded a glacier-draped mountain, and a valley dotted with evergreens came into view, snow still covering the earth in the shady spots. A walled outpost rose from one end of the valley, the surrounding area cleared of trees, leaving lush green grass and a stream that ran straight through the compound on its way toward a waterfall a couple of miles away.

The fliers coasted toward the outpost, then, as the momentum faded, the pilots flipped switches, and the propellers turned off as thrusters ignited in a display of engineering that left Lilah wondering at the mathematics. She doubted the technology would have been possible without the yellow power crystal that glowed from a casing inside the cockpit. From what she'd heard, the army denied that they were magical, instead, promising they were completely natural phenomena. Lilah had always doubted that, being intimately familiar with the earth's natural fuel sources.

Sleepy landed beside Ridge atop a large, flat roof on a big, two-story building made from stone. Soldiers patrolled a wall, complete with towers and large artillery weapons, including cannons and shell guns. It looked like the kind of outpost one would find on the coast nearest to the Cofah empire, rather than some remote mountain deep within Iskandian borders. Lilah glimpsed some bare-chested men fighting in the courtyard and thought of the criminal-miners Ridge had warned her about. Perhaps they were permitted an evening exercise session.

"Ma'am?" Sleepy had already hopped out of the cockpit and was offering her a hand down.

Lilah lowered her gear to him, then climbed out on her own.

"Why is that man fighting every time I show up here?" Ridge grumbled from a few steps away. He and Kaika were also on the ground, Kaika shouldering the duffel bag—it didn't look like she had taken more than a few items out of it after Ridge had ordered her to lighten the load.

"It's what he's good at, sir," Kaika said. "At least this time, it doesn't look like an insurrection is going on." She jerked her thumb toward the courtyard. Now that the propellers had died down, Lilah could hear the jeers of men and the smacks of fists striking flesh. "That's just how Therrik winds down after a hard day of not killing people."

"It would be nice if he'd wind down by coming up to greet us," Ridge said. "I *know* he didn't miss our arrival. Fliers aren't exactly stealth craft."

Lilah walked to the edge of the rooftop, curious to see the man of whom they spoke. Maybe it would be wiser *not* to be curious, but uncurious scientists did not make many discoveries.

The fight broke up as soon as she poked her head over the edge, though she doubted it had anything to do with her. Half of the men were kneeling or sitting, grabbing arms or shoulders and grimacing in a manner that suggested they regretted participating in the first place. Another lay on his back, his palm protecting what promised to become a black eye. The men were shirtless, muscular, and didn't *look* like they would be easily defeated, but none of them had any fight left. Except for one.

A brawny, broad-shouldered man stalked across the courtyard, his shirt dangling in his hand. Every line of his musculature stood out, like one of the marble statues of ancient warriors in the courtyard at the university, though the dagger tattoos on his forearms wouldn't be found on many statues, at least not in her town. Another tattoo darkened one pectoral muscle, though she couldn't tell what it depicted from here. It seemed thorny or barbed. Definitely prickly. He looked prickly, too, with short, thick black hair speckled with gray, a square jaw, and dark, intense eyes.

Built to kill and to like it, the phrase popped into her head, a line used frequently in the *Time Trek* novels to describe Commander Asylon, the hero of the series. Commander Asylon was an honorable man under the rugged exterior. She had no idea if this fellow would turn out to be similar.

He looked toward the rooftop, a fierce—or maybe fiercely annoyed—expression on his face. If he smiled, she imagined many women would call him handsome, but he didn't look like someone who did that often. Lilah found herself stepping away from the edge, uncomfortable holding his hard stare.

Ridge came up beside her and looked down as the big man approached the outside stairs leading up to the rooftop. "You better not be out of uniform when you get up here, Therrik. There are ladies present." He elbowed Lilah and whispered, "The promotion was worth it just so I could outrank him."

"Kiss my tattooed ass, Zirkander," the man called up as he started up the stairs.

"Does he *know* you outrank him?" Lilah asked.

"He has a hard time remembering it. Too many blows to the head during his career." Ridge turned toward the stairs, clasping his hands behind his back as he strolled across the rooftop.

When Colonel Therrik came into view, he had donned his shirt, a black short-sleeve one that did little to hide the musculature of his torso. He seemed to be missing the uniform jacket that typically went over the shirt. Lilah told herself it was silly to appreciate that lack, especially when the officer seemed to have the personality of a premenstrual porcupine. Definitely not Commander Asylon.

"What do you want, Zirkander?" Therrik asked, sparing Lilah a glance but nothing more. Surprisingly, he offered Kaika a nod.

It was almost cordial, at least in comparison to the glower he fixed upon Ridge.

"We got Bosmont's report on the dragon burial site," Ridge said.

"It's not a damned burial site. It's just some bones wedged into some rocks. Stopping to worry about them is delaying our mining preparations for that part of the mountain. It's probably going to impact how many energy crystals your pilots are going to get this winter."

Ah, Sleepy had been right. Therrik seemed someone more likely to eat academics than to work with them. Lilah was glad Ridge had orders from the king.

"Nevertheless, I've brought you a paleontologist to examine the site and the bones and determine if they can be safely excavated or if we'll have to work around them."

"A paleontologist." Therrik frowned at Lilah. At least he'd pronounced the word more easily than Sleepy had, albeit with less respect.

"Allow me to introduce Professor Lilah Zirkander." Ridge extended a hand toward her.

She started to offer the man her hand, but Therrik's eyebrows flew up. *"Zirkander?"* The name came out of his mouth like a curse, a very distasteful curse.

For once, Lilah had a feeling that being related to the famous pilot might not be a boon. Oh, well. At least he wouldn't be asking her to talk Ridge into autographing his undergarments.

"She's my cousin," Ridge said, "but don't let that fool you. She's much smarter than I am."

"That wouldn't take much."

"I expect you to treat her better than you treat me."

"That wouldn't take much," Kaika said with a smirk.

"No kidding," Ridge said.

Therrik's nostrils flared.

"Since I know you sometimes have trouble honoring *my* orders," Ridge said, eyeing Therrik's torso long enough to make it clear he had noted the missing jacket, "I've brought handwritten orders from the king."

"Of course you have," Therrik said.

Ridge handed him the paperwork. "Will you have any problems being hospitable to your guest?" he asked, his tone cooling a few degrees. He glared at Therrik, managing the challenging eye contact that Lilah had shied away from. Usually, she could face down anyone, but there was something about Therrik that made doing so seem more dangerous, as if violence simmered beneath the surface for him, waiting for an opportunity to boil over and destroy anything—or anyone—nearby. She was surprised Ridge didn't back away from him, superior rank or not.

"Is she a witch or dragon in disguise?" Therrik asked.

"Nope."

"Then I won't have a problem." Therrik accepted the envelope with his orders without further comment.

"Where shall we put our stuff, sir?" Kaika asked. "Same quarters as last time?"

"You're staying?" Therrik raised his eyebrows.

"To make sure none of your grubby miners or soldiers manhandle the professor, yes, sir. I believe the king mentions me in the orders he wrote up."

Therrik grunted. Or maybe it was a grumble. He waved his hand. "Take whatever you can find open. Some of the bones are in the artifact room. Lots more still stuck in the rocks. Bosmont can show you whenever you're ready."

"Some have been removed already?" Lilah grimaced, imagining the damage that a bunch of unschooled soldiers might have done to ancient fossils. "I would have preferred to have looked at them in place."

"Be happy you can look at them at all. Some grimy thieves tried to filch them right out of the mountain."

Ridge frowned. "How did grimy thieves know they were *in* the mountain?"

"Your father isn't around, is he?" Lilah asked.

Ridge gave her a flat look. "As far as I know, he's only interested in lost treasures, not lost dragon bones."

"Do what you want," Therrik said and walked away. "I have work to do."

"And the rest of your uniform to find," Ridge called after him. Therrik trotted down the stairs without acknowledging him.

"Are you *sure* you outrank him?" Lilah asked.

"*I'm* sure. I'm not sure *he's* sure."

"He's a difficult man," Kaika said, shouldering her huge duffel bag and ambling toward the stairs. "Come with me, Professor, and I'll show you what kind of luxury accommodations this place offers."

Sleepy climbed up and retrieved the rest of Lilah's bags for her, including the tool box she'd brought, with gear for examining fossils. He also handed down the hunting rifle she had, at the lieutenant's suggestion, retrieved from storage for the trip.

"Lilah?" Ridge asked. "Sleepy and I won't be staying, at least not for the long-term, but how do you feel? Do you want us to wait until tomorrow to go back? Or until after you've looked at the bones?"

"I'm sure we womenfolk will be fine without you." Lilah patted the rifle case. "Besides, Colonel Therrik didn't seem to like you very much." She didn't mention that he had looked like he wanted to spit his teeth out when he'd heard that she was related to Ridge. "It's possible he would be more hospitable toward us if you weren't around."

Ridge snorted. "That does seem likely."

She gripped his arm. "It was good seeing you. Thanks for thinking of me for this project." She kept herself from calling it an adventure, even if she hoped it would become an educational and enlightening start to her summer.

"You're already thinking about those bones, aren't you?"

"Maybe so."

He offered her a salute. "All right. Be careful, and find Captain Bosmont if you need anything. He knows the outpost better than anyone here. If you need to get word back to me, he'll make sure your report goes out with the supply ship. There's supposed to be a radio tower in construction around here too. I saw it when we flew in."

"I'll be fine, Ridge," she said, shooing him toward his flier.

"Yes, good." Ridge waved and shouted, "Take care of her, Kaika, or I'll tell everybody back home your first name."

"What? Who told *you* my first name? You're bluffing!"

"Am I? I have sorceresses, dragons, and sentient swords for housemates now, remember. And they're all nosey telepaths."

"That begs an explanation," Lilah murmured as Ridge vaulted into his cockpit.

"You probably shouldn't miss the family picnics," Kaika said, waiting at the top of the stairs.

The pilots did not start their engines until Lilah headed that way too.

Lilah followed Kaika down the stairs and around to the front door, pausing there to take in more of the facility. Buildings were spread around the edges of the courtyard, interspersed among towers supporting tram cars. Closed doors in the ground lay next to those towers. Was that where the miners worked? Down shafts beneath those doors? She shivered to imagine herself in some dark tunnel with the only exit closed off up above her. Did the prisoners sleep down there too? Several of the buildings looked to be barracks, so she hoped that meant they were allowed to come up at night.

A few dirty faces peered in her direction from one of the tram towers, the only one with the shaft doors next to it standing open. Even from across the courtyard, she felt the brazen appraisal as the men's gazes dipped to her chest. It made her shudder and hustle through the doorway, realizing that Ridge had sent along a bodyguard for a very real reason.

She found Kaika waiting for her inside, keeping an eye on her. It was the expected thing, Lilah supposed, but strange, too, to have a bodyguard. She thought of all the battered men who had been outside, having apparently lost their sparring match with Therrik. Would Kaika truly be able to stand up to him in a brawl if he decided that something should happen to his visiting paleontologist? Lilah could imagine the tall woman clobbering one of the gaunt, dirt-smudged miners who had been looking her way, but there was nothing gaunt about Therrik.

"Ridge said you would be better able to handle Colonel Therrik than a lot of the men in your unit," Lilah said quietly as she followed Kaika down a first-floor hallway laid with cracked tiles that had to be several decades old. "Is that true?"

"Hm, possibly."

"Because you're faster and cleverer than he is?"

"Because I know where all of his tattoos are." Kaika smirked at her, then stopped at the end of the hall and poked her head through a doorway. "This one's empty and has two bunks. You all right with sharing? I think it's what the general had in mind, though I doubt any miners are going to wander into headquarters to harass you. All of the officers bunk on the first floor in here, and then the barracks on that side—" she pointed out the window, "—is for the soldiers. You shouldn't walk around the compound on your own here, though, especially after dark."

Kaika entered the room without waiting for a response and slung her gear on the bunk on the left side. Judging by the way the duffel clanked, very little of it was devoted to spare clothes and toiletries.

"I will let you know if I need to walk anywhere."

Lilah put her toolbox, which also clanked, on the floor at the foot of the other bunk, and dropped her bag on the thin mattress. There was only one four-drawer dresser for them to share, so she was glad she had packed lightly, much as she had when she and her husband had gone on safari. *He* had usually been the one with all the gear, bags full of art supplies so he could draw and paint out there on the savannah. Even if he had been the one to first get her into hunting, he'd always seemed as pleased to paint a portrait of a lion as he had been to shoot one.

She shook her head, wondering why she was thinking of him this afternoon. She opened one of the dresser drawers to tuck her toiletries away, but paused.

"Is there indoor plumbing?" She made a face, imagining waking Kaika up in the middle of the night to escort her to some outhouse.

"Yup. I told you the accommodations are luxurious." Kaika had checked her rifle and her pistol, and now pulled out a cleaning kit and sat on the edge of her bunk. "Just one lavatory, though, that we share with everyone in the building. How are you at using urinals?"

"Ah. Rather unpracticed."

"Kidding. They're optional. Do you want a tour when you're done? Probably a good idea to do it before dark. There's always a guard on the miners' barracks, but nobody pays much attention if the men sneak out for liaisons with the female prisoners. Or if female prisoners sneak out for liaisons with the soldiers. I suspect either sex would sneak out for a liaison with you if given a chance."

"You make it sound like I'm some nubile young virgin here for a sacrifice." Lilah opened the case for her hunting rifle, since she had stuffed socks into it to conserve space. She tossed them into a drawer.

"Trust me, you're a lot more nubile than the female prisoners. And female soldiers don't even get sent up here, unless there's a dragon to slay and they have some special talent." Kaika patted her bulky bag.

"Ah, and what exactly *is* your talent?" Lilah assumed she was excellent with those firearms and perhaps in hand-to-hand combat, but she didn't think that either would be useful against a dragon.

Kaika squinted into the barrel of her disassembled pistol and poked a bore brush through it as she answered. "Demolitions, explosives, explosive ordnance disposal, languages, firearms, unarmed combat, and, oh, I'm wicked with my tongue."

Lilah glanced over at her, expecting another smirk or perhaps a leer, but Kaika merely blew specks of carbon out of her pistol barrel.

"Is that useful against a dragon?"

This time, Kaika did grin. "I don't know yet. But they can shape-shift into human form, and I have a deal with Ang—with my lover that if I get a chance to sleep with a dragon, I get to take it, no questions asked, whether it's mission-critical or not."

"Does he get to watch?" a dry voice said from the open door.

Lilah jumped, dropping the panties she had been about to put into a drawer. They hadn't closed the door, but she hadn't expected company, certainly not company that would be standing out there and listening in. Of course, Kaika was the one who had been speaking of tongues, not she. *She* did not drop anything on the floor. She merely grinned over at Therrik as she stuffed her bore brush back into the barrel.

"He can join in, if he wants," she said. "I've been trying to broaden his horizons."

Therrik's face twisted into something between bemusement and horror. Both were better than the expression of flinty, barely-controlled anger that he had worn on the rooftop. He had since donned his uniform jacket, the dark blue material ironed and pressed, the sleeves rolled up and buttoned below his elbows. He looked more like a soldier now than a random thug, though the tattoos—were those daggers dripping *blood*?—still lent him a malevolent air.

"That's more information than I needed."

"Walk up on a women's barracks room, and that's usually what you'll get," Kaika said.

Therrik dropped his head and pushed a hand through his black hair. Unlike the rest of him, it looked soft, touchable.

He looked up, his gaze locking onto Lilah, and she almost jumped again. Why was she having such thoughts? She barely noticed men at all anymore, at least around campus, and he was far rougher—and ruder—than anyone she would ever consider.

"I can show you the artifact room now," he told her. "It'll be dark soon, so the field trip around the mountain will have to wait, but the bones in there ought to keep you busy for a while." His gaze flicked downward, to where her panties still lay on the ground.

She had forgotten about them, too busy thinking about touching hair. She forced herself to calmly reach down, pick them up, and toss them into the drawer, instead of hastily snatching them up and sticking them in her pocket or somewhere else inappropriate but out of sight. Kaika, she imagined, wouldn't have been embarrassed by panties. She probably would have twirled them in the air before putting them away. Lilah settled for shutting the drawer.

"I'm ready now," she said, meeting his eyes, wondering if she would catch a smirk there.

But all of the almost-humor he had displayed in bantering with Kaika was gone, covered with an impassive mask. His gaze did perk slightly as he noticed the rifle case on her bunk, the weapon still half hidden by socks.

"That's a Brasingher 980, isn't it?" he asked.

"A 960. My husband had the '80, but I always liked the lever-action reload better than the pump."

Therrik walked in, uninvited, though his gaze remained on the weapon, rather than roaming inappropriately around the room. He had yet to give Lilah the hip-to-chest appraisal that she usually got from men, though her long-sleeve shirt, buttoned to the collar, didn't invite a huge amount of speculation. She moved aside so he could approach the bunk.

Therrik reached for the rifle, but paused. "May I?"

Kaika made a choking sound. Lilah raised her eyebrows as she waved for Therrik to do what he wished with the rifle.

"He's not usually so polite," Kaika said.

"You're not supposed to be polite with soldiers," Therrik said. "It confuses them."

"Yes, *confusion* is the reason why your house on base gets vandalized by disgruntled privates."

His face hardened, his jaw tightening, but he did not respond. He merely examined the rifle, running his hand along the decorated wooden stock. Taryn had painstakingly carved lions and elephants into it as a birthday gift to her, and she was relieved when Therrik did not mock it. He did pick up the box of ammunition, arching his brows at the caliber.

"You planning to hunt bears while you're here?" he asked.

"Lieutenant Sleepy implied I might need to defend myself against a grumpy commander the *size* of a bear."

Kaika snorted, amused, but a different emotion flashed across Therrik's face, first surprise, then irritation, his mouth turning down into a scowl. Standing this close to him, the change was alarming, and Lilah had to brace herself to keep from stepping back.

"Zirkander's pilots are a bunch of cloud-humping prisses, just like he is." Therrik returned the rifle to the case and walked out, saying, "The artifact room is this way," as he disappeared into the hallway.

"I knew that politeness wouldn't last long," Kaika said.

Lilah felt a flash of indignation on the colonel's behalf and found herself wondering what he was like without any of his soldiers around. But then, *she'd* been the one to irritate him, not Kaika. She had meant the comment as a joke, not realizing until afterward that it was a dig at his honor, if he *was* a man of honor. She did not know at this point.

"I better go look at his room," Lilah murmured.

She grabbed her toolkit and walked out, aware of Kaika snapping her firearm together and following her. Lilah wasn't sure whether to be relieved or not that she would have company. With her knack for offending people, being alone with Therrik might not be a good idea, especially since he apparently possessed a special hatred for Zirkanders.

* * *

On the second floor of the headquarters building, Vann unlocked the door to the artifact room while he waited for the professor to join him. His own office, complete with a never-ending pile of paperwork on the desk, stood open at the end of the hall. It would be a damned shame if the supply ship forgot to include reams of paper the next time it floated into the valley. Unfortunately, he needed to get back to that paperwork. He'd taken more of a break than he should have for his evening exercise session. His muscles, less tense after going a dozen rounds of wrestling and boxing, thanked him for the diversion, but General Zirkander's arrival had added to what should have only been an hour delay. Vann would be going over reports by lantern light tonight.

Professor Zirkander's head appeared as she climbed the stairs, her reddish-brown hair falling about her shoulders. He'd outpaced her, his strides irritated after the implication that he was someone whom women needed a rifle to fend off, but there weren't many places to get lost in the rectangular two-story building. A long hallway on each level granted one access to all of its rooms.

Kaika ambled after the professor, appearing relaxed, if not bored, but she'd had much of the same training as he'd had, and he knew she was always alert and ready to react. He clenched his jaw, feeling irritated anew that she—or maybe the professor—thought her services as a damned bodyguard were needed inside of the headquarters building. Of all people, *Kaika* ought to know that he wasn't going to maul a woman, not a civilian woman, anyway. He tried to treat soldiers the same way, regardless of sex, though he always felt uncomfortable forcefully demonstrating combat maneuvers with women on the training field. He was relieved he hadn't had to deal with them as soldiers for his first fifteen years in the army. Only when he'd gotten promoted to colonel and had been taken from the field to the academy to teach unarmed combat to all upcoming officers, not just infantry ones, had he encountered mixed genders. As he would admit to nobody but himself, he had been equally inept with men *and* women when it came to instruction. He missed fieldwork like a lost limb. He felt more than a little envious of Kaika for still being sent on covert missions, though he allowed himself a bit of a smug smile as she approached with the professor. He knew she must hate this little mission and would look forward to its end. Bodyguard duty. How tedious and unexciting.

"They're in here," Vann said when the women stopped in front of him. He pushed the door open, his gaze snagging on the cracked window, a cracked window which would require more paperwork, since every bit of inventory that came up from the capital had to be accounted for. He grumbled to himself.

The professor, who had been walking past him on her way into the room, must have caught the noise because she glanced up at him in alarm. Vann smoothed his face. He'd been told his under-the-breath grumbles weren't much different from his growls, for which he was infamous, and he hadn't meant to alarm her. Kaika quirked an eyebrow at him as she passed. Vann tightened his jaw and said nothing, not sure how he felt about her being here. Oh, he didn't mind her as a person or as a soldier. They had been in the same elite forces unit for years, and had crossed paths often, even sharing a few missions. She was the one female soldier he had encountered in infantry, apparently there because of a special exemption from the king. What bothered Vann was the idea that she had been assigned to protect the professor not just from the prisoners but from *him*, as if he were some sex-starved troglodyte who would assault a woman. There was absolutely nothing on or off his record that justified that, and he knew he had General Zirkander to blame for the insinuation. And apparently, Lieutenant Sleepy. Damned pilots. They were the biggest whiners at the academy, just wanting to fly and not wanting to learn how to be *real* soldiers.

He managed to keep from grumbling again as he followed the women into the room. Lilah beelined for the tarp on the table. Vann grimaced at the mess he had left the bones in, but he rubbed his fingers, remembering that there was a reason they hadn't been organized.

Kaika looked around the room, her gaze lingering on the cracked window, then watched the professor for a moment before shrugging and walking to the wall beside the door. "Guess I'm on lamppost duty for the rest of the night."

The professor—Lilah, Vann decided to call her, if only in his mind, because he didn't want to be reminded of her last name—had already pulled a journal, several tools, and a loupe out of her kit. She hunched over the bones, her back to the doorway, immediately engrossed.

"Just the night?" Vann asked.

"Hm." Kaika considered her charge, who gave no indication that she heard them. "Until she collapses? How long do you figure she'll last?"

Vann's mind went to something that had nothing to do with standing up and looking at bones, and he glared suspiciously at Kaika, suspecting the double entendre, since most of what came out of the woman's mouth was sexual.

"I bet she can go until lunch tomorrow," Kaika said, smiling innocently.

He didn't even remotely believe that innocence, and he kept

his mouth shut, refusing to be drawn in to joking about the woman.

"Though I suppose academics aren't known for their stamina," Kaika went on, her eyes twinkling, clearly not needing help to continue the joke.

Vann was half tempted to defend the professor—and her stamina—especially since she was right there and could hear them, assuming she was paying attention. All he said was, "Zirkander should have sent a more professional bodyguard."

He grabbed a box of matches and walked into the room to light the handful of lanterns sitting on the tables and shelves. The remote outpost wasn't plumbed for gas lighting, so it got quite dark after the sun went down. He didn't know if the professor would be able to continue with her studies, stamina notwithstanding, but he brought the lanterns over to the table and perched them where they might help. He eyed the bones warily, wanting to ask her if magic was something to be expected when it came to dragon remains, but he was reluctant to sound stupid in front of a professor. A year ago, hardly anyone had believed in magic and witches, and he wasn't sure if that had changed outside of the select few who had been dealing with the Cofah sorceress and the handful of dragons that had reappeared in the world.

Lilah looked up when he set a lantern near her, seemed startled to find him there—or maybe to realize that anybody was still in the room—but recovered and smiled. She had a pretty smile, and normally he would have at least nodded in acknowledgment, but he thought of General Zirkander and the way his smiles were always mocking, at least when directed at Vann, so he caught himself staring at the woman as he tried to decipher whether hers was sincere or not. Her expression faltered, and she looked down, determinedly picking up another bone.

He scowled at himself. Glaring at a woman, Vann? Not classy. He groped for a way to apologize without admitting that he had done anything wrong—it wasn't *his* fault that she was related to General Mouthy.

"Do they look normal?" he asked.

She peered up at him, her brow furrowed, and didn't respond right away. It was either a stupid question, or she'd thought their interaction was over. Maybe it ought to be. He couldn't contribute anything here, and he had work to do.

"The bones," he added.

Kaika stood quietly by the door without commenting, as a good bodyguard should, but the way her eyebrows lifted seemed to imply she thought he was being weird. No, he was just curious about the damned bones and whether they were a threat. Maybe he was *slightly* curious about Lilah, too, even if her relationship to Zirkander sounded alarm bells in his brain. He shuddered at the idea of having anything to do with that family. Even if he hadn't loathed Zirkander, one had to consider his witch and that crazy dragon that followed her around.

Still, Lilah was an attractive woman, and undesirable relatives couldn't keep him from noticing that she had lovely curves that the long-sleeve shirt and trousers couldn't entirely hide. She also had full lips and green eyes that contrasted noticeably and appealingly with her thick, reddish-brown hair, hair with a lustrous sheen that made a man want to run his hands through it.

"Actually, they're fossils," Lilah said. "The organic part of the bone, including blood cells, collagen, and fat, broke down long ago—it'll be difficult to determine exactly how long without access to my lab. What remains are minerals that seeped into the inorganic material from what I presume was the sedimentary rock they were found in. So, you see, what we have here is far more rock than bone."

"So are the *rocks* normal?"

Kaika snorted.

"I'm not sure what you mean by normal exactly, Colonel, but I haven't had time to determine much of anything."

Lilah bent back over the bones, and Vann decided that had been a suggestion to leave her alone. Running his hands through her hair wasn't likely to happen. He snorted at himself and walked toward the door, wondering if Bosmont wasn't the only one around here who'd been without female companionship for too long.

"I'll be in my office if she needs anything," Vann told Kaika, whose eyebrows were being entirely too expressive.

"I'll let you know the results of the stamina test," she called after him.

Grumbling again, he strode into his office.

Chapter 4

Lilah finished copying her most important notes onto a fresh piece of paper and pushed her chair back, leaving her journal open on the table so she could come back to it. Morning light streamed through the broken window. Good. Now, she could find someone to take her out to the dig site, where she could investigate more than the fossils. She hadn't gone to bed, having given up on that idea when the sky started to brighten again, but she couldn't imagine napping now, not when such a momentous find might be waiting for her. Besides, at one point when she had dozed off, her arms pillowing her head on the table, she had woken from a dream with a start, her heart racing, memories of being captured and eaten alive by a dragon fresh in her mind. That had dissuaded her from going back to sleep.

Kaika, who had stayed in her spot by the door all night, aside from leaving briefly to find them food and water, stirred and yawned. A couple of times, she'd seemed to be dozing, but if she had been, it had been done standing up.

"Time for some sleep?" she asked.

"Sleep? No, I need to see the dig site."

"Oh. I guess picking out a room was an unnecessary side trip then."

"Perhaps the colonel could assign some of his soldiers to wander around behind me, being bored."

"I wasn't bored last night," Kaika said. "I had my daydreams to keep me entertained."

"Was that before or after you started snoring?" Lilah waved the paper to dry the ink and headed for the door.

"I wasn't snoring. I know I don't do that when I'm standing up. Occasionally, it happens when I fall asleep with my head hanging off the side of the bed, but I think that's understandable."

"Perfectly. Do you know where this Bosmont might be?" Lilah asked. "Is it necessary to bother the colonel? I have some preliminary notes that could go back ahead of me, if a ship is due in soon."

"You may have to bother the colonel either way. He probably keeps Bosmont busy. As I recall from my other stay here, the outpost is perennially short-staffed, so I'm not sure if he'll give up his engineer easily." Kaika yawned. "I'm also quite positive he doesn't have any replacement bodyguards to offer you. Besides, I'm irreplaceable."

"Is that so?"

"Very so."

"Perhaps this Bosmont could just point us in the right direction, and we could find the site on our own. You sound like you could handle thieves if they're out there, and I can take my rifle and handle wild animals." Lilah supposed Kaika could handle wild animals, too, if not with her rifle then with whatever explosive ordnance she carried in that pack.

"That would be fine with me, but we should still check in with Therrik. He's responsible for us, and it wouldn't go well for him if you disappeared and he didn't know what had happened. Or if you disappeared and he *did* know what happened."

"I don't plan to disappear, but even if I did, he shouldn't be held responsible."

"That's not how the army works. If you're the outpost commander, you're responsible for everything that happens on your outpost."

Lilah hesitated, frowning down at her report. Therrik hadn't been rude to her, unless one counted that first exasperated outburst when he'd learned her last name, but she sensed that he didn't care much for her and was probably annoyed to have a scientist roaming around his outpost. He hadn't looked like he'd been enlightened or excited by her explanation of what fossils were, that was for sure. At least she'd kept herself to the *short* explanation, as non-academic people seemed to prefer.

"He seemed to be somewhat interested in the bones—fossils," Kaika said. "He might appreciate your report."

"He seemed *interested?*" Lilah stared at her.

Kaika knew the man better than she did, but Lilah hadn't gotten that impression at all. Mostly, she remembered the way he had glared at her when she'd smiled at him. She had been on the cusp of thanking him for lighting the lanterns, but the glare had made her falter.

"Well, he asked if they were normal."

"That denoted interest? I didn't even know what he meant. What would an abnormal fossil be? I mean, I guess I can think of some scientific examples, but I can't imagine a layperson would have them in mind."

Kaika shrugged. "You've obviously found something." She nodded to the paper. "Let's give him the report and see if he minds if we go out on our own."

"Would you consider going out even if he *did* mind?" Lilah asked, curious whether the bodyguard she had been assigned had instructions to follow her orders or whether she had to obey the outpost commander since he outranked her. She had no idea how special assignments like this worked in the military.

"If it was to save you from risking your life, probably, but listen." Kaika held up a hand to block the doorway, even though Lilah had stopped walking several moments ago. "Don't put me in that position, please. Therrik is all right when you're properly respectful—as long as you don't have any dragon blood in your veins—but sometimes, it's hard to predict how far you can push him. And when he snaps, he's scary ferocious. I don't want to be in front of him if that happens. You asked if Ridge picked me because I can beat him in a fight. Hells, no. He just likes me more than most of his soldiers, so he's less likely to clobber me if I irk him, but I don't go out of my way to irk him."

"You're not making me want to go talk to him," Lilah said, smiling to lighten the tone. Kaika hadn't displayed much of a serious side during the brief time Lilah had known her, so seeing her this way was discomfiting. "But I wouldn't want to cause you to irk him, so I *will* talk to him." She was less willing to dance around the man and worry about being properly respectful, but there was no reason to go out of her way to rile him.

"Good." Kaika extended her hand toward the hallway. "Shall we see if he's in his office this fine morning, or if he's out pummeling some hapless private?"

"Is that actually encouraged in the military?" Lilah stepped into the hallway. Her limited experience with the military came from novels and the handful of chats she'd had with Ridge over the years. She gathered that pilots were in their own special division and perhaps not representative of the common experience. The fictional Commander Asylon also might not be representative of the common experience.

"He usually offers pointers while he's pummeling you. Yes, he likes to take out his aggression in the boxing square, but he genuinely seems to want his soldiers to improve their skills. He's from the old-fashioned school of thought that people best learn to avoid fire by being burned. It's not untrue. It's just..."

"Violent?"

Kaika shrugged and nodded toward the door a few feet away, the one at the end of the hall. Lilah hadn't realized Therrik's office was so close. She bit her lip, wondering if she should have spoken more quietly. If he was in there, would he have heard them talking about him?

Not obviously concerned about this, Kaika knocked on the door.

"What?" came a growl from within.

Lilah wouldn't have considered that an invitation, but Kaika opened the door and strolled in.

"The professor has some preliminary results," she announced.

Therrik stood behind a desk, a pen in one hand and a coffee mug in the other, his jacket on the back of his chair. Once again, he wore the black shirt that so nicely conformed to the powerful muscles of his torso. Lilah reminded herself that he didn't like her and that Kaika's information made that a relief rather than a disappointment. The pen was a poor fit for him. He looked like he should be flipping daggers, perhaps similar to the ones tattooed on his forearms. Seven gods, he looked like a man out of a prison yard, not someone a wholesome and distinguished teacher of students should be eyeballing.

"What is it, Professor?" Therrik asked, his tone not quite as surly.

She jerked her gaze up to his face, realizing that she had been, despite her silent admonitions, staring at his chest.

"I'd like to take a look at the dig site this morning," Lilah said, speaking quickly as if that could distract him from the wandering eyes that she hoped he hadn't noticed.

"I can't spare Bosmont to take you out there today. There was an incident this morning, prisoners attacking soldiers and trying to escape. They managed to break one of the machines that run the tram. I've got Bosmont fixing that. It's a priority, and I get to write a report explaining why two more prisoners are dead." He scowled down at the papers on his desk.

"I understand that you're busy, and I'm sorry to hear about the incident," Lilah said. "Since Captain Bosmont is busy, Captain Kaika and I are prepared to go out on our own, if you'll give us directions."

He frowned at her and then at Kaika, as if this might have been her idea. "I'm not going to have our guest roaming the mountainside without a guide. You've never been outside the fort walls and tunnels, Captain."

"No, sir. The rest of the place was still covered with snow when I was here," Kaika said. "But I'm sure we can make it to the site without running into any trouble we can't handle."

"But not without running into trouble." He snorted. "There may be more thugs wandering around out there trying to steal those bones. Those *fossils*," he corrected, glancing at Lilah. "Wait until tomorrow. Bosmont should be done then."

Should be?

"Colonel," Lilah said, using her firmest, brooking-no-arguments teacher's voice. "I don't plan to spend my entire summer break up here waiting around for men to be available to serve me. Captain Kaika has offered to watch my back while I poke around, and she seems sufficiently capable for the task. We *will* go out to research the site today." She met his gaze, trying not to think about Kaika's comments regarding his temper.

Therrik's eyebrows rose slightly. Captain Kaika stood with her hands clasped behind her back and facing his desk. She didn't argue further on Lilah's behalf, but she didn't deny that she had made the offer.

"Fine, go," Therrik said. "I'll walk you to the end of the valley and show you the trail, such as it is."

Lilah wanted to protest and say that he need not leave his office at all, but there could be dozens of trails out there. It would be best to know for sure which one to head up.

"Thank you, Colonel."

"What's the hurry?" he asked, glancing at the report in Lilah's hand. "You find something that implies a need for urgency?"

She hesitated, remembering the way he had asked if the fossils were *normal*. For some reason, she also thought of her weird dream.

"I don't know about urgency, though I would of course like to complete my studies before more thieves show up, but I did find something potentially interesting. And unique. The bones didn't all come from the same dragon. They're from at least three. Dragons didn't—don't—die that easily. Usually only dragons kill dragons, but even that would be rare. They are the highest-level predator that has ever existed, but there have never been that many of them. We estimate that there were a thousand or less in the world even at the peak of their dissemination across all of the major continents. They also don't seem to have always been here, if that makes sense. Some of my early research focused on trying to find the missing link, as we call it, the evolutionary ancestor to the dragon. I never did find that. Even with modern science and with the world largely explored, it's been rare to find the fossilized remains of dragons. To find three—at least three—in one spot is remarkable and may, indeed, hint of a burial site, but we don't have any prior evidence to suggest that dragons buried their kin in the equivalent of our cemeteries or mass graves."

Lilah paused, noticing Therrik looking at Kaika.

"Was there an answer to my question in there?" he asked her.

"I'm not sure, sir. I don't speak scientist."

"The *urgency* is that this may be a first, historically speaking. I wish to check the site before it's disturbed further. So the results won't be compromised for my paper." Lilah set her report on a mostly bare corner of his desk. "This can go back to... whoever decided to have me brought out here." She didn't want to say Ridge's name, since the merest mention of it irritated Therrik. Besides, she wasn't sure he had been the one ultimately responsible.

"A paper," Therrik said. "Ah."

She looked at his face, trying to determine if she was being mocked. These things sometimes went over her head. He hadn't joined in with Kaika the evening before in making jokes about her stamina, but she didn't know if that meant much.

"Let me be blunt, Professor," Therrik said. "All I need to know is if the fossils can be moved so my people can continue mining into the front of the mountain, which will apparently be a much more direct ingress point into the old witch stronghold than where we've been digging." He waved toward the courtyard and perhaps the tram cars. "I also need to know if the miners would be in danger at all."

"Danger? From fossils? I can't imagine how they would be dangerous."

He hesitated, then bunched his shoulders and said, "They're not magical?"

"Magical? Fossils?"

"*Dragon* fossils. Dragons are magical, right? Not long ago, we had Cofah aircraft attacking the continent, and those aircraft were powered by dragon blood."

"Oh." Lilah hadn't heard anything about that, and it surprised her. She wasn't one of those scientists to completely disregard the idea of magic and to say it didn't exist, but she had also never encountered it. Certainly not in the fossil record. "If any of the dragon-related fossils I've looked at retained some degree of... magickness, I was never aware of it. I don't know how you would tell."

"My fingers tingled when I held one of those bones," Therrik said.

Lilah shook her head. She hadn't experienced any tingling.

"Does... that sort of thing run in your family?" She hesitated to ask if he had ancestors with mysterious gifts, since that was grounds for hanging or drowning in rural areas of the country.

"*What* sort of thing?" he asked, his voice taking on that growl again, and his eyes closing to slits.

"Being able to sense magic. Or—" She wriggled her fingers, not wanting to come outright and say *perform* magic.

"*No*," he said—almost snarled, clenching his fists. "There aren't any witches in *my* ancestry." The pen in his hand snapped, and he cursed, ink smudged all over his fingers.

Kaika shifted her weight.

By the time Therrik picked up the pen, tossed it in the trash bin, and found a handkerchief to wipe his hands, the fury had faded from his face. "Something about those bones is odd," he said calmly, meeting her eyes. "It's *not* me."

"I'd like to see some more reports on dragon blood before accepting that dragon anatomy is inherently magical—I'd always assumed the feats they're able to perform were a mental ability rather than anything integrated in their physical bodies. Even if their blood and bones had some magical element to them, I find it unlikely that it's something that could be retained in fossil form. Not only do fossils take a minimum of ten thousand years to form, but as I said yesterday, little of the original bone remains." She pointed over her shoulder toward the artifact room. "Those are essentially rocks at this point. I—"

A crash came from somewhere outside of the room. Kaika whirled toward the door, her hand dropping to her pistol. Therrik vaulted around the desk and charged past them and into the hallway. He turned straight for the artifact room, as if he knew that the noise had originated from there. Maybe he had better ears than Lilah had.

Therrik cursed. Lilah started after him, but Kaika held her back with a hand and went first. She peered down the hallway—it was empty—then entered the artifact room. Flapping noises came from within, and Lilah refused to remain out of the way. She trotted to the doorway and peeked inside.

A broken lantern lay on a rug at the base of the table where she had been working. Therrik had removed his shirt and already smothered the flames, though the rug smoldered, smoke wafting into the air. He picked up the cracked lantern and frowned over at Lilah.

"Sorry," Lilah murmured. "I should have cut it out when it got light. I didn't move any of the lanterns, though. That was left where you placed it last night. I don't know how it could have fallen."

Therrik glanced toward the window, toward a crack in one of the panes. "Because odd things are happening around these bones." He set the doused lantern on the table. "Come with me, will you? I want to show you my sword."

Kaika snorted. "Do you think that's appropriate, sir? You've barely known her a day."

"Funny, Captain," Therrik growled, striding toward the hallway.

"Just noticing that you've managed to have your shirt off a lot around her," she called after him.

"I thought you tried not to irk him," Lilah said, passing Kaika and following Therrik down the hallway. He took the stairs several at a time, quickly descending out of sight.

"Sometimes, I can't help myself. It's a flaw." One she did not regret much, judging by the smirk.

Lilah hurried to catch up with Therrik since she didn't know where his room was. Or where the armory was. Maybe that was the place one stored one's sword.

He waited at the bottom of the stairs, then led her toward the same hallway where Kaika and Lilah had claimed a room. He chose a door at the end that was not locked. He stepped inside, revealing not an armory but a bedroom, this one with a single bunk larger than the ones in the guest quarters. He opened the shutters on the window, and daylight flowed inside, brightening a dresser identical to the one in her room, a wooden chest at the base of the bed, and a few shelves on one wall. A couple of small framed portraits rested there, though Lilah's eye was drawn to the wall next to the bed where several weapons hung: an intricately made Cofah scimitar from the Rogavian Dynasty, a morning star that had to be close to a thousand years old, and an early muzzle-loading rifle with a silver inlay etched with a dragon's tail sweeping in and around it.

Lilah stepped closer to the weapons while Therrik tossed the shirt he'd used on the lantern into a bin and opened a drawer to pull out a new one. There was only one sword. The scimitar was handsome, a work of art even, but she couldn't imagine what it had to do with dragon fossils.

"Not that," Therrik said, tugging his shirt over his head.

Lilah stole a glance at the ridges of his abdomen before he pulled the hem down. He didn't seem to notice. He dropped to his knees and looked under the bed.

"Is this a King Menotok morning star?" Lilah asked. "It's too old to be a replica." She touched one of the spikes on the head of the weapon. "You can tell from the way these were attached, and the handle is tiger wood from the Zangier Islands. We were fighting a war during his reign and occupied the northern islands, so it was popular to get wood from there and incorporate it into the weaponry. Of course, the Cofah took those islands from us nine hundred years ago when they invaded the continent and drove us back to these very mountains."

Therrik had pulled a wooden box out from under the bed, but paused to stare up at her while she spoke.

"Sorry," she said, remembering that he hadn't been impressed with her explanation of fossils. "I have a tendency to fall into teacher mode, whether it's welcome or not. It's odd, really, when you consider how little I actually enjoy teaching. I much prefer my lab and my books. And my old dead things, as my friend Tatia calls them. She's a humanities professor." She clamped her mouth shut, realizing that she was babbling and also that Therrik was still on one knee and staring up at her. Gaping, almost.

"You know about weapons," he stated. He wasn't exactly incredulous, but he did sound surprised.

"Historical ones, yes. I took all manner of history classes while pursuing my degree. And, uhm, some that I didn't need for my degree. It took seven years for me to finish my studies, since I had eclectic interests and didn't decide on paleontology right away."

Therrik rose to his feet, removed the morning star from the wall, and handed it to her. "This one isn't just from the Menotok reign; it belonged to King Menotok himself. There was a Lord Knight Therrik who fought at his side. He died trying to repel the Cofah invaders and saving the king's life. Menotok had his favorite weapon sent to the knight's son as a thank you. It's been in my family for centuries."

"The craftsmanship is lovely." Lilah slid her hand along the smooth tiger wood, the exotic grain still vibrant after all these years. It had been well cared for.

Therrik grew still, watching her hand, and she stopped, feeling self-conscious. And also aware of his closeness.

He shrugged and picked up the case. "It cracks skulls open well too."

"Functionality is important, I understand." She returned it to the wall. "Are you also related to Piontor Therrik, the dragon slayer from the Third Century Before Dominion?"

"Another ancestor, yes." Therrik unclasped the lid on the box, but not before she glimpsed the symbols carved on the top—words in Old Iskandian and also in Middle Dragon Script. That would make the case even older than the morning star. "If having noble blood still meant anything, I'd be serving at the king's side right now, instead of being here." He jerked his chin toward the window. "These days, anyone can become an officer, and the journalists are far more likely to fawn over some impoverished common fop who scrapes his way through the academy."

"To become a famous pilot?" Lilah asked, more amused than offended. She had several colleagues with titles that didn't mean much anymore, and they, too, were often bitter about the way their family's influence had eroded over the past couple of generations.

Therrik had the grace to look a little sheepish as he glanced at her, probably realizing that she must have the same roots as Ridge.

"An *infamous* pilot, I'd say. Here's my sword." He flipped open the lid to the case, glancing toward the doorway as he said sword. Kaika hadn't come in, but her sleeve was visible as she stood guard in the hallway.

She poked her head into the room, but not to make jokes about his weapon. "Sir, do you smell that? Seems like something might be burning out in the courtyard, and it's gotten quiet. I'm going to check on it."

"Good," Therrik said, waving for her to go.

Her eyebrows twitched upward, but she did not comment further. She trotted out of sight.

Lilah looked down at the sword nestled within a velvet-covered cutout. It wasn't as aesthetically appealing as the weapons on the wall, but its craftsmanship was amazing. She ran a finger along the sleek side of the blade, the smoothness broken by more Old Iskandian and Middle Dragon Script engraved in the steel. Yes, steel. Even though it had to be at least two thousand years old, dating back to the era when smiths had made steel more by intuition than through any scientific understanding of the amounts of iron alloy and carbon needed, it was a perfect example.

"You're able to touch it," he said, his voice coming from deep in his chest. It sounded like a rumble of approval.

"Yes... Can't you?"

"Witches can't. It zaps them. It glows when it's around them or when it's around dragons. It glows faintly around the fossils. That's what I wanted to show you. When I had it up in the artifact room, the sword made me want to destroy them, the same way it makes me want to destroy witches and dragons."

She almost snorted at the idea of a sword having some kind of sentience, but she held it back. His face was utterly serious. Serious, but not as fearsome as it had been when they first met. The notion flashed through her mind that maybe he *was* a Commander Asylon, gruff and dangerous on the surface, but an honorable and loyal comrade underneath it all. She'd always found Asylon to be the most appealing of the characters in the series. All right, *more* than appealing. Even if it was silly to daydream about a fictional hero.

"I'm glad you're not a witch." He sounded genuinely relieved, as if that had been a likely possibility.

"I told you we don't have any witches in the family. It's an impressive blade." Lilah lifted her hand from the engravings.

"I had that translated," Therrik said, surprising her by how close he was standing. His chest brushed her shoulder as he pointed at the symbols. "It's supposed to be a warning to dragons that the sword is prepared to kill them."

"I'll take your word for it. I recognize the language, but I'm not a philologist. I could make a rubbing and take it to a friend to verify it if you're curious."

"I'd like that," he said, his gaze shifting from the blade to her face. "Its name is Kasandral. I used it to kill a sorceress that was trying to kill the king. It can cut through magical defenses."

His eyes were intense, and she could feel the heat from his body. It occurred to her that his opinion of her, whatever it had been before, might have changed when she'd shown some interest in his weapons. She should probably step back and ask why he'd brought her down here instead of retrieving the sword by himself. She doubted he'd had anything salacious in mind, even if he was still gazing at her, his intensity somewhere between alarming and appealing. She couldn't bring herself to move back. If anything, she found herself wondering what it would be like to touch someone with a body like that. Her husband had been as much of an academic as she, and her best friend in every way, but he hadn't been someone who hurled weapons—or soldiers—around to improve his musculature. Before that... well, she'd not crossed paths with many military men during her academic studies.

Still, Kaika's warnings about his temper flitted through her mind, and she'd already seen for herself that he had a rough demeanor. She couldn't imagine what he'd be like in a relationship. Those moods would be abysmal to deal with on a day-to-day basis. Of course, it wasn't as if people didn't have sex just for the sake of having sex, without thoughts of long-term dealings in mind. *She* wasn't typically one of those people. She tended to think things through, imagine consequences and repercussions, rather than simply reacting on instinct. And in her youth, she'd spent so much time rebuffing men that it had become a reflex. Few eligible colleagues even approached her anymore.

"I'll take you out to the dig site," Therrik murmured, his chest brushing her again. This time, it did more than brush—it stayed there, pressed against her shoulder.

"Today?" she whispered, shifting toward him, drawn closer even as her mind told her to step back, that he should be avoided.

"Today," he agreed, his hand coming to rest on her waist.

She felt the heat of it through her shirt, heat that flared through her entire body. His head lowered, his lips parting, and she rose on her tiptoes, leaning against his chest in order to reach those lips. It was like leaning against a statue chiseled from marble, but much warmer than cold stone. Much more alluring.

A hair's breadth before their lips met, a shout came from the courtyard. Was that Captain Kaika?

Therrik jerked away from Lilah, releasing her and racing for the door. He grabbed a rifle that leaned against the wall next to it, then disappeared into the hallway.

The air around her seemed terribly cool after his departure. Disappointingly so. She shook away the memory of his warmth, telling herself that she barely knew him and that what she knew wasn't heartening. It was a relief that they'd stopped, that they'd *been* stopped.

Reminded that some trouble might be approaching, Lilah peered into the hallway. A few soldiers ran past, not sparing her a glance. Should she remain in the room? After the last of the soldiers passed, she decided to return to her quarters and grab her hunting rifle. Just in case.

Before she had taken more than a step into the hallway, a boom came from somewhere outside. At least, she *thought* it came from outside. Tiles trembled beneath her feet, and something crashed to the floor in a nearby room. More shouts came from outside. Had they been attacked? And if so, by whom? Some enemy from the outside? Or prisoners trying to escape?

A loud clang came from the courtyard, followed by more shouts. Whatever was happening, it wasn't good.

As soon as the floor stopped trembling, Lilah ran to her room, grabbed her rifle, loaded it, and trotted for the front door. She did not rush out, since she wasn't a soldier, and both Therrik and Kaika would berate her if she needlessly put herself in harm's way, but she wanted to see what was going on. She pushed the door open with her shoulder while keeping her rifle in her hands, and she peered into the courtyard.

Smoke roiled from a nearby building, one that was now

missing a wall, the wooden boards torn—or *blown*—out. Kaika crouched at the corner, peering into the dark hole. With the smoke flowing heartily out, Lilah couldn't tell what that building was for or what might be stored inside—fortunately, it did not look like a barracks. She hoped people hadn't been caught in the explosion. Bits of wood and cardboard and warped metal lay in the dirt outside. She thought she spotted the casings of rifle cartridges gleaming in the sunlight too. Soldiers raced about, several securing a set of tram doors. Another set stood open, and men scampered out of a tram car, dirty men in torn and faded clothing. A soldier fired a rifle over their heads, but they did not stop. They ran toward the outpost's exit across the courtyard.

"You try it, and you die," came Therrik's hard voice from somewhere beyond the smoke.

Lilah couldn't see him from her position. She eased away from the doorway and headed toward the corner of the building, keeping her back to the wall. She wouldn't go far, but she wanted to know if Therrik was in trouble. Only Kaika was braving the smoke—she'd risen from her crouch and stepped inside the damaged structure, using the gaping hole as a doorway.

When Lilah reached the corner of the headquarters building, Therrik came into view. He stood in front of the double doors of the outpost. Those big iron-bound oak doors were closed, but a group of eight miners approached him. They carried improvised clubs, pickaxes, and shovels, gripping them with white-knuckled fists as they shared nervous glances.

A fight had broken out at the entrance to one of the other mine shafts, men surging out from the doors before they were fully closed. The soldiers in the courtyard turned to deal with them first. Up on the wall, more soldiers ran toward the exit and pointed their rifles at the pack of prisoners approaching Therrik. Lilah rubbed the stock of her weapon. Should she aim to protect him too? This wasn't her fight, and he might not appreciate a civilian jumping in to help.

"Sir?" one called down. "Do we shoot?"

Therrik glared at the miners, his rifle in hand but still down at his waist. He raised a staying hand toward the men on the wall without taking his gaze from the crowd. "Turn around, you fools. You're not getting out of here alive."

Someone fired from one of the buildings near the agitated pack of men. It was as if that had been a starter's pistol, sending runners leaping into action. The men charged toward Therrik.

Lilah stepped away from the building and lifted her rifle, aiming for a man's thigh. Before she could squeeze the trigger, a hand clamped onto her shoulder.

"Look, a civilian," the person behind her blurted.

"Get her. We'll use her as a shield."

Even as they spoke, Lilah lunged forward and swung her rifle around. The wild-haired man standing behind her released her shoulder, but he caught her weapon in mid-air, a calloused hand wrapping around the barrel.

"Don't let her get away, Bremmy," a smaller man behind him ordered.

Lilah couldn't shoot with the brute holding the rifle barrel, but she tugged at it to get his attention focused on it, then lunged in and stomped on his instep. He yelped in surprise, releasing the rifle. Lilah spun it around and clubbed him in the side of the head. The second man ran forward, and she scrambled backward, spotting a knife in his hand. She didn't know if he meant to use it on her or just scare her, but his eyes seemed crazy—desperate—and fear for her life surged through her. She started to raise her rifle, but her heel caught on some debris from the explosion, and she tumbled backward before she could catch her balance.

She landed hard on her back, but she didn't let go of her rifle. The man leaped after her, that knife raised. From the ground, she fired straight at his chest. He was leaping through the air, and she thought her shot struck, but that did nothing to still his momentum. She flung herself sideways, rolling away. He hit the ground inches away from her, dust springing into the air.

Not certain what had happened to the other man, but positive that clubbing him in the head hadn't stopped him, she scrambled to her feet. The big man was less than three feet away. He snarled and lunged for her.

As she whipped her rifle up, pulling the lever to chamber the next round, she knew she would be too late, that he would grab her first. Then something akin to a tornado slammed into the man from the side, amid a roar of fury. The miner was lifted off his feet and hurled against the stone wall of the building. Therrik came right behind him, like a battering ram. The miner was almost as big as he was, but his attempts to punch back were smashed aside. Therrik slammed the man against the wall several times, until his eyes rolled back into his head. Therrik dropped him and spun toward Lilah.

Rage curled his lips, and she stepped back, but he only glanced at her in his scan of the area. A pile of miners lay crumpled in front of the oak courtyard doors. None of the men had come close to opening them and escaping. Lilah couldn't tell if they were dead or unconscious. Elsewhere, soldiers had captured the other miners, forcing them to kneel with rifles pointed at their backs.

"Captain Kaika," Therrik roared.

After a moment, Kaika stepped out of the still-smoking hole in the building, soot smearing her hands and one of her cheeks. "Sir?"

"What is this?" Therrik pointed at Lilah.

"Ah, that's a professor, sir."

"Aren't you supposed to be *guarding* her?"

Kaika grimaced. "Yes, sir, but I figured you'd want to know about the explosion, and I also thought she would stay inside and admire your sword."

The excuse only seemed to enrage Therrik further. Blood rushed to his face, and he clenched a fist. Hells, this wasn't Kaika's fault. Lilah *should* have stayed inside. She groped for something soothing to say that might calm him down.

"Get over here and stay with her, and do your damned duty before I—"

"Colonel Therrik," Lilah said, speaking loudly and firmly enough that she hoped it would cut over his words. Unfortunately, because of her residual fear or just because the teacher in her wasn't good at soothing or cajoling, her words came out sterner than she intended. "I appreciate your help with those two men.

Captain Kaika is correct in that I should have remained where I was. This isn't her fault." She spread her hand toward the man she'd shot, a man who wasn't, she noted with a queasy sensation in her stomach, moving. Had she killed him? Seven gods, she'd only meant to defend herself. She wasn't a soldier. She wasn't supposed to kill people. Hunting was one thing, but this was... She shook her head and rubbed her fingers, as if there was blood on her hand that she might wipe off.

"Are you all right?" Therrik asked brusquely. He winced as soon as the words came out. Maybe he wasn't good at soothing tones, either.

"I'm uninjured." Lilah wasn't sure she could claim to be "all right," but she would consider her mental state later, in private.

"Sorry, Professor," Kaika said, stepping around the dead man to join her. "I shouldn't have left you. I didn't know you'd get bored with the colonel's sword so quickly."

"Can you say anything that isn't sexual?" Therrik snapped. He still sounded irritated, but he'd lost that alarming enraged edge.

"I can, but how would that be fun?" Kaika patted Lilah on the shoulder, and despite her irreverent mouth, Lilah had the impression that she was genuinely sorry.

"Sir?" a young soldier asked, walking up and saluting. "We've subdued all of the troublemakers. Should there be any punishment or extra duty for the ones who survived?"

"Surviving and being stuck here is punishment enough," Therrik grumbled, waving the man away. "Clean up the mess, send the injured ones to the doctor, and put the rest back to work."

"Yes, sir."

"Captain Kaika, did you discover who lit that explosive?"

"I discovered... something." Kaika nodded toward the building. "Will you follow me, sir?"

Therrik followed her, and Lilah followed him. He glanced back but did not object to her trailing along. How could he? Her bodyguard was leading the way, and he had already berated Kaika for being separated from Lilah.

The building turned out to be an armory. Instead of leading them through the new hole in the wall, Kaika took them through a front door, down a short hall, and to an iron door with thick rivets running along the frame. She tugged at the handle, but it did not budge.

"You'll note it's locked," Kaika told Therrik.

"There are only four of us with keys." Therrik pulled a ring out of his pocket and held it up.

"You and three trusted officers, I presume?"

"Yes."

"Then only you and those three officers could have entered the armory."

Therrik nodded. "Everything's been reinforced and made more secure since the rebuilding." He stuck the appropriate key in the lock, but paused before turning it, perhaps realizing Kaika was staring steadily at him. "You're saying that nobody walked in there to detonate a charge, unless Kanz, Sayormoon, or Bridge did it."

"Or you, sir. Even if one of the others did, he would have needed to use a delayed fuse, left, locked the door again, and then disappeared before it went off. Possible but..."

"Why would one of our people do it?"

"Exactly, sir."

Therrik pulled open the door while Lilah debated the ramifications. Did that mean they believed some weapon had exploded of its own accord? Spontaneous combustion? She'd heard of such things with grain silos, but with military armories? Surely, weapons and explosives were stored with the utmost care.

Lilah paused inside the doorway while the other two went to explore. Plenty of light came in through the hole, but that wouldn't usually be the case, since there were no windows on that or any other wall. The locked door should have been the only way into the room.

Captain Kaika murmured to Therrik, pointing to shelves and crates, some damaged and some not. Lilah had nothing to add since she had no experience with explosives, other than fireworks and primitive charges made with gunpowder. And most of her experience with *those* was through books. Still, the two officers circled back and faced her expectantly.

"Yes?" she asked.

"Kaika has convinced me that this just *happened*," Therrik said, "much like the lantern falling and the window breaking in the artifact room."

Lilah looked back and forth between the two of them. "Are you suggesting that the *fossils* have something to do with this?"

"These strange occurrences started happening yesterday, after I returned with them. Lieutenant Kraden claims the radio hasn't been working since the fossils were originally unearthed out on the mountainside."

"I don't know what to say. We have fossils at the university. Nothing has ever exploded or broken in their presence."

"In retrospect, perhaps Sardelle would have been the better expert to bring out here," Kaika mused.

Lilah flushed at this insinuation that she couldn't handle this problem, if there *was* a problem. She wasn't convinced that these mishaps had anything to do with the fossils.

"We're going out to the dig site," Therrik said, "and we're going to figure out what's going on. Right after I wrap those bones up and hang them in the middle of the forest, far away from the outpost walls."

He stalked out of the room without so much as a glance at Lilah. She tried not to feel as if she had disappointed him by not having the answers he wanted.

Chapter 5

VANN TOOK THE LEAD ON the way to the dig site, with Kaika, Lilah, and Captain Bosmont trailing behind him, everyone armed and carrying a pack of supplies that would let them stay out there for a few days, if needed. He had work to do back at the outpost, but he'd elevated this new... *situation* to priority status. He wasn't superstitious, and he didn't believe in curses, but it was hard not to see a connection between the arrival of the bones and the incidents in the fort.

That damned explosion... Kaika had pointed to the remains of a keg of gunpowder, the circle of soot burned into the cement floor all that remained of the receptacle itself. They had been lucky, extremely lucky, that the explosion hadn't reached the crates of dynamite on the other side of the room. If that had happened, the entire outpost might have been blown up, not just the wall of a building.

He glanced back at the people following him, Lilah in particular. She hadn't spoken much since she'd shot that man, and he didn't know if that had distressed her or if she should be resting. Killing had never bothered *him*, but he'd been told by more than one woman that he wasn't normal, and that such a reaction wasn't desirable.

He felt a little proud that Lilah had fought off her attackers— he suspected she would have thwarted the second one without his help, had he not been able to finish dealing with the miners trying to get past him to escape. He hadn't expected a civilian woman to be able to handle herself against criminals willing to do anything to anyone to escape. He was pleased that she had, much as he'd been pleased that she knew her historical weapons. Admittedly, he'd been a little too pleased at that, letting his body respond in a way that he shouldn't have. Had he truly been thinking of kissing her? He couldn't imagine that she would want that. Hadn't she mentioned a husband? Seven gods, what would she say when she returned home? She would probably tell her husband and her cousin that Vann had plied her with unwanted affections. Zirkander would share that information with his chain of command, and Vann might very well end up stuck out here for the rest of his career.

He grumbled, reminding himself that there were dangers out here and that he had better stay focused on his surroundings. He was not going to give his superiors or the king reason to keep him out here any longer than necessary. Lilah was off limits.

The forest grew quiet as they came within a mile of the dig site, and Vann paused to listen, remembering that the same thing had happened at about this spot when he and Bosmont had come out. That time, he'd assumed the birds were disturbed by the mining. This time, he did not hear any scrapes or voices drifting down the trail. Some predator might have caused the stilling of the forest, but he doubted it. All he could make out was the distant chatter of a creek somewhere down the slope from them.

"It's still another mile or so," Captain Bosmont said, coming up behind him.

"I'm aware of that."

A rock shifted under Lilah's foot as she approached, and she flailed for balance. She had already found that balance when Bosmont reached out, catching her arm.

"Careful, ma'am," he said, smiling warmly at her.

Vann felt his eyes narrow to slits. She had been perfectly capable of navigating the slip by herself. She did not need Bosmont grabbing her arm, especially since he hadn't let go of her arm yet.

"No railings out here on this trail," he added.

"I'm fine." Lilah looked down at his hand, hopefully implying that she didn't want it there. "I've been over rougher terrain than this plenty of times." She nodded to Vann. "It got quiet all of a sudden, didn't it?"

He nodded, pleased that she'd noticed.

"Is there a lot of rough terrain at a university?" Bosmont let go of her arm, but he looked like he hadn't wanted to. Vann recalled his complaints about how long it had been since he had shared a bunk with a woman. Lilah, with her appealing curves, would be tempting even to a man who had access to frequent bed partners.

"No, but my husband and I used to go on safaris in the south every summer. We did some mountain climbing, now and then. Mastmonsoro is down there, a big extinct volcano with a miles-wide grassy caldera where many types of animals evolved independently of the surrounding ecosystem. It's amazing."

"Husband?" Bosmont mumbled, his shoulders slumping.

She pursed her lips and turned toward Vann instead of answering the question. "Do you suspect there's something dangerous out there?"

"We'll see," he said, starting up the trail again.

He didn't want to mention magic or curses again. He'd already felt foolish admitting that he believed something otherworldly was going on back in the outpost. As a scientist, Lilah probably thought it silly to jump to conclusions without evidence. Even if she was married and he definitely wasn't going to pursue anything physical with her, he did not want her to think him silly.

The forest remained silent as they drew closer to the dig site, the only sounds their own footsteps on the rocky trail and the breeze occasionally stirring the branches.

"They're being awfully quiet," Bosmont said.

"Who?" Vann asked.

"The men I sent out here last night."

Vann halted. "What? I didn't think Lieutenant Kraden had gotten a team together yet."

He could just make out the cliff through the trees, and if anyone had been digging, he would have seen them.

"Lieutenant Kraden mentioned his problems, and I took it over myself, sir. I thought posting some guards was a good idea, since I have a bunch of equipment out here. Might not be as portable as fossils, but it's worth a lot, and I wouldn't want it vandalized on account of those thieves feeling vengeful." Bosmont looked at Vann but was bright enough not to point out that Vann's rough treatment of the thieves might have caused them to feel vengeful. Thieves deserved rough treatment, especially when they threw dynamite at military officers.

"Who did you send?" Vann asked.

"Corporal Savit and a couple of privates. They liked the idea of camping out and escaping the outpost for a couple of days."

Camping out? That wasn't quite what Vann had been thinking when it came to finding people. He would have grumbled to himself, but he continued forward instead, an uneasy feeling spreading through him. If there were three men out here, he ought to hear signs of some activity.

When he entered the cleared area next to the cliff, pickaxes and shovels lay on the ground where the thieves had left them, and it did not appear that anyone had been out here since the morning before. He peered into the recently started tunnel, which was deeper than he realized, but he could see to the end, and there wasn't anyone inside, nor did he spot anyone around the equipment or the clearing. He walked until he could see the creek meandering through the trees at the bottom of the slope. That area, too, was devoid of life. The entire forest stood quiet, uncomfortably still.

Lilah stepped past Kaika and Bosmont and headed straight to the dragon skull lodged in the cliff.

Kaika elbowed Bosmont. "The men you ordered to come out here... Did they *know* they'd been sent out?"

"I didn't actually see them walk out the gate." Bosmont propped a fist on his hip as he gazed around the clearing. "I suppose it's possible someone waylaid them and put them on some other task."

Vann continued to walk around, this time looking for less obvious signs of disturbance.

"No, they were here last night." He stopped beside a log and picked up an empty tin from one of the prepackaged army food packs. "Someone enjoyed some sardines."

"I don't think anyone *enjoys* sardines, sir," Kaika said.

"That might have been out here before," Bosmont said, waving at the tin. "My team had lunch here on the day we were moving the equipment out. Told everyone to clean up after themselves, but you know how privates are. Might have left a wrapper or two."

"And did they also leave a uniform jacket or two?" Vann strode farther down the slope and plucked up a jacket draped in the shade on another log. He had missed it on his first perusal of the area.

"Ah, that would be less likely."

"Savit," Vann read off the nametag.

If something odd had happened out here, caused by the magic in the fossils still in the rocks, then maybe the men had been spooked and fled. But if so, why wouldn't they have fled back to the outpost? Why run off into the woods?

Vann tossed the jacket back onto the log and debated whether he wanted to start looking for tracks and try to discover where the men had gone. Since the thieves had run off just the day before, it might be hard to distinguish the soldiers' tracks from those of the others. He decided to see if Lilah needed anything first. Most likely, he wouldn't be of any use with the fossils, so he could search once she started working. Currently, she was standing in front of the cliff, staring up at the dragon skull.

"This place feels creepy," Kaika said, gazing out at the mountains rather than at the cliff. "It's too quiet out here."

Vann walked past her to stand beside Lilah, wondering why she wasn't moving. He had expected her to throw open her toolbox and spring into action, hacking bones out of the rocks.

"Problem?" he asked quietly.

"A perplexing one, yes," she said not taking her gaze from the cliff, though she looked up and down and from side to side along the rock.

"Explain?" Vann eyed the dragon skull, not caring for the way it seemed to leer out at them. The thieves had already carved it halfway out of the rock, giving it an ominous and lifelike aspect.

"I'm impressed that your looters managed to pry any fossils out of this rock at all, because this, my brawny friend, is granite." Lilah rested her palm on the rock and faced him.

For a few seconds, he was too busy being simultaneously pleased that she had noticed his brawn and disappointed that she'd chosen the word friend for him. Still, it was less formal than colonel. Maybe he should invite her to call him Vann. No, he had better not invite familiarity.

She was looking at him as if waiting for him to figure something out or to nod sagely in agreement.

"Granite is hard," he hazarded.

"Yes. It's also not a rock in which you ever find fossils. Granite is formed when molten masses cool off, molten masses underneath the earth's surface where living things aren't present. Even if they were, the conditions would destroy any organic matter."

"Oh?" Vann eyed the dragon skull again.

"Either the fossils are fake, which would surprise me since I had a good look at them under magnification, or..." She looked at the rock in puzzlement.

"Or?"

"Or someone stuck them in here, and no, I have absolutely no idea how that could be done." She ran her hand along the lumpy surface of the cliff. "There are some cracks here and there, but it doesn't look like the rock was previously broken and then stuck back together with the fossils inside. I can't even imagine how much effort that would require or who would bother making that effort. What would be the point? To flummox your soldiers? To make you do exactly what you did? Stop digging in the area and call a scientist in? If so, to what end? Even one of my students could have identified granite and known this was an improbable if not impossible scenario." She thumped her palm against the hard rock. "If you've ever dreamed of seeing a paleontologist stymied, you can now say that you've seen it."

"Paleontologists rarely feature in my dreams," Kaika said, her thumbs hooked into her utility belt as she ambled up beside them. "You, sir?"

"Not until recently," Vann murmured, then glanced at Lilah and was relieved that she appeared too lost in thought to notice his words. "Bosmont, how come you didn't know this was granite?"

"I knew it was granite, sir," the engineer said, walking over to rap his knuckles against the hard rock. "Didn't know about the rest of the special science-y stuff."

"The fossils themselves are still of interest," Lilah said, "but I'm disappointed because it's quite unlikely that this is a dragon burial ground. It seems more plausible that someone robbed a museum, grabbing all the fossils from a collection that was composed of past finds and then brought them here and..." She frowned at the granite. "I still have no idea how they could have been embedded, and so seamlessly at that." She slid her finger along the top of the skull where it lay nestled perfectly into the cliff.

"Magic," Vann grumbled.

She looked skeptically at him.

"Makes sense to me," Kaika said. "I've seen dragons hurl fire, and I've seen Sardelle's sword melt rock. What if someone used magic, hot magic, to melt the granite, the way you were saying happened underground, Professor, and then thrust the fossils in when the stuff got cool enough but before it hardened all the way?"

Lilah's lip curled up in an expression of further skepticism. "I think this rock would look different if it had been formed a couple of weeks ago." She walked a few paces down the cliff, then climbed up to a small ledge, where she plucked up a chunk of moss growing out of the dirt. "Can dragons also cause dirt to form in crevices and make things grow?"

"Uhm, maybe?" Kaika shrugged. "Maybe it's been longer than two weeks. Sir, maybe you should send a report back and see if Sardelle can come out here. Or her dragon, Bhrava Saruth."

"That dragon is *weird*. I'm not inviting it anywhere."

"But I bet he'd be the one to let us know if this was possible and if it had been done."

"You just want your chance to lure him into bed," Vann grumbled.

Kaika grinned. "He *does* seem to be the most likely dragon for that."

Lilah stared over at them as she climbed down, her expression quite bemused. Vann reminded himself that most of the population was only vaguely aware that dragons had returned to the world. A few months ago, he also would have found this conversation strange. He *still* found it strange.

"The next supply ship isn't due until next week," Vann said. "That's the soonest I can send back a request for help, unless Lieutenant Kraden gets that radio working."

Bosmont scratched his jaw. "I still wonder if some of our problems with that might have to do with these bones being unearthed."

When the lieutenant had shared Bosmont's hypothesis with him back at the office, Vann's first inclination had been to dismiss it, but what did he know? "So far, strange things have only been happening in proximity to the fossils. The radio tower is over five miles away."

"We don't know what all is behind that rock," Kaika said. "There could be a higher concentration of bones here. Maybe there's more magic and it can affect equipment that far away."

"I'd like to reiterate," Lilah said, "that, as far as I've seen in my years of research, fossils of dragon bones aren't magical. Or cursed. There's an entire skeleton assembled at the First Age Museum in the capital, and strange things don't happen there. Every day, children wander up and touch the fossils."

Vann sighed. "I hate to admit it, but we do need someone with knowledge of magic out here."

Kaika smiled.

"Sardelle. Not the damned dragon."

"You're crushing my dreams, sir."

"I thought you wanted to share those dreams with Angulus. Wouldn't he be disappointed if he didn't get to watch?"

Lilah's eyebrows arched to her hairline at the name. Vann supposed Kaika's relationship with the king was a secret, but it wasn't as if Kaika was the most discreet person. *He* knew about it, after all.

"Guess I'll have to invite Bhrava Saruth to the castle for tea someday," Kaika said. "Once construction finishes."

"I hate magic," Vann grumbled as he turned his consideration to the rock again. Was it possible these bones were close enough to affect the outpost? "If someone put these fossils in here to keep us from drilling into the mountain, then I want them out, and I want to know what's behind this cliff."

"Getting the fossils out of solid granite without damaging them will be difficult," Lilah said. "The thieves were probably working at this for some time."

"There wasn't any sign of the thieves when I first brought the equipment out, and my team started digging a little under two weeks ago." Bosmont walked to the cliff and patted some of the spots where rock had recently been sheered away. "It's amazing they got so many fossils out in such a short time."

"Perhaps those fossils were placed near the surface so they would be easy to discover," Lilah said.

"And so their magic would ooze out and affect my outpost?" Vann sneered.

Lilah looked toward the ledge where she had plucked out the piece of moss, but she did not say anything.

"If you just want the fossils gone, I imagine we could handle that." Kaika smiled and patted the rock.

"By blowing them up along with the rock?" Vann asked.

Lilah's eyes bulged in horror. "You can't blow up the fossils. If these were stolen from a museum collection, that museum will want them back. Even if they weren't stolen, they're historically significant. They should be studied, magical attributes or not."

"Yes, and I don't need a museum railing at the army over this, especially not when I'm the outpost commander here." Vann lowered his voice and shook his head. "I'm never going to get promoted as long as there's magic in my world." He could already foresee getting in trouble for what had transpired thus far, especially if something had happened to those three soldiers. He needed to resolve this, or at least get his people working on a solution, so he could go look for the men.

"Didn't know that was an aspiration of yours, sir," Bosmont said.

"Isn't it for you?"

"Nah, just want to hit my twenty years and retire. Go down south somewhere and lie on a beach. A beach overflowing with beautiful women."

"That being their natural environment?" Kaika asked.

"In my dreams, it is."

Retirement. On the more frustrating days, Vann did entertain the idea. He had already hit his twenty-year mark. But what would he do if he left the military? He wasn't even forty-five yet. He wasn't ready to lie on beaches. And in the civilian world, he wouldn't be able to pummel people regularly. How would he let off steam?

"Do you have any aluminum powder back at the fort, Bosmont?" Kaika asked. "I know you've got plenty of iron oxide. I saw the rust in your machine shop."

Bosmont snorted. "What do you have in mind?"

"Making some thermite to burn out the fossils."

"Eh, rock is a poor conductor of heat," Bosmont said. "The reaction would probably finish and cool off before cutting into much of the granite. There's a creek down there, and I have a hydraulic rock splitter in my machine shop. You know, under the rust."

"We could bring both back."

"You won't be happy unless you burn something, will you?"

Kaika slapped him on the shoulder. "You already know me. That's nice."

Bosmont smiled hopefully at her, glancing at her chest oh-so-briefly. Maybe he thought she would be easier to lure to bed than the married professor. Brave man. Vann wouldn't make an attempt on her these days, not when she was sleeping with the king. Vann had already irked Angulus often enough for one lifetime.

Kaika ignored Bosmont's glance and nodded to Vann. "What do you think, sir?"

"Go ahead." He waved to both of them. "Go back to the outpost and collect what you need. Come back, and let's get started on the fossils tonight. I want them out of here and wrapped up in a tarp next to the other ones." Far, far away from the gates of his outpost. Vann decided he would move the first collection farther away when he got a chance, just in case the magic embedded in them *could* affect things for miles around.

"Kaika, bring Kasandral back with you too," Vann said. "The sword is in my room."

"Oh, it can cut through rock, can't it?"

Vann had only been thinking that he would feel better with the weapon nearby if there was magic in these fossils, but he paused to consider the question. "If there's a dragon or a witch on the other side, it can. I'm not sure the bones would excite it enough to bring it to full power."

"Your sword doesn't get excited by bones? Good to know, sir. And probably healthy too." Kaika winked.

"I feel like I should write you up for disrespecting a senior officer."

"You can just beat on me in the boxing square later, sir."

"I'll look forward to it."

"Of that I have no doubt."

"Professor, do you want to go back with them or stay here?" Vann thought about simply telling Lilah that she would remain here with him, because he didn't want her staying in the outpost without her bodyguard around, but he didn't know if she would feel comfortable alone with him. She had to have noticed that he'd been close to kissing her earlier.

"There are a few hours of daylight left. I'll stay with the fossils." Lilah laid a hand on the dragon skull.

Vann noticed that she spoke of staying with the fossils, not with him. Well, what did he expect? She was married. Something he had better keep in mind. Not everyone was like General Chason, making a habit of jumping into non-matrimonial beds. He suspected the gold chain sometimes visible beneath the collar of Lilah's shirt was a marriage bond necklace, something he should have thought about when he'd been entertaining sexual fantasies involving her back in his room.

"I'm going to look for the tracks of my missing men," Vann said, as Kaika and Bosmont headed back along the trail, already arguing about explosives and thermite reactions, "but I'll stay within earshot. Yell if anything happens."

"I will," Lilah said.

Vann walked away, very pointedly *not* looking back to admire her assets from behind.

***

Lilah studied the embedded fossils, trying to determine both if they were real and how they had been embedded, until it grew too dark to see them. She turned away from the cliff to find that the sun had long ago dipped behind the ridge, and deep twilight shadows blanketed the mountainside. At first, she didn't see anyone and thought Therrik had decided to go track his missing soldiers after all, but then he came out of the gloom carrying an armload of wood.

"Campfire time?" Lilah rubbed her arms. A fire sounded excellent. It might be summer, but they were at a high elevation, and the temperature had dropped dramatically as soon as the sun disappeared.

"I was thinking of it as a signal fire." Therrik nodded toward the trees, in the direction he said the men had gone.

"You're worried about your soldiers?" She wondered how wise it was for her and Therrik to stay out here tonight when something disturbing had presumably happened to his men. Maybe returning to the outpost would be a good idea. Of course, it would be fully dark well before they reached it. She should have returned with the others earlier if she hadn't wanted to spend the night out here. But she had only just arrived when Kaika and Bosmont had gone back. She'd been too interested in studying the fossils to contemplate leaving then.

"If they weren't smart enough to run in the direction of the outpost, they don't deserve my worry."

He spoke gruffly, as he so often did, but nevertheless, he piled up more wood than would have been necessary for light and warmth just for them. He soon had a blazing bonfire going, the flames high enough that they should be visible from far downslope and also from the mountain opposite them. He returned to the trees to gather more wood.

Since there was nothing more she could do with the fossils—

not that she had done much even when there had been daylight—Lilah ambled into the trees and picked up a few branches to help. She had only grabbed a couple when he called to her.

"Come here." Therrik pointed at a log next to the fire.

She paused, debating whether she wanted to rebel over his presumptuousness. She wasn't one of his soldiers, sworn to obey the commands of superior officers. Deciding she was too tired, she shuffled back to him, though not without comment. "Please."

"What?"

"Come here, *please*. I'm not one of your men." She propped her foot on the log and gave him a challenging look.

He stared back at her, his face even harder to read than usual, thanks to the shadows. "That's not a word I use."

"No? It's only one syllable. Much easier to say than igneous rock or paleontologist, neither of which you had trouble with."

"Just sit down, will you? You were up all night, right? I'll get the wood." He waved to the log again, then disappeared into the shadows between the trees.

Realizing he had called her over because he'd been thinking of her needs, Lilah blushed and sat down. Now she wished she hadn't been difficult. A part of her wanted to help, regardless of his request, but with the sun down, her fascination with the fossil problem waned, and weariness caught up with her. She eyed the ground, thinking of lying down with her back to the log and her face to the fire, but her stomach growled, so she pulled over her bag and rummaged for one of the packaged meals they had brought.

Therrik continued to bring wood until full darkness covered the mountain. He must have planned to keep the signal fire going all night.

"Did you find sign of your men?" she asked as he added wood to the stack.

"They hared off in three different directions. I'll have to wait until morning to track them." He cast a sour look toward the forest, then settled on the log next to her.

"Salted chicken, diced and canned?" she asked, reading the label off the tin before handing it to him.

"Sounds appetizing, doesn't it?" He accepted the can and used his utility knife to open it.

"I had mine already and can attest to the excellence of the cuisine."

"I bet."

"Here are some beans too, if you want them. I didn't finish them."

He accepted the open can silently. Apparently, thank-you wasn't a word, or a term, that he used, either.

She didn't know what to say after that. A part of her wanted to lean against his shoulder and close her eyes, but that seemed overly familiar when she had known him for less than two days. She eyed the spot on the ground again, though to claim it now would mean sleeping with her head under his legs. That also seemed familiar. And it could be dangerous if those beans had the typical effect.

"What?" Therrik set the can of beans on a rock by the flames to warm it.

"Hm?"

"You're grinning."

"No reason." She grinned wider.

"Just delighted by my company, eh?"

"Clearly."

"Kaika and Bosmont should be back within the hour," Therrik said, nodding toward the trail. "It shouldn't take them that long to gather supplies."

Lilah nodded, though she hadn't been worried about being alone with Therrik. Was that odd? That she trusted him after less than two days? Even if she hadn't started to get the sense that he was honorable under the gruffness, she would have expected an army officer to act ethically. After all, the soldiers in the *Time Trek* stories often wrestled with questions of morality when they traveled into the past, and they tried to do the right thing. She smiled, wondering if Therrik had read any of the books and what he would think of her comparing him to Commander Asylon.

"Have you always been a soldier?" Lilah asked. "Since you were old enough to sign up?"

He hesitated, stirring the beans before answering. "Almost."

"Was it something you dreamed of as a boy?"

"Not really. I didn't think I'd make it into adulthood."

She frowned at him. "What does that mean?"

He stirred the beans some more.

"Sorry, I'm prying. I was just trying to think of something to talk about."

"Aren't you tired? You could go to sleep."

"I didn't want you to be lonely."

He snorted. "I'm alone a lot. I'm used to it."

She almost said that was as sad as a boy not thinking he would make it to adulthood, but managed to stop the words from tumbling out. He didn't seem like someone who would want or appreciate pity. Besides, around here, teasing seemed the more acceptable response to a person sharing his feelings.

"It could have to do with the yelling," Lilah suggested, offering a smile.

"Oh? I thought it was my pummeling people." He removed the can from the fire and took a bite.

"The pummeling probably doesn't help. Though I am relieved that you beat back the man who attacked me. We've been so busy that I forgot to say thank you. Thank you."

"You would have handled him if I hadn't gotten there in time."

Lilah wasn't so sure, but she accepted what probably passed for a compliment from him. At the least, he believed she had some competence, though she wasn't sure what she had done to earn that opinion from him. She had been falling over backward as she shot the man she'd killed. Maybe if she hadn't been, she could have chosen a less vital target. Had he deserved death for trying to escape? She wasn't sure, but she couldn't believe the conditions in those mines were appealing. If she were in the prisoners' place, she might risk her life trying to escape too.

"My father was an asshole," Therrik said, his gaze toward the fire.

She blinked and looked at him. She wasn't sure what that was apropos of, but she made an encouraging noise. Thus far, he hadn't shared anything about himself, and she found herself curious about him. What had caused him to end up in this remote post? From the comments she'd overheard, she got the impression it was doled out as a punishment assignment, as rough on the soldiers as it was on the miners.

"To me, to my little brothers, to my mother," Therrik went on. "I planned to kill him as soon as I was old enough to be able to overpower him. He wasn't that big of a man, but he was wiry and strong." He flexed his arm and smiled—the smile didn't reach his eyes. "Runs in the family. I knew they'd arrest me when I succeeded, give me a death sentence, but I figured it would be worth it, so he'd leave my mother and brothers alone."

"He hit you?" Lilah guessed.

"All of us. He was always mad. Mean. Cruel. He gambled a lot, lost a lot, got beat up by underworld thugs a lot, since he didn't always have the money to pay when he lost. He couldn't get back at them, so he took it out on us. When I was little, I thought it was my fault, that I was a disappointment. By the time I was nine or ten, I figured out the truth, and I just started to hate him then. That's when I developed my plan and went to bed dreaming about enacting it every night."

"That's... Couldn't your mother get any help? Go to the authorities?"

"She tried. They wouldn't do anything. He was still Lord Therrik, even if having a title didn't mean much anymore. Nobody who wasn't of noble blood was going to cross him, nobody except the mobsters. All they care about is if you owe them money. They're not intimidated by anyone." Therrik shrugged. "When I was twelve, I made a serious attempt to kill him. Looking back, if I'd waited another year, I might have succeeded. I grew a lot at thirteen. Too late then."

"What happened?" Lilah asked, her weariness driven away as she imagined the scenario.

"He'd just beaten my mother so hard that she couldn't get up. My carefully calculated plans disappeared. I just had this black rage swallow me. I barely remember grabbing a kitchen knife and jumping at him. If I could have kept to my plan to take him from behind, maybe it would have worked out. As it was, I did some decent damage for a scrawny kid. Must have cut him ten places and nearly took out his eye before he got the knife away from me and threw me against the wall. Nearly knocked me out. Think he would have killed me, but my mother crawled over and covered me with her body. He stabbed *her* instead. He had better aim than I did."

"Gods, Therrik." She gripped his arm, not knowing what else to say or do.

"He ran, the coward. Left me holding her. She died in my arms. I didn't know what to do after that. Walked my brothers the ten miles to the capital and looked up an aunt I'd only met a couple of times in my life. My mother's sister. I thought she might take us in, but she didn't have any money. Ended up putting us in an orphanage. My brothers were younger and less... angry than I was. More confused. They did all right. I never did. Ended up on the streets, running with some older kids. Learned to steal, to survive. Later on, I learned to kill. Those in rival gangs, scum for the most part. Same as me." His mouth twisted with wry acknowledgment.

"Then some innocent man got caught in the crossfire, and the police cared enough to hunt us down. I think the two boys I was with probably ended up here." He jerked a thumb toward the mountain. "I hadn't been responsible for the shooting, not that time. Just an accomplice, as they called it. Anyway, I said who I was, and someone recognized the family name. At first, they didn't believe me—guess my father had finally gotten himself killed by some mobster the year before, so the estate was unclaimed, and they thought I was trying to lie my way into nobility. But my story checked out, and then the aunt remembered me and said I was who I claimed. I swear I wasn't trying to get out of anything, but the judge overseeing my case was from a noble family, and when he heard my story, he offered me jail for twenty years or the army for ten. I'm not sure he quite realized I was only sixteen at the time. I'd grown a lot by then. Did a couple of years in the regular army, took to it, and ended up getting sent to the academy to become an officer."

For the first time since he had started speaking, he looked at her. He shrugged and spread his palm. "So the very long answer to your other question is no, I'd never considered the army until I was given the choice between it and jail."

"It seems like it was the right choice."

Therrik nodded. "At least I get to channel some of my aggression into killing the nation's enemies. I *used* to be able to do that, anyway. When I got sent out on missions and encountered imperial soldiers. Lately, I've been stuck teaching young fools or commanding the rejects of the army." His thumb jerk toward the mountain was more frustrated this time, though he soon clasped his hand in his lap, as if to quell his irritation. More calmly, he said, "You teach, I assume. How do you deal with it?"

"I'm actually not very good at it, and I also get frustrated with young fools."

His eyes widened. Had he expected her to get poetic about the joys of teaching?

"Especially the ones that don't want to be there," Lilah added. "They take the class because it satisfies some degree requirement and they think it's easier than other options. Because how can studying old bones be difficult? Or require math?"

"You sound bitter." He actually smiled, like he enjoyed hearing about it.

"It's the research I love. The teaching is required, fortunately fewer classes now than I used to have to endure. But I got into this to be in the lab or out in the field making discoveries. Do you know that I have over forty-seven articles published in well-respected academic journals? In the last five years, I've filled in several branches of the phylogenic tree for mammals, linking extinct species with modern animals. When I was in school, I thought *I'd* be the first Zirk—first person in my family to bring a degree of fame to our name. Granted, it would have been in small and erudite circles, but still. We aren't noble, not even close, and most of the men in the family are drunks. It would have meant something." She tossed a stick into the fire. "Ridge beat me to fame by spinning upside down in the air and shooting things. It's petty, and I know it, to begrudge someone else his success, but I can't help but be exasperated sometimes at what society decides is worth admiring. Do you know that I regularly have students, male and female, come up and ask me to get his autograph? We don't even live in the same city."

Therrik's smile stretched wide. It was almost alarming, since it was so out of place on his usually dour face. "You don't like him."

"What? No, that's not true. I mean, I don't *not* like him." Lilah rubbed her face. Did that even make sense? Why was she complaining about this after that horrific story Therrik had told her? As if her academic aspirations mattered that much in the grand scheme of life. "Honestly, I don't know him well enough to like him or dislike him as a person," she said, feeling his gaze still upon her, and that he truly seemed pleased, or perhaps amused. "I've just been slightly irked with him from afar over the years."

"Half the reason I want a promotion is so he won't outrank me," Therrik said. "Pilots make me crazy, and he's the worst. They're so damned lippy, and they get away with it because the king and everyone else is convinced the fate of the nation rests on them and their flying buckets."

Lilah snorted. She could see through the unspoken words that Therrik would prefer it if the fate of the nation depended on him and his muscles.

"But I might be crazy for wanting to get promoted," he went on, his expression sobering. "I've barely been able to stand colonel. Too much organizational busy work, teaching, babysitting, keeping track of wayward soldiers." He flicked a disgusted finger toward the trees where his men had disappeared. "I miss going on missions. Shooting people is much easier than turning them into model soldiers."

"Anyone ever tell you that you're a bit of a ghoul, Therrik?"

"Many people. Mostly women. And I think you can call me Vann now."

"Ah. Good." Lilah leaned against his shoulder.

He grew still, and she thought he might wrap an arm around her. It would not have been unwelcome. But he kept his arms down. At least he didn't move away from her, so she could use his shoulder as a pillow. Too tired to decide if it would be an imposition or not, she closed her eyes, thinking she might fall asleep there.

A loud snap came from the cliff, and she jerked upright, her butt almost slipping off the log.

Therrik—*Vann*—steadied her, resting his hand on her thigh. The fire still burned high, and light and shadows danced on the granite cliff. If some rock had shifted, Lilah couldn't see it, but the noise had been ominous. A cliff shouldn't be susceptible to a rockslide, and yet, all the moss-covered boulders littering the area suggested one had happened long ago. She still couldn't imagine the scenario that Kaika had described, someone with magic melting igneous rock and re-forming it into granite, complete with fossils inside. There would have been evidence if that had happened within the last few weeks or even within the last few decades. Surely, such heat would have destroyed vegetation and trees in the area.

An eerie moaning sound came from the forest. Or was that a howl? It didn't sound natural, whatever it was.

"That's just the wind, right?" Lilah asked, trying to sound nonchalant, though the noise was creepy.

"I don't know. Something scared my men off last night. I spotted a few prints from what seem to have been large wolves when I was looking for tracks, but wolves shouldn't have scared grown men with rifles."

"I'll hope it's just wolves. I would rather deal with animals than anything otherworldly." Lilah felt foolish speaking of such things as if they were real, but she didn't know enough about how magic worked to guess at what could and could not be done with it. She looked toward the skull leering out at them from the cliff.

"As would I. At least for now. The others will be back soon, and Kaika should have my sword. It loves slaying the otherworldly."

The idea of a sword having a sentience and loving anything was disturbing, but if there was some strange evil out here, Lilah approved of having a weapon to use against it.

The howls faded, and the only snaps came from the wood in the fire. As the strangeness of the moment passed, she grew aware of Vann's hand on her thigh. In the chill of the night, the warmth of it felt good through her trousers. She wondered if he had plans to move it at all. Should she encourage that? He had seemed on the verge of kissing her back in his room, but he hadn't taken advantage of the fact that they were alone around a campfire now. She hadn't minded his touch even before he'd shared his past, and now she wanted to wrap an arm around him and comfort him, even if he hadn't sounded like he needed it after all this time. That must have been thirty years ago for him.

Lilah's mother was still alive and working as a humanities teacher who proofread her papers before she sent them off to her peers to evaluate. She had lost her dad in the same accident that had taken her husband from her, but she barely missed him. He had never struck any of the kids, but he'd been drunk more often than he'd been sober, and even after his death, she had never been able to forgive him for being the one who had been driving that ridiculously modified steam wagon—or talking Taryn into going for a ride in it with him.

Vann had been peering into the darkness, toward the direction where those howls had originated, but she must have made some noise, because he looked back to her now, then down at his hand. He released her quickly, as if he hadn't realized it was there and was chagrined to find it so. A twinge of disappointment ran through her.

"I'm going to walk around the perimeter." Vann grabbed his rifle and stood up. "You should get some rest. Once Bosmont arrives with that rock splitter, sleep won't be easy to come by."

Lilah watched his broad back as he headed into the gloom, wondering what had changed since they had stood so close in his room, admiring his weapons. Had she offended him? Surely, he wouldn't have shared his story with her if he was mad at her. But maybe he hadn't meant to share so much and now felt uncomfortable about what he'd revealed. She could understand that, especially from someone for whom sharing was probably a rare thing. Still, as she pulled her jacket close about her and lay down between the log and the fire, she kept running the conversation over in her mind and wondering if she had said something wrong.

Chapter 6

THE EERIE HOWLS CONTINUED TO drift up from the forest, sounding slightly like something from a wolf's throat but too sonorous to have come from any native creature. Vann had spent enough time in survival training courses and out hunting in the wilderness to be familiar with what stalked these mountains. If he were a kid wandering through a cemetery at night on a dare, he would be thinking that some restless spirit was haunting him, but he had never seen anything in his life to suggest that such things happened anywhere other than in people's imaginations. The gods knew he'd killed enough men that their souls would be haunting him every day if they could.

He paused in his patrol with the fire at his back, and he gazed down the dark trail toward the outpost. How many hours had passed since Kaika and Bosmont left? Six? Seven? Even allowing that they would need time to gather their equipment and, if Kaika had her way, mix up a batch of thermite, they should have been back by now. As the strange howls continued to meander through the trees, raising the hair on the back of Vann's neck, he worried that something had happened. Perhaps these cursed fossils, or whatever he was dealing with, had created some new problem. Maybe he and Lilah should have gone back to the outpost, too, and waited until morning to return.

Fortunately, she seemed to be sleeping, able to ignore the howls. He circled back to check on her for the fifth or sixth time, refusing to acknowledge that his interest had anything to do with admiring her as she slept, the curves visible beneath her clothing and the way her thick hair tumbled about her shoulders, a lock snagged on a nub on that log...

No, he wasn't admiring those things. He was just making sure she did not need anything and wasn't scared being out here. Women got scared in situations like this, didn't they? If that happened to her, he might have to gather her in his arms and make her feel protected.

Vann snorted at himself. So far, she had not appeared any more alarmed by anything than he had. If anyone in the group needed cuddling, it was Bosmont.

A noisy clatter arose somewhere up the trail, and Vann spun around. A rockfall? He almost sprinted in that direction, but he couldn't leave Lilah without a guard. Besides, he had been wandering around without a lantern, and on a dark night like this, he might end up causing a rockslide himself if he raced up the trail without a light.

As he dug out his lantern, he debated whether to wake Lilah. If he meant to go check on that noise, he had better take her with him.

"Sir?" came a distant call from the trail. Captain Kaika.

"Here," Vann called back.

Lilah lifted her head.

"Need some help, sir," Kaika responded. Her voice did not sound too alarmed, but that might not be an indicator of anything. She could stay calm in the midst of a firefight, while hurling grenades with one hand and loading her rifle with the other.

"Will you come with me?" Vann asked. "I don't want to leave you here alone."

Lilah pushed away from the log and grabbed her hunting rifle. He allowed himself a quick smile. No, she did not seem like someone who needed protective cuddling.

With his lantern lit, he led the way up the trail. They found Kaika kneeling next to a pile of gear and looking over a ledge, a ledge that had not previously existed. Before, the goat trail had run alongside a steep, rocky slope, but now a large hole gaped open, dropping away into darkness. On the other side, four soldiers with more gear stood or knelt, peering over the ledge on their side. One corporal cursed as he unraveled rope from a coil hanging from his pack.

"Bosmont?" Vann asked, stopping behind Kaika.

"Down here, sir," the engineer called up from what sounded to be at least thirty feet below. "I'm hanging from a branch with one hand and trying not to let go of the rock splitter that's in my other hand. It's, uhm, difficult."

"We're hurrying," Kaika called, then snapped her fingers at the soldier unraveling the coil. "You got my rope yet?"

"Almost, ma'am."

Vann had a bundle of rope attached to his own pack. He set down the lantern and shrugged off his gear. With the corporal already lowering his rope, a second one probably wasn't necessary. Still, some light might be useful. He tied one end of his rope to his lantern and waved Kaika back so he could lower it into the hole.

"What happened?" Vann glanced at the rock-littered slope, what remained of it. He couldn't remember exactly what the spot had looked like before, but he could smell freshly revealed earth and see evidence of a slide.

"Oh, nothing strange, abnormal, or disturbing," Kaika said, "such as the trail picking the exact moment to give out that the man carrying the rock splitter was crossing it."

"What are you implying?" Lilah asked softly from behind them. "That something sentient is trying to keep us from extracting those fossils? Even if magic were used, I've not heard of anything that could do what you're describing." She spoke firmly, but she also gazed nervously toward the steep slope that descended immediately to the side of their trail.

Vann said nothing, only lowering his lantern until the light revealed Bosmont and his tree. It was more of a bush growing out of the nearly vertical rocky slope, its roots penetrating the unyielding earth. It did not look like something that could hold the weight of a grown man indefinitely. At least there was not a sheer drop underneath him. He would probably survive if he fell. Not breaking any bones and finding a way back up to the group would be another story, especially while toting the rock splitter.

"Next time, carry that thing on your back, Bosmont," Kaika called down. "Then you could be hanging onto the bush with two hands."

"I'm sure that would be *much* better." It was hard to tell whether Bosmont's scowl was for her or because the rope the soldier dangled down did not quite reach him.

Vann shifted his own rope, trying to make it swing toward the engineer. With the lantern on the bottom, providing some weight, it acted like a pendulum.

"Grab mine, Bosmont," Vann called. "You're closer to this side."

"And we need you and your big tool on this side," Kaika added.

"We have the hose over here, ma'am," a private with a hose coil on his shoulder said, sounding slightly indignant.

Vann hoped to get *everybody* over to this side, but with a good fifteen feet of the trail missing, it would be a challenge. He grumbled to himself. Who didn't enjoy a challenge at midnight?

"I'm never sure if you're growling or talking to yourself when you do that," Lilah said from behind him.

"Does it matter?" Kaika asked, a grin in her voice. "It's alarming either way, isn't it? Unless you're in bed. In that context, I chose to take it as complimentary."

Vann glared over at her. He didn't know if Kaika had already blabbed to Lilah that they had slept together once, but it wasn't something *he* would have chosen to mention, especially not here. This was hardly the place for such revelations. Besides, it had been years earlier, and they had both been drunk at the time. Sleeping with lower-ranking officers in one's unit tended to be frowned upon.

"I see," Lilah said, her voice quiet and subdued. Disappointed?

No, that didn't make sense. She was married. Why would she be disappointed if he had slept with her bodyguard? Admittedly, he had been tempted to see how dedicated she was to her marriage when she had been leaning against him on that log. He remembered the feel of her leg beneath his hand and how badly he'd wanted to let that hand drift higher. He had only meant to reassure her when he'd touched her, but his hand had a mind of its own and had wanted to linger. But no, it was bad enough he had slept with Chason when she was married. She'd instigated that, and he'd known he had been one of many. He didn't make a habit of breaking up people's marriages.

A sudden weight on his rope nearly pulled Vann over the edge. Cursing, he braced himself and lowered into a squat for stability. That would remind him of the price for not paying attention to what he was doing.

"You got me, sir?" Bosmont asked, worry in his voice.

"Yes." Vann bit back a comment about the engineer's weight and that he had been scarfing down too many of the cook's brick-like pancakes in the mornings. He didn't want Lilah to think he had any trouble dealing with the burden. "You ready?"

"Yes, sir. I've spent as much time communing with this bush as I care to. And the rock splitter isn't getting any lighter."

Ah, right. The thing probably weighed an extra fifty pounds. No wonder the sudden weight had nearly upended him. Vann stepped back with one leg, found a strong stance, and started pulling, his muscles straining but up to the task. Physical exertion was almost as pleasing of an outlet as combat, if not quite as exciting.

"If we can help, please let us know, Vann," Lilah said.

"Our job is to catch him if he slips," Kaika said, probably oblivious to the fact that Vann was slightly irked with her for blabbing about their past. It was hard to get a good glare off in the dark, especially when his only lantern was attached to the engineer thirty—no, it was twenty feet below now. "We'll grab the back of his belt there," she added.

"Won't we just fall in after him?"

"Nah, I'm sure the two of us together weigh more than he does."

"Wouldn't we have to weigh more than him and Captain Bosmont combined?" Lilah asked.

"Hm, you may be right. I guess we just wave to him as he goes over the edge. Maybe that bush can support both of them."

"Lilah?" Vann asked, his voice strained as he continued to haul Bosmont and his big tool up. "Next time you come to visit, maybe you should request a bodyguard that talks less."

"I will keep that in mind."

Kaika snorted noisily. "A fine thing to say when I went to your room and got your sword for you." She pointed toward her back, where Vann could barely make out the hilt poking over her shoulder.

"It won't help here."

"No, not unless Bosmont's bush turns into a dragon, I imagine."

Kaika grabbed the end of the coil of rope growing behind him and tied it to the nearest tree. Now that Vann had his mind focused on the task, he wasn't concerned about dropping Bosmont, but he gave her a nod, glad she was working instead of talking.

The light grew as the lantern rose higher, and a hand wrapped around the rope above it came into view. Vann stepped back farther, giving Bosmont room to climb up. Since he still held the rock splitter, Bosmont struggled to clamber up, and Kaika eased around Vann to help him. There wasn't much room on the goat trail for maneuvering, but together, they managed to get him onto solid ground, or at least ground that was solid for the moment. Vann eyed the area above the trail again, aware that what had happened once might happen again.

"Is there something you can tie our rope to over there?" Vann asked the soldiers lined up on the other side. He removed the lantern and tossed the end over to them so they could grab it. Their end remained tied to Kaika's tree, and he envisioned the rope connecting the two sides.

"Boxcar has a real thick neck, sir," one man in the back said.

"I see you brought the jokesters," Vann muttered to his officers.

"We brought the people willing to do a five-mile march while carrying heavy equipment," Bosmont said. "Though I think Private Boxcar only came because Kaika showed him her butt."

"All I did was bend over to pick up that bottle of aluminum powder," Kaika said dryly.

"Yes, while he was watching. He liked it."

"Clearly, he has good taste." Kaika peered past Vann. "Which one is he, again?"

"I think he's the one with a rope around his neck," Vann said.

"We found a tree," a soldier said. "Are we sending the gear across first and then following? Or..." His voice lowered, directed at his comrades rather than Vann. "I guess there's no way to get it across without us carrying it, is there?"

Vann clenched his jaw, irritated that he had a bunch of weaklings that didn't think they could make it across with a pack, but he refrained from saying it aloud, mostly because Lilah was still standing behind him. That made him want to be less of an ass. He grunted. Maybe his soldiers would prefer it if he always had a woman around.

"Drop anything you can't carry," he said. "I'll come over and pick it up."

The soldiers shuffled about and muttered to each other. The first one swung onto the rope, hands and ankles hooked over it, without removing any of his gear. Huh. Now he just had to hope they were strong enough and that he hadn't embarrassed them into doing something stupid. Sighing, Vann inched close to the edge, so he could grab the man if he got close but didn't make it.

The tree behind him creaked. The soldier paused halfway across.

"How's that knot, Kaika?" Vann asked.

"The knot is excellent. The tree is old."

"Nothing to worry about," the soldier muttered and picked up his pace.

A low-pitched howl drifted through the forest once more. Vann sighed, wondering if this was all worth it. What would happen if he simply left the bones where they were and told Bosmont to find another spot to mine into the mountain? At least until Sardelle came out to take a look. Still, the idea of needing a witch to come help made him grind his teeth. He would prefer to resolve this on his own. At the least, they could get all of the fossils out and move them to someplace in the valley, someplace far from the outpost and the radio tower.

The soldier reached the edge, and Vann grabbed him, hauling him onto solid ground. He waved for the next man to go. The tree creaked again as the second soldier scaled his way across. Vann had an image of the rest of the trail giving way, with his whole team falling to their deaths. He gritted his teeth again, second-guessing himself once more. He barely knew the names of the soldiers, but he would lament losing them nonetheless. He would lament losing Kaika and Lilah even more.

Rocks fell away as the soldier reached him and crawled onto the trail. A few more inches of dirt crumbled and disappeared down the mountainside.

"Kaika, take everyone on this side and continue down the trail to the camp," Vann said over his shoulder as he waved for the next man to start across.

"Sir?" Kaika asked.

"In case this section of the trail falls in too."

The third soldier proved agile and light and skimmed from one side of the gap to the other in seconds. So far, nobody had left his equipment behind. A hose for Bosmont's drill tried to tangle around Vann's boot as he helped the soldier onto solid ground, but nothing more upsetting happened. He shooed the man down the trail and waved for the last person to cross.

The rope groaned and dipped as the big man clasped onto it, his legs clenched around it so tightly he could have cracked walnuts. A bulky pack sagged from his shoulders.

"This must be Boxcar," Vann said.

"Private Boxin, sir," came the voice from the other side, an alarmingly squeaky voice for a man of such size. He hadn't started across yet.

Vann bit back a comment of, *Get your ass over here, Boxin,* and groped for something encouraging to say. General Mendatson at the academy was always telling him that young soldiers needed encouragement. He suspected a solid thump on the side of the head did more to get them in line, but he could feel Lilah's gaze on him from farther up the trail and, once again, sublimated his natural inclination to be callous and brusque.

"You make it over here in twenty seconds, and we'll get Captain Kaika to show you her ass again, Private," Vann said. Possibly, that wasn't exactly the kind of encouragement that General Mendatson had been talking about, but Vann owed Kaika a dig for talking about their past where Lilah could hear.

"Really, sir," Kaika said from much closer than he expected.

He scowled over his shoulder. The three privates had disappeared down the trail with their equipment, but for some reason, Kaika, Lilah, and Bosmont loitered. "Didn't I tell you three to get moving?"

The rope bounced and wobbled as the heavy soldier groaned and strained his way across, his fingers slipping more than once. Maybe his walnut-clenching grip with his legs was a good thing. He hurried, but the tree creaked ominously under his weight.

"We did move, sir," Kaika said. "I stepped back a whole meter. Bosmont ran back three meters. The professor only went a foot. She seems worried about you. Were you wooing her with your masculine wiles around the campfire?"

"Don't be ridiculous, Captain," Vann said. "I—"

Wood snapped behind him. The tree.

Boxcar yelped as the rope slackened. Vann grabbed it, almost missing in the dark. Once again, he braced himself, leaning back, using his weight to tighten it again.

"Hurry, Boxcar," he said.

Something slammed into the back of his shoulder. Part of the tree. He skidded forward, his front foot going over the edge. He let go with one hand, twisting and lunging backward, knocking the tree aside. He ended up on his knees, facing away from the hole, the rope still gripped in his hand. He grabbed it with the other hand, too, as he hunkered down like a turtle. The rope bit into his shoulder as he leaned forward, trying to counter the soldier's weight. Even without his gear, the kid would have weighed more than he did, but Vann added sheer determination to his side, refusing to budge, even though he lacked anything to grab onto or brace himself against.

The rope vibrated, and Boxcar's alarmed panting filled the air.

A figure came into sight on the trail in front of him. Bosmont.

"Grab my hand, sir. I'll add my weight to yours."

Vann glared at that hand. He would have to let go of the rope with one of his own to reach for it, and he wouldn't do that. Bosmont ended up grabbing his shoulder, for all the good that would do. Vann merely hunched lower, imagining himself sinking into the ground, embedded like a boulder, unmoving.

"Almost there," Boxcar said. "I—help?"

"Bosmont," Vann barked. The weight on the rope had not lessened, so he didn't dare let go yet.

The engineer crawled past him. Rocks scraped, slid, and tinkled down the side of the mountain. Bosmont grunted as something fell on him—Boxcar, perhaps.

"Got him, sir," Bosmont said, on the ground now. "You can let go."

The weight disappeared from the rope, and Vann allowed himself to kneel back. "If I do that, our end falls into the hole. Kaika, any more trees you can tie this to?" He pulled up the chunk of bark at the end of the rope, all that remained of the last tree, the rest having disappeared over the side of the trail.

"Not close enough, sir. Maybe Bosmont can come up with something."

"How about letting the rope go and finding another way back to the outpost?" Bosmont suggested.

"That the kind of brilliance they taught you in engineering school, Captain?" Vann asked. He had exceeded his capacity for providing encouragement. It wasn't a substantial capacity to start with. "Drag a big rock over here, so we can wedge the end of the rope under it for now."

"Yes, sir."

Vann climbed to his feet so Bosmont and Boxcar could squeeze past him on the narrow trail. He remained in place, holding the end of the rope and eyeing his surroundings. As Kaika had said, there weren't any more trees close enough to reach.

"Big rock," Boxcar grumbled, looking upslope as he walked along the trail. "Where's a good big rock?"

Vann rubbed his face, ignoring the grit and dirt that stuck to his palm. He had all of the geniuses out here tonight.

"Sir," Kaika said, a dark shadow farther up the trail. "Do you want to—"

Several snaps came from under Vann's feet. Rock rumbled on the slope overhead. Cursing, he let go of the rope and ran up the trail toward the others. The ground shifted under his feet, and rocks tumbled down from above. He was sprinting by the time he reached the others and might have bowled through them, but they were running too. He found solid ground a second before the crashing and banging grew cacophonous behind him. He kept running. Everybody did.

Vann did not stop until the trail widened and the drop-off grew less steep. He looked back. Though the darkness hid much, enough stars were out that he could see the outline of the terrain. What had been a fifteen foot hole had to be a fifty foot gap in the trail now. The odds of making it back across were dubious at best, even if someone had brought a grappling hook. He would have to hope that, as Bosmont had suggested, they could find a route back when they finished, but he questioned if that would be possible without climbing equipment. Vann berated himself for not thinking to pack some.

"Are you all right?" Lilah asked, stepping up and touching his arm. The others had kept running, probably all the way to the camp to warm their hands around the fire.

He gripped her shoulder, appreciating that she had lingered to check on him. After nearly falling down the mountainside, his blood surged through his veins, the familiar mix of exhilaration and fear still riding him. He had the urge to pull her into his arms and kiss her, to prove that he was still alive and to thank her for caring. And because it would feel brilliant to have her soft curves pressed up against him, her lips against his, hungry, eager...

Instead, Vann cleared his throat and let go of her shoulder. "Yes," he said, his voice raspy. "But I'm really starting to hate your fossils."

She stared up at him, probably wondering if that was a joke or if she should be offended. He hadn't meant to offend.

"Paleontology isn't for everyone," she said. "Just those with lots of patience and a quirky sense of humor. Say, what do you call an extremely old joke?"

"What?"

"Pre-hysterical."

"That's, uhm." Vann quirked an eyebrow, wishing he had

opted for kissing her instead of talking to her. At least he knew she wasn't too rattled by the night's experiences if she had come up with that gem.

"Yes, that's the typical response to my jokes." Lilah bumped him with her arm. "I'm afraid I don't have any specifically about magical fossils."

"Good, because I don't find those fossils to be funny at all. If I learn who put magic in those rocks, I'm going to wring his neck."

"Or perhaps throw him off the side of the mountain?" she suggested.

"Only after I've wrung a neck or two."

"You're a violent man, Colonel Therrik." Fortunately, she sounded more amused than alarmed.

"Just determined." He reached out, touching her shoulder and pointing her up the trail. Some of her soft hair tickled his fingers, and he gritted his teeth, once again sublimating the urge to do more than touch her, though it was hard not to think about such things. With the others out of sight, he might have pushed her against the stone wall and kissed her senseless as he slid his hands under her shirt to cup her—

He shook his head. Seven gods, he was just as horny as Bosmont.

"Determinedly violent?" she asked lightly, unaware of his libidinous thoughts.

"Whatever you want me to be, Lilah," he murmured. He took a deep breath, trying to force his muscles to relax. *All* of them.

"Really? I didn't know I had the power to control you."

"Few do. I'm not sure it's a gift. It's like a lion tamer with an unruly charge."

"Hm," was all she said, finally heading up the trail toward the others.

Vann looked back, worried about what else might befall his people while they were cut off from the outpost.

Chapter 7

Lilah slept an impressively long time, considering a pump was vibrating a few feet away, and cracks and snaps kept sounding as Bosmont split rocks. She didn't wake until it was fully light out, which was a good thing, since the temperature had dropped further during the night, and Vann had let the fire burn down. She wasn't as cold as she expected to be and found an extra garment draped over her, in addition to the jacket she wore buttoned to her throat. Someone's army jacket. She smiled, recognizing the smell of Vann's shaving soap mingled with his... determinedness. Her colleagues in the science department would have denied that such a thing could have a scent, but it was distinctly his. She was tempted to stay there, burrowed under the jacket for a while, to enjoy its warmth and the fact that Vann had thought to drape it over her during the night. When she had first met him and seen him curling a lip and uttering *Zirkander* with distaste, she wouldn't have thought he possessed the ability to be considerate.

The continued bangs, cracks, and thumps convinced Lilah to poke her head out from under the jacket, along with Captain Kaika saying, "Just let me burn a *little* away."

"Get back with your evil torch, woman," Bosmont said, his teeth rattling as the rock splitter pounded away at the granite.

Worried about the safety of the fossils, Lilah tightened the boots she hadn't removed to sleep, then hustled over to what looked like a construction zone. Several canvas tarps lay around the rubble, one pinned down with a huge rock that held the dragon skull. The fossil was still embedded in the granite; they had simply cut around it and extracted the entire lump. Several smaller rib and leg bones had received the same treatment. She spotted a second skull, the crown just visible in a newly revealed piece of rock.

"Morning, Professor," Kaika called, waving a metal tube with a canister attached to the back. She lifted a welding mask that had been protecting her eyes. "Did you sleep well?"

A loud crack sounded as Bosmont pressed deeper into the cliff.

"Or at all?" Kaika added.

"More than you would think. I was tired." Lilah wondered if *Kaika* had slept. She had been up the previous night, just as Lilah had been. She must be exhausted, unless burning things kept her feeling cogent and perky.

Around the camp, the other soldiers had been pressed into dragging or rolling the smaller rocks away and tossing them down the slope toward the creek.

"Make sure none of those have fossils in them," Vann said, striding out of the woods with three more soldiers in tow. The missing men from the day before presumably. All of them had ragged, haunted features, their uniforms torn and stained, and their shoulders hunched with fear or shame.

Vann wore his black shirt, his muscled forearms bare to the chill air, and Lilah was torn between feeling guilty that he had given her his jacket and wanting to admire his powerful form. In addition to the rifle he'd had slung across his back the day before, he now carried that sword in a scabbard, also on a strap that let it hang across his back. She wondered what he thought he would find to hack at out here. Not her fossils, she presumed. He had *better* not be thinking of hacking at them.

"Sit." Vann pointed at the log by the fire. "Eat something and rest, because you're about to become scouts. We need someone to find another way back to the outpost."

The beleaguered men did not object. One even looked enthused at the order as he plopped onto the log, either at the notion of eating or perhaps at getting to go back to the barracks. All of them could use showers and a bunk.

"Already checked before letting them tote the boulders away, sir," Bosmont said. "We're tossing the boneless rocks in that pile and the boners in that one there."

"Boners? Really, Bosmont?" Kaika asked. "There's a lady

present. Though I guess she's made a career out of liking bones, so maybe it doesn't matter."

"I've already heard every joke that can possibly be made about fossils," Lilah said.

"I think she just called you unoriginal, Bos."

Vann grabbed his jacket from the log and came to stand beside Lilah. There was a tuft of moss sticking out of his dark hair, and he'd lost his cap the night before.

"Where did you find your wayward soldiers?" she asked.

"Way down the mountain. They said that giant black wolves chased them off, herding them away from the tunnel, and then not letting them circle back so they could find the trail to the outpost again."

"Why didn't they shoot the wolves instead of letting themselves be herded?"

"Apparently, these were cursed wolves that couldn't be killed," Vann said, his tone flat with disbelief.

"Ah."

"Anything interesting going on?" He waved at the cliff and the tarps.

"Would you believe that your officers are less mature than my seventeen-year-old students?" Lilah asked.

"Yes, but that's not interesting. It's just pathetic."

"We heard that, sir," Kaika said, as she fired up her stick, turning it into a torch. The flame melted some rock, but it appeared less efficient than Bosmont's rock-splitting tool.

"I just woke up," Lilah said. "I'll take a look at what they've pulled out and determine my interest level."

"Good." He donned his jacket, then started for the tunnel.

Lilah had taken a peek into it the day before, but it had been unimpressive, and she had been told that only one fossil had been dug out of the shaft. The others were off to the left of it. If the soldiers had started their tunnel two feet to the right, they might never have found the fossils. Vann probably wouldn't have minded that.

"Wait a second." Lilah plucked the moss out of his hair and dropped it before waving for him to continue.

He frowned and scraped his fingers through his mussy black locks. "Anything else sticking up that I should know about?"

"Not that *I'm* aware of." She bit back a smirk, feeling daring for making the innuendo—and then wondering if he would catch it. So many of her attempts at jokes fell flat.

The corners of his mouth twitched upward, and he nodded at her before waving at Bosmont. "Join me in here, Captain. I want to hear your plans for after the fossils have been removed."

"Yes, sir." Bosmont switched off his tool and leaned it against the wall. "Don't touch," he told Kaika before following Vann into the tunnel.

"You don't let any women touch your tool, and you're doomed for a lonely life, Bos," Kaika called after him.

Lilah looked at her, remembering her comment from the night before, the one that had affirmed what Lilah had suspected, that Kaika had slept with Vann. She had a hunch Kaika had slept with a lot of men and wondered if her liaison with him had meant anything. She also wondered if they still... liaised.

"Believe it or not, I think I was more mature at seventeen," Kaika said with an easy smile. "I've spent my whole career being the only woman in all-male units. You either make the same jokes they do, or you set yourself up as an outsider. You have to give as good as you get, and not be offended by the getting, to make it out with your sanity."

Lilah was one of the few women in her field too. Her colleagues were perhaps less raunchy and blunt than the soldiers, but she'd definitely felt like an outsider many, many times. Would she have felt less awkward if she had done as Kaika had? Made all the dirty jokes before the men could? The gods knew it was hard to ignore the whispered comments about her feminine attributes and the assumptions that since she had them, they should be made available for the men's use. Even worse had been the insinuations that because she had boobs and a butt she couldn't possibly have a brain. Most of the papers she had published were listed simply as L. Zirkander, since she had noticed early on that it was easier to get them approved and printed if her gender wasn't apparent.

"You want to play with his tool?" Kaika asked.

"Pardon?" Lilah wasn't sure what expression had been on her face, but it had probably involved a scowl.

Kaika smiled and waved to the rock splitter, maybe trying to lighten her mood. "It's fun, probably more fun than his other tool."

"I heard that, Kaika," Bosmont's voice echoed back from the tunnel. "And don't even think of cracking rocks while we're in here."

"I'll let her try it on a boulder we've already extracted. One of the boneless ones."

"Honestly, I'm more interested in the ones with bones," Lilah said, walking toward the tarp.

"I'll pass that along to the men, if you like," Kaika said, winking at one of the soldiers within earshot. The young man picked up a rock that should have been rolled by two people. He did an admirable job of flexing his muscles and looking like he wasn't in danger of throwing out his back. "You can have your choice here, you know. If you decide you need a little relaxation mixed in with your work."

"I'm just here to study the fossils and make a report." Lilah knelt next to the dragon skull and did her best not to think of Vann.

"Oh, right. You said you were married, didn't you? I suppose you wouldn't be shopping for wares here, but if you change your mind, I can be discreet. I'll stand guard in the hall outside of your door. Or whichever door you end up behind."

"Mm," was all Lilah said. She hadn't corrected Bosmont about her marital status and wasn't sure she wanted to correct Kaika, either. She still wore the promise necklace her husband had given her, even if she usually kept it tucked beneath her shirt. When she needed it, she could pull it out to use as a silent barrier against flirty strangers or visiting professors who thought they should have a relationship since they'd read one of her papers and since their own wives were a couple hundred miles away.

Lilah walked to her toolbox and pulled out her chisel, hammer, and brush, but almost dropped them when a thought occurred to her. Did *Vann* think she was married? She realized she hadn't said that she wasn't, and if he'd noticed her necklace, he might have assumed she was. Not that Bosmont had. Still, Vann seemed observant. Was that why he hadn't touched her the couple of times she'd thought that he might want to? Such as in his room on the base and again the night before, after he'd nearly been pulled off the trail? She'd wanted so badly to run over there and help, but she'd been powerless to do anything except watch as he struggled to keep his soldier from falling. Afterward, he'd treated the moment as if it had been nothing, but even he must have feared for his life at some point.

She carried her tools to the fossils, debating whether she had a problem or if it would be wiser to simply go on pretending her husband still lived. She fully admitted she was attracted to Vann, but she had never been the kind of person to leap into bed with someone just to satisfy carnal pleasure. There had to be a potential for a future together, and what kind of future could she have with a soldier stationed in the middle of nowhere? Besides, she wasn't sure what Vann felt for her, besides attraction, one that might have more to do with being stuck in a remote place with few women around. They barely knew each other, and they certainly weren't similar types of people, unless one counted an interest in old weapons and a shared irritation toward Ridge. Not to mention that he was very open about the fact that he'd apparently killed people—a *lot* of people—in his career, and he seemed to like it.

She had never been overly emotional and had a tendency to underreact or make a sarcastic comment when handed alarming news, but the scientist in her couldn't help but wonder what such a man could be capable of in a dark moment. She'd already seen hints of his temper, and Kaika had warned her that it could get worse. Did he have a history of taking his anger out on those he was in a relationship with? She had the impression that he wasn't married. Was there a *reason* women avoided him?

"Is it all right?" Kaika asked, crouching beside her.

"Pardon?" Lilah had been staring at the pile of fossils without seeing them.

Kaika waved at the skull. "We tried to be careful not to damage any of them while removing the rocks."

"Oh. No, they're fine. I mean, I haven't looked that closely yet, but I appreciate you extracting them for me. I don't usually have soldiers around to do that." She smiled and nodded toward the rock splitter still leaning against the cliff. "I actually have something similar in my lab back home. People have these notions that paleontologists run around with toothbrushes, carefully whisking away specks of dirt. You usually have to break a *lot* of rock to get to fossils. Granted, it's usually sandstone or limestone rather than granite, but it's rarely easy."

"Ah, good. You looked kind of concerned."

"I was thinking about... something else." Lilah considered Kaika, wondering if she might be a source for information on Vann's history when it came to women. If she was seeing someone else now—had that Angulus Vann had mentioned been *King* Angulus?—then her interest in him should be in the past.

And yet, Lilah couldn't bring herself to ask. She ought to have a frank discussion with *him*. That would be better than getting gossip from some past lover, wouldn't it? It was always possible he wouldn't be honest with her, but if anything, he trended in the other direction, toward blunt to a fault.

"That would happen to me a lot if I studied rocks for a living." Kaika thumped her on the shoulder, a sign that she was teasing, Lilah assumed.

"I can see where it wouldn't be as exciting as blowing up rocks."

"Exactly." Kaika remained crouched beside the tarp, her eyebrows lifted. "Can I help with anything?"

Temptation teased Lilah's tongue. Maybe she could ask for just a few tidbits about Vann, not necessarily to encourage gossip, just to gain more information so she could make a logical and rational decision about him. Maybe it was her imagination, but Kaika almost seemed to be offering that.

"Professor?" Vann called from within the tunnel, his voice muffled by the walls.

"Maybe later," Lilah said and stood, half-relieved he had called in time to squelch her curiosity. What would he think if he knew she was out here asking questions about him? She headed to the entrance of the tunnel, wondering what Vann and Bosmont had found to talk about back there for so long. She peered into the gloom. "Yes?"

"Will you join us?" Vann asked. "And bring a lantern?"

"Yes…" Her curiosity roused, she hurried to find a couple of lanterns and light them. They might not be able to return to the outpost for more equipment easily, but the new soldiers had brought quite a bit with them, including food and light sources.

She almost grabbed her hunting rifle, but that was silly. What could she possibly need to worry about in a little stub of a tunnel?

With a lantern in each hand, Lilah headed into the passage. In the beginning, the squarish tunnel showed signs of tidy machine-led excavation, with the walls shored up by beams at regular intervals. That stopped about a third of the way in, where someone had dug a hole in the wall. Perhaps the first fossil had been found at that point? Beyond that, the sides of the tunnel were irregular and hadn't been shored up. Rubble littered the ground. Had the thieves Vann had spoken of extended Captain Bosmont's passage?

The shadows lay thick at the back, and she was more than halfway down the tunnel before Vann and Bosmont came into sight. They were prodding something along one stone wall. Had they found another fossil?

Vann waved for her to join them, stepping back to make room for her. He pushed Bosmont back, too, so she could see the section of wall that they had been examining. The chiseled rock of the tunnel came to an end only a few feet beyond them, several large boulders blocking the way. Lilah handed Vann one of the lanterns and kept the second one, lifting it toward the wall.

Everywhere else, the tunnel was composed of the same granite they had dealt with outside. Here, a smooth gray stone reflected the flame of her lantern. She slid a hand along what felt like glass under her fingertips.

"Oh," she said, a memory popping into her mind. "I've seen this before."

"Good, because I haven't," Bosmont said.

"Nor have I," Vann said, "but I don't spend a lot of time looking at rocks. What is it, Li—Professor?"

Lilah smiled at the slip. It wasn't the first time. She should have invited him to use it, since he had given her his.

"A Referatu tunnel," she said.

"Witches," Vann snarled and spat.

His vehemence surprised her, especially since whoever had used magic to mold and shape the old stone wall had likely lived hundreds, if not thousands of years earlier. But he'd made it clear before that he didn't like magic. It was, she supposed, the typical Iskandian response. Somewhat familiar with Referatu history, Lilah knew that most sorcerers in the past had been helpful people rather than evil souls. A few had gone rogue, but mostly, fear and superstition had turned them into something the common man feared. There were countless tales of witch drownings from centuries past, and the newspapers sometimes mentioned recent incidents, too, especially out in rural areas. She admitted a hint of disappointment at Vann's stance. For some reason, she had thought him someone who wouldn't give in to superstition, perhaps because he was so casual about this supposed curse originating with the fossils.

"Huh," Bosmont said. Surprisingly, he was the indifferent one. "So that's what one of their tunnels looks like before it collapses?"

"I helped with an excavation of one of their ancestral homes along the eastern cliffs in Mindovia—there used to be a dragon rider outpost in the caves along the ocean. It was quite interesting to see some of their ruins, though the valuable artifacts had long ago been pillaged." Lilah patted the wall. "Similar construction style."

She ran her hand along the gray glassy stone until it halted, the tunnel ending in more granite boulders, boulders that had fallen from the ceiling sometime in the past. It was almost as if someone had intentionally collapsed this tunnel.

"Oh," she said, a new realization coming over her. "Is this..." She blinked and stared at the men. Would they know? They *must*.

"Was this mountain the last Referatu stronghold? Erakusuth?"

Vann stared at her as if she were speaking gibberish.

"One of my historian colleagues would know more about it, but a few old books point to it being in the Ice Blades. Of course, most books with information on the Referatu have been burned over the years by those who feared anything to do with magic—" she tried to keep the judgment out of her tone as she spoke, noticing that Vann's expression remained quite icy, "—but our university has managed to preserve a couple over the years."

"This is where Sardelle came from," Bosmont said. "She's that, I think. Refer-whatever. A sorceress."

"Well, the last of the Referatu were wiped out three hundred years ago," Lilah said, "so she couldn't be one of them, but—"

"No, she really is. She was—oh, I forget what it was called. But I was here, working in the outpost, when she was found. She'd been in some magical sleep for three hundred years. We found a book with her picture in it from back then. She was the last of her people who survived some kind of secret invasion and attack that brought down the mountain and crushed everyone inside. I guess it was just luck that she survived." Bosmont rubbed his head. "I don't think anyone ever told me how. General Zirkander was here as the commander then. Had someone less, uhm, open-minded been in charge—" he was wise enough not to look at Vann, but his gaze did momentarily slide in that direction, "—she probably would have been killed. Good thing she wasn't, as she helped us fight off a nasty Cofah shaman."

Lilah listened as Bosmont spoke, enthralled by this unexpected source into a part of history that had been lost by time and obfuscation. "So... the military has always known the Referatu were here? And that's why they—you—claimed this mountain and started mining? To find old Referatu artifacts?"

That was surprising, but maybe the army had thought they could use some of the old magical items as weapons. Still, wouldn't the soldiers have had as much fear and hatred toward magic artifacts as the common Iskandian subject?

"Not sure how it all started, ma'am," Bosmont said, "but the mines are here because of the, uhm. Is it all right to tell her, sir?"

"Probably not, but she'll figure it out on her own, anyway, I suspect," Vann said.

Lilah frowned at his comment, and he added, "It's supposed to be top secret," by way of explanation.

"I signed a non-disclosure agreement before coming up here," Lilah said.

Bosmont shrugged. "Good enough for me. Usually, nobody gets to know what's in this mountain except the soldiers stationed here and the miners, and the miners don't ever leave. It's a death sentence for them. The soldiers... well, I guess someone comes after you later, if you blab. It was a good secret for a long time. This is where the energy sources that power the military dragon fliers come from."

Lilah thought of her ride out here with Sleepy. She distinctly remembered that glowing crystal up in the cockpit.

"So," she reasoned, "they're some tool that the Referatu made with magic in great enough quantity that we've found hundreds over the years, and early on, some team in the military science department decided they weren't so disturbed by magic that they couldn't find a way to use them as power sources? They hooked one up to what must have been a prototype flier at the time and found that these devices could power the craft? Then the army set up the mines, keeping it all a secret so that our enemies wouldn't discover the place and try to take the power sources for themselves?"

"That's about what I reckon, ma'am," Bosmont said. "And the rumor I heard is that they were originally lamps."

"Lamps? Ridge is flying around in an aircraft powered by a lamp?"

"That's what I heard, ma'am. Also heard that we inadvertently set up our outpost and started our mine shafts on the *back* side of the mountain. The witches had their headquarters on the front. We found some power sources back there, sure, but apparently *this*—" Bosmont waved to include the area under their feet and above them, "—is closer to where their front door was. Actually, that's a couple of miles that way." He pointed even further from the direction of the outpost. "But that was crushed when the mountain was blown up. Er, blown up the first time, three centuries ago. We blew it up again, the back side, a few months ago, trying to trap a dragon."

"Soldiers like to blow things up," Lilah commented, trying to gauge what Vann thought of the story. He wasn't speaking, and she didn't know if that was because Bosmont had been here longer and knew the tale better, or he just loathed all this talk of sorcerers and magical artifacts.

"Yes, ma'am. Blowing things up, shooting them, it's our job. Captain Kaika was the one who rigged the explosions that were supposed to trap the dragon, an evil dragon that'd been terrorizing the fort and some villages in the foothills. And that's why the shafts under the outpost are still an unholy mess. That mess is a big part of what motivated us to try and make a side incursion *here*. Figured we'd only be dealing with one layer of collapsed mountain and it might be easier to find more power sources."

"The collapse from three hundred years ago."

"Yes. Soldiers of the time did it, according to Sardelle, though I don't care to believe that supposition, ma'am. As much as we like to blow things up and shoot things, we aren't monsters. Sardelle said there were hundreds if not thousands of her people in the mountain when it happened. I don't know many that would sign up for mass genocide, even if witches were involved." Bosmont looked to Vann, perhaps silently asking for confirmation. "Anyway," Bosmont continued when Vann did not speak, "Sardelle said she was busy running to some stasis chamber after the alarm went off, and she couldn't know for sure who was responsible for the attack, just that nobody else made it to those chambers, and everybody got flattened."

"Thus ending the Referatu presence in Iskandia," Lilah murmured, "if not the world."

She had read hypotheses on what had happened to the magically inclined people before, but the one book she'd chanced across on the topic had not mentioned the specific location or who had been responsible. In fact, the author had suggested that a disease wiped out the Referatu, a plague delivered by the gods as punishment for using magical powers to harm others. The prejudice and fear toward sorcerers had been a very real thing, even back when some of them had been working for the throne.

"Bosmont," Vann said, "finish pulling out all of the fossils, and then I want this wall down." He pointed at the jumble of granite at the end of the tunnel. "We'll see if there are any witch tunnels, crushed or intact back there, and get as many crystals out as we can while we're here. That's our job, not standing around and speculating about the past."

"Yes, sir," Bosmont said as Vann walked out without another word.

Lilah watched his broad back as he strode away, realizing with a jolt that the pommel of that sword was glowing a faint green. Magically. How could a man who loathed magic and witches—and who hadn't objected to the idea of genocide when it came to them—justify walking around with a sword that glowed?

She shook her head and turned back to the smooth gray wall before following Bosmont out. Speculating about the past might not be *their* jobs, but it definitely was hers. A three-hundred-year-old mystery might not be in her usual repertoire as a paleontologist, but since none of her Post-Dominion-studying colleagues were along, she would do her best to find out what had happened here, and perhaps what had happened back then. If she found some actual evidence, she could even write a paper.

Was the world ready to know what had happened to end a race of people? She wondered.

Chapter 8

Vann pushed rocks around, clearing room for Captain Kaika, who whistled cheerfully as she set explosives against the granite at the end of the tunnel.

"You're just going to blow this open, right?" he asked, rolling a boulder out of her way. "Not bring down this tunnel and everything that might be back there."

"What's back there is probably just more rocks." Kaika pulled a fuse out of one of the pouches on her utility belt.

"Probably, but that doesn't answer my question."

"I'm not using charges designed to collapse the mountain again, I assure you. As to the tunnel, I'm reasonably sure the section Bosmont and his team hollowed out can withstand some explosive attention." Kaika waved toward the front of the passage, the part reinforced with beams and posts. "This back half is a mess. More of it may fall down, but we have Boxcar and his thick neck to clear the rubble."

"It's me and *my* thick neck that are clearing things for you right now."

"That's your choice, sir. You seem unable to sit still for more than two minutes without hurling something heavy around."

It was more that Lilah had been pursing her lips in disapproval at him since Bosmont had shared the story about the witches getting crushed, and Vann wanted an excuse to avoid her. What had she expected him to do? Shed tears for people who had died three hundred years ago? People who preferred using magic to more honorable means of dealing with problems? Perhaps he should have tried harder to keep his thoughts to himself, but he hadn't expected Lilah to be some... witch sympathizer. Bosmont didn't seem to care one way or another about witches, and Vann could accept that, but to be sad that the dreadful people had been taken from the world? He couldn't abide such thinking, not after what he'd endured at the hands of someone with that kind of power.

All he said to Kaika was, "I can sit still for *five* minutes at a time."

"I'm sure that's why I always find you *standing* at your desk to do paperwork."

Vann pushed another boulder out of her way, heaving with his muscles, enjoying the sensation of physical exertion. He did hate the desk. The paperwork didn't bother him so much, as long as he didn't have to spend an entire day at it, since he liked having the power to keep things orderly, but he hated what came with the paperwork, being responsible for hundreds of men, men who always had some complaint or another or some ridiculous request. He'd had three requests for leave come in the day before, as if this was the kind of duty station where one could hop on a train for a ride home for the holidays.

"What do you think of Professor Zirkander?" Kaika said, kneeling to attach her fuse to a charge.

"Don't say that name."

"Professor Lilah then." She grinned back at him.

"I don't think anything of her."

Such a lie. Even if she was a witch sympathizer, that couldn't keep him from stealing glances at her backside whenever he walked past while she was bent over her work. And the front side was even better. Why did she have to be such an attractive woman? It would have been much easier to ignore a homely girl, but no, he kept having fantasies of undressing her and getting a much better look at all of her sides. Even if she had been homely, he might have thought of her. How many women had he run into in his life that could name the eras the weapons in his collection came from? Not many *men* could do that. She wasn't anything like the usual women he met, other soldiers and the girls who worked in the bars and brothels near the army fort.

He never had trouble finding company, but women—those kinds of women—always seemed to think of him as someone to have fun with for a night, or in the case of the soldiers, as someone to date briefly on a dare. Nobody ever had marriage in mind or even a future. He'd gradually come to accept that his demeanor was too off-putting. People liked to ride the beast now and then. Nobody wanted to go through the effort of learning how to live with it.

Now and then, he wondered what it would be like to have someone to rant to, so he didn't always have to turn to the gym to take out his anger. He hadn't been so angry all the time when he had been younger, when he'd been sent out on missions alone or on small teams. A lot of his perpetual frustration with life had come with the responsibility of more rank and of having to command. And teach. Gods, he hated the teaching. It amused him to think that Lilah did too. He didn't know what he would do—what he would be qualified to do—if he left the military, but wondered what she would think if he showed up at her classroom door someday in civilian clothes and asked her to go on a date.

Kaika laughed. "You're thinking of her right now, aren't you?"

He stared at her, the tunnel coming back into focus around him. "You made me."

"Uh huh."

"It's moot, anyway. She's married."

"Is she?" Kaika asked. "Hm, you might want to check with her about that. I got the impression that was no longer the case."

"Oh?"

Kaika shrugged. "Look, it's none of my business. I'm just curious since you seem... calmer out here. Less gruff. Are you trying to impress her by not yelling at anyone?"

He hesitated, remembering that he *had* curtailed a few imminent diatribes because of her presence. "I thought the way to impress a woman was by walking around with your shirt off."

"You *do* do that well." Kaika gave him a leer that would have been more flattering if she hadn't been giving Bosmont a similar one earlier.

Not for the first time, he wondered what Angulus saw in her. Kaika wasn't unattractive by any means, but she wasn't a real beauty, either, and as king, he could have anyone in the kingdom at the wave of a hand. He probably got plenty of feminine attention even without waving anything. Vann supposed that a woman who knew what she wanted and didn't play games could be appealing to someone like him. Probably rare for him to encounter too.

"Well, if you *are* interested in her, and you can keep from scaring her away with your temper and standoffishness, I think she might be a good match for you."

Vann meant to say that his temper and standoffishness weren't topics that a captain should be bringing up with a senior officer, but what came out was, "You do?"

"She doesn't seem to be scared of you, for starters."

"I don't go out of my way to intimidate women, Captain," he said dryly.

"Maybe not, but you're scary in general."

"Has Angulus mentioned how appealing your bluntness is?"

"Yes."

Vann paused, not having expected that answer. "Was he lying?"

"I don't think so."

"Remarkable."

Kaika snorted. "I believe we were talking about Professor Lilah and that she'd be good for you, assuming you could control yourself and be good for her."

"I've never *not* controlled myself with a woman," he growled. How had he allowed himself to be drawn into this conversation? Just because he'd known Kaika a long time didn't mean she should be advising him on his love life. Still, he found himself wanting to share this information, just in case she was also chatting about him to *Lilah*. "You pummel men. You protect women. Those are the rules."

"Oh? Did your mother teach you that growing up?"

He fought back a snarl. Unlike Lilah, Kaika did not know what had happened to his mother. That was not a story he told often.

"I learned that from her, yes," he said, forcing himself to answer calmly.

"Maybe if you mounted someone regularly, you wouldn't feel the need to pummel men so much, either." Kaika stood up and dusted her hands off.

"I'm not exactly virginal, Captain," he said stiffly. The advice-giving had grown a little too personal.

"Fine, maybe if you mounted someone you *cared* about regularly, it would help your outlook on life."

Vann held back a sigh. There might be something to that.

"I can't believe General Chason aroused warm cozy feelings in you," she added while pulling out a match. "She's got a reputation for eviscerating privates who don't bring her morning coffee quickly enough."

Vann stared. How in all the levels of hell had she known about *that* relationship? She wasn't even on base that often.

"She used to brag around the officers' club that she had you on a leash," Kaika added. Surprisingly, she wasn't grinning as she said it. She actually appeared annoyed. On his behalf? Huh, he hadn't realized she cared. "Shall we blow up these rocks? Then you and the professor can go exploring together."

"And will you and Bosmont then go exploring together too?" He gave her an arch look.

"Not the same kind of exploring. I told Angulus I'd be a good girl unless I got my dragon chance."

"Does he demand goodness?" Vann asked, somewhat curious about their relationship, even if he didn't normally care two nucros who Kaika slept with. Angulus was a good man and his king.

"No, he doesn't demand anything. He's been very clear about that, but I know he'd be hurt, even if he didn't say anything. That's why I'm scheming to lure the dragon back for *both* of us." Her eyes crinkled with something akin to glee.

Vann couldn't keep from curling his lip in disgust. Or maybe distress. "I don't want to hear about that."

"You better stay up here in this hole then, because if I get a dragon into bed, I'm telling *everyone*."

"Just don't pick that one that thinks he's a god."

"No? I thought he might be my most likely bet. Have you seen him in human form? He's gorgeous. You'd want to get him into bed too."

"I highly doubt that."

"We've got all of the fossils dug out," Bosmont called, peeking down the tunnel.

"Thank the gods." Vann hustled away before Kaika could go into lurid details about her fantasy. It was impossible not to choke on the idea of their staid and proper king having a threesome with a dragon. "Blow up those rocks, Captain."

"Gladly, sir," Kaika said, sounding entirely too chipper.

***

"Is this good, ma'am?" Corporal Hetty lifted a lumpy rock with dragon vertebrae half carved out of it.

"Yes, be very careful as you get closer to the fossil," Lilah said.

"Yes, ma'am."

Next to him, Private Boxcar worked in silence, slicing away stone with precise strokes of a chipping hammer. He had extricated three fossils from their granite prisons in the time Hetty had done half of one. Who knew some brutish soldier with a neck the size of a tree trunk would have a deft hand for this? Neither of the men was older than her average student, but they called her ma'am and kept their glances at her bosom to a minimum. She found herself wishing she had some soldiers enrolled in her classes.

"This reminds me of *Time Trek*," Boxcar announced out of nowhere. He hadn't spoken a word to Lilah, so this random statement surprised her.

Hetty groaned. "Not your comics again, Boxcar."

"They're not comics. They're books. Novels. There aren't even any pictures."

"I'm familiar with them," Lilah said, smiling at the big man.

He fumbled the hammer, almost dropping it. "You've read them, ma'am?"

"I have."

"All of them?"

"I have the latest one in my room back at the outpost. I was hoping to read it on the way out here, but apparently, I get queasy when I'm in the back of a flier, so I haven't had a chance yet."

"I've heard that happens to a lot of people who ride with General Zirkander." Hetty grinned evilly and glanced toward the tunnel where Kaika and Vann were working.

Lilah didn't bother informing him that she had ridden with Lieutenant Sleepy. She wondered which one of the officers had prompted the grin—she hadn't noticed that Kaika had been green or wobbly-kneed when she had hopped out of Ridge's flier.

"The last book is cracking, ma'am," Boxcar said. "My mom sent it to me in a care package. I just finished."

"Don't tell me the ending, please. I'm waiting to see if Sashi finally captures the Cofah time wizard."

"I won't say a word, ma'am."

Vann and Kaika jogged out of the tunnel, Kaika wearing a grin. Vann wore his usual stony facade of determination. He looked toward Lilah as they came out, nodding as he met her eyes. She nodded back. Before she could wonder if he and Kaika had been discussing anything in particular in the back of that tunnel, an explosion rattled the mountainside. A cloud of dust flew out of the passage, and rocks clattered down from the cliffs above.

Lilah jumped to her feet, the rockslide that had wiped out the trail fresh in her mind. The area they were working around was flatter and much wider than the trail, but she could still envision it being buried in rubble.

Boxcar also leaped up. He placed himself between her and the rocks, resting a hand on her shoulder and putting his back to the mountainside. She wasn't a short woman, but her head only came to his collarbone, so he made an effective shield.

A couple of boulders tumbled down, and smaller rocks clattered off the ground like hail, but nothing more dangerous happened. When the dust cleared, Lilah found Vann standing next to her and giving Boxcar a flat look. The private let go of her shoulder.

"We're helping the professor, sir."

"I'm sure."

"She's real nice to work with. And she's read *Time Trek*."

Vann blinked. "What?"

Lilah felt her cheeks warm. "They're novels. They're popular on campus." Usually more with the students than the professors, but there was no need to mention that. It wasn't as if she went to the costume parties.

"A team of soldiers and scientists use a time machine to go back a thousand years to use modern technology to drive back the Cofah invasion, so that Iskandia was never taken over," Boxcar said, speaking more in that sentence than he had since Lilah had met him. "There's adventures, and romance, and Commander Asylon gets his own dragon in the third book."

Vann stared at the young soldier as if a third eye had sprouted from his forehead, then he raised an eyebrow at Lilah. "You've read these?"

"Yes, the author comes and speaks at the university from time to time," she said, refusing to feel silly for liking them. "They're quite well written."

"The romance doesn't involve the dragon, does it?" Vann's lip curled as he looked toward Kaika. She was peering into the tunnel as the dust settled and did not notice.

"No, sir," Boxcar said. "It's been Commander Asylon and the scientist he works for—Sashi Silverton."

Lilah rubbed her face, not sure she would have done quite so much summarizing for someone who hadn't read the books.

"He works for her, eh?" Vann asked.

"Well, it's a joint expedition between the military and the university, but Sashi always ends up knowing more than the commander, so she's kind of in charge."

"Are they written by a civilian?" Vann asked, his tone dry.

"What, you wouldn't be willing to work for me?" Lilah asked, glad he sounded amused rather than derisive. She had encountered numerous negative reactions at work. Most of her colleagues dismissed the books as juvenile.

"I suppose it would depend on what kind of remuneration was involved." The corners of his eyes crinkled.

"How is it that you can use big words like remuneration but not little ones like please and thank you?"

"It's the mystery of me."

"Bos, come check this out with me," Kaika called, waving toward the dwindling dust cloud.

"Why don't we wait a few minutes to see if those cursed fossils get twitchy and cause additional cave-ins?" Bosmont asked. "It's been a whole six hours since anything creepy happened. We might be due."

"I'll take my chances. I can always blow myself out." Kaika patted the pouches on her utility belt, then ambled into the tunnel.

"She better be careful if she wants to live long enough to seduce that dragon," Vann said.

Lilah grinned and swatted his arm. She much preferred Vann-with-a-sense-of-humor to Grumpy-Vann. He looked down at where she had swatted him, raised his eyebrows, then wriggled them at her. It was the first flirtatious look he had given her, and a tingle of warmth flushed her body. Playful-Vann was something she hadn't seen before, but she promptly decided she wanted more of it.

"Sir?" came Kaika's call from the back of the tunnel. "You and the professor may want to see this."

Vann nodded at Bosmont. "Think it's safe to take her back there?"

"I don't think it's safe anywhere on this mountain, sir," Bosmont said.

"In that case, we might as well go exploring," Lilah said.

Vann snorted but did not disagree. He grabbed a canteen and a pack with food tins in it, slinging both over his shoulder to hang next to his rifle and sword. Curious as to what he expected to find back there, Lilah trailed after him. She assumed it would just be more cleared rock, but maybe he had an inkling of something else?

He grabbed a lantern on the way in and strode toward the back of the tunnel. Dust lingered inside, dulling the light of his flame, but Lilah could see surprisingly well. A faint yellowish-white light came from the back, from what had been nothing but a dead end before.

Kaika came into view amid piles of rock. She pushed a boulder aside, and more light flooded into the tunnel. If Lilah hadn't been warned that Referatu tunnels filled the mountain, along with whatever artifacts they'd left behind when they had died, she would have been flummoxed.

"Is that a power crystal?" Vann asked.

"Yes, sir." Kaika leaned against the gray wall, a wall that now extended much farther, and pointed around the rubble pile that took up most of the tunnel. Vann would have to flatten all of his muscles to squeeze past. "I can see two of them. They're just hanging on the ceiling down there. General Zirkander will be so pleased with you."

A rumble came from Vann's throat at Ridge's name. "Zirkander can suck my—" he glanced back at Lilah, "—toe."

"What a treat that would be," Kaika said, then squirmed out of sight, disappearing between the wall and the top of the boulder pile. Rocks shifted, tumbling and clacking on the other side.

Without hesitating, Lilah climbed up to the opening and squeezed through after her.

"Lilah," Vann protested. "It's going to be dangerous back there. Don't you want to wait back in camp while the soldiers investigate?"

"Not in the least," she called back, excitement dancing through her veins as a wide tunnel came into view, a completely intact tunnel.

Long ago, a portion of the ceiling had collapsed, dropping granite boulders to block the passage, but after about twenty feet, the ceiling continued, as flat and gray as the walls and floors. Lilah patted one of those walls, again noticing the smoothness. She wondered if the Referatu had melted the existing rock of the mountain somehow to create the tunnels. Though the gray was oddly uniform, the passage reminded her of lava tubes, such as she had clambered through on her way to the crater in Mt. Mastmonsoro that she had told the others about.

More rocks shifted, this time behind her. Grumbling as he squeezed through the gap, Vann scraped his way up to join Lilah, the tip of his sword scabbard and the muzzle of his rifle thumping and clanking against the rocks. Kaika had already reached the end of the cave-in and stood on the gray floor, looking up at an angular crystal mounted to the ceiling. It provided so much light that no shadows remained in the passage.

"This is wonderful." Lilah gripped Vann's hand, wanting to smooth the irritated crease on his forehead. "An unexplored historical site. What a gift."

"We'll see how much of a gift it is. This mountain hasn't treated us well lately." Despite his gruffness, his brow did, indeed, smooth in the face of her unfeigned enthusiasm.

"If these are just hanging around, stuck to the ceiling, we might get a whole ton of them, sir," Kaika said, now dangling from the light fixture with one hand while she prodded at the seam with a dagger. "You might get that toe-sucking after all."

Vann's lip curled again, and Lilah laughed.

A thump and a pained grunt came from behind them. Bosmont was almost as big as Vann, if not quite as brawny, and he would have a hard time pulling himself through too.

"Captain," Vann said. "Grab a couple of the men and most of our supplies. We'll take a look around in here and see if we can extricate a few preliminary energy crystals to take back. Leave a few people to guard the camp. Tell them not to touch the professor's fossils while she's not there to watch them. And also tell them not to get scared and run off again."

"I'll relay the message, sir," Bosmont said.

"Leave them some explosives too," Vann added. "In case there's another rockfall, I'd like someone back there who can dig us out."

"Uh, are you sure you want them to do that? Corporal Hetty is the highest-ranking one, and I doubt he's ever used dynamite. Certainly not any of the more sophisticated stuff that Kaika brought."

"Are you volunteering to stay behind, Bosmont?"

"It would be an honor to extricate you from a cave-in,

sir." Judging by the sound of his voice, Bosmont was already retreating.

"Uh huh." Vann met Lilah's eyes. "I better keep you with me. I think he'd let me stay buried in the cave-in, but I'm reasonably certain he'll go through great lengths to rescue Zirkander's cousin."

"It's not too late to say something nice to him so he wants to rescue *you* too."

Vann sighed. "I don't know what nice thing I would say that would be sincere. Nice thoughts don't pop into my head."

"As a teacher, I have to get creative to find them in mine sometimes," she admitted.

He smiled slightly. "Are you married, Lilah?"

Her mouth dropped open. Where had that come from? True, she had been thinking that she should let him know that she wasn't, but she doubted he was a mind reader.

"Got it," Kaika announced before Lilah could answer. She dropped to the ground with the foot-long energy crystal—the foot-long lamp—cradled in her arms. She saluted them with her dagger, then strolled toward the next crystal.

"We might want to leave some of those until we're on our way out," Vann commented as the shadows around them deepened.

"Yes, sir," Kaika said without looking back, "but I thought you might like some soft mood lighting."

Vann grunted. More rocks scraped beyond the granite pile, and Lilah remembered that he'd told Bosmont to send some of the soldiers along.

Lilah started after Kaika, waving for Vann to walk beside her.

"I was married," she said. "My husband and my father passed away at the same time five years ago." Passed away. Such a bland euphemism for that fiery death. "It was a vehicle accident. My father was driving." She didn't usually tell people that, but Vann had told her about his vile father. If anyone would understand how disappointing her own father had been, it would be he. The man had not possessed any mean blood in his veins, but he'd been so worthless, leaving her mother to raise her and her brothers by herself while he spent his days tinkering with steam vehicles and drinking at the pub.

"I'd say I'm sorry, but it would be a lie," Vann said, "and I already told you that insincerity doesn't come easily to me."

Lilah wasn't sure whether to find his honesty endearing or alarming. His bluntness aside, it secretly pleased her that he wanted her to be unmarried. Available. But in the future, she would have to make sure never to ask him a question she didn't want a sincere answer to.

"It was a good marriage," she said quietly, following Kaika around a bend in the passage. They walked under a power source that had burned out, but more lit the way up ahead. "We were both academics. Friends first. A good match. I never thought I'd look for anyone else. I thought we'd both have brilliant careers, children eventually..." Her throat tightened. She had thought she had come to terms with the passing of that dream, but five years wasn't as long ago as she sometimes thought. Funny how when she'd been younger, five years had seemed an eternity, but these days, some of those memories still seemed so fresh. Like yesterday.

She shook her head, done sharing, at least for now. All he had asked was if she was married. He hadn't wondered about the quality of that marriage or if her husband's death had left her with any crushed dreams.

"I always thought I'd have children," Vann said. "My youngest brother has three. They're noisier than a pack of agitated coyotes, but tolerable if you wear them out."

Lilah imagined Vann ushering toddlers through some military obstacle course, then ordering them to give him twenty push-ups.

"I let them swing from my arms and ride on my shoulders. They seem to like that." He shrugged. "I can't imagine myself being a very good father, but as odd as it seems, given the way of my own father's demise, I'm the heir to the family title and the estate. I didn't even know we had property anywhere until a lawyer found me when I was in my twenties, reported that my great uncle had died without heirs and that since my father was dead, I was the next in line. That's when I found out I had a crypt full of dead relatives, along with this sword." He tilted his thumb toward the hilt. "There was a lot of history that I'd known nothing of as a boy, since my father hadn't cared to share it with us. One of my brothers lives out there now. He's trying to turn it into a blueberry farm if you can believe it. But the land would be mine if I ever wanted it, or had someone to share it with." He glanced at her. "I've only been out there a few times. It's not really home."

Lilah didn't get the feeling that he was giving her the information to impress her, though there was the suggestion that he wouldn't mind getting married someday. Was it strange that he was talking to her of such things? When they had known each other such a short time? Maybe he had been lonely out here, an outpost commander with nobody of his rank to speak plainly to, and nobody from the civilian world that he might converse with, either. Loneliness did have a way of making one ponder if one would ever find someone, as did reaching a certain age.

The voices of the two soldiers trailing them drifted toward her, two young men making jokes about the shapes of the power crystals.

She snorted softly and shook her head. Perhaps this wasn't the time for sharing stories or thinking of futures. She offered Vann a smile, so he would know she was acknowledging his words, even if she doubted she could imagine herself living on some rural estate, miles and miles from the nearest university. Nor could she see spending significant time up here in this remote outpost. Or following a soldier around from duty station to duty station, her life and livelihood depending on him. She loved her career. It was nonnegotiable. Vann's attention was flattering, but there wasn't any hope for a future for them, not practically speaking, and she didn't do the impractical. She never had.

A low whistle came from up ahead. Kaika had stopped at the mouth of a tunnel, the walls opening into a larger space.

Distracted by Vann's words, Lilah hadn't been paying much attention to their surroundings—that was surprising, since she was excited to explore. She hurried ahead now, eager to see what awaited them.

Vann trailed behind more slowly, and she wondered if he had sensed a rejection in her silence.

"Not sure what I was expecting," Kaika said, "but that wasn't it."

She pointed to old bones scattered around a chamber made of the same smooth gray stone. The chewed remains of a faded carpet formed a circle in the middle. Lilah crouched next to a skull with teeth marks around the eyeholes. A leg bone lay nearby, snapped in half, the marrow licked out by some predator. She shivered, wondering what animals larger than rats might be in here and how they would have gotten in.

Vann walked the circumference of the chamber, his rifle in his hands now. Three other tunnels opened up at what Lilah thought might be the cardinal directions. Two stood dark, and one was lit by power crystals.

"It was a man," Lilah said, lifting the skull to see if any cracks might have accounted for a killing blow. Had this been a Referatu sorcerer? Someone who had been down here when the tunnels had collapsed? She frowned. But these tunnels hadn't collapsed.

Something clinked inside of the skull and fell out onto the floor at the same time as she spotted a small hole in the back. The object rolled several feet before coming to rest against the edge of the carpet. Vann reached it first, squatting to pick it up.

"Musket ball?" Lilah asked, having glimpsed it rolling.

"Musket ball with an old Iskandian Guard stamp on it." Vann held it between his fingers. "0.75 caliber. Big."

"A good size for hunting sorcerers?" Lilah stared at the lead ball.

"I haven't seen a bullet hit a sorceress yet. They make shields around themselves. The dragons do too."

"Uh, I don't think that fellow was a sorcerer," Kaika said from across the chamber. She picked up a dusty jacket, mostly intact despite its age. She spread it out and showed it to them.

"That's from an old army uniform," Vann said.

Something clanked to the floor as Kaika shook the dust out of it. At first, Lilah thought it might be another musket ball, but it was something flat.

"Tags." Vann walked over to join Kaika.

She picked them up and squinted at the old metal. The round disks had probably been hand engraved back then. "Captain Troyar Molisak."

"Molisak?" Vann asked.

"That's a noble family," Lilah said, also recognizing the name. "I guess that makes sense. Back then, all officers came out of the nobility."

"And being noble actually meant something," Vann said.

"I wonder if his family ever had any idea what happened to him," Lilah said.

"What *did* happen to him?" Kaika rifled through a pocket. "There's something poky in here."

"He was shot," Vann said.

"But by whom?" Lilah wondered.

"The witches defending this place, obviously."

"Uh, *is* it obvious?" Kaika asked. "Witches with muskets? I've never seen Sardelle use a firearm."

"Because she's got a sword that can melt a man's balls off."

The words prompted Lilah to glance at Vann's crotch, though she quickly averted her eyes.

He must have noticed because he firmly said, "My balls are intact."

"Smooth, sir," Kaika said. "If the professor wasn't interested before, she's sure to be now."

Vann glowered at her. "I know better than to manhandle a witch."

"Your wisdom only grows with the years."

His glower deepened. "What *does* Angulus see in you?"

She grinned. "I'm the only one around him who doesn't fire with the safety on."

"What a treat."

Kaika unbuttoned one of the pockets in the dusty jacket and extracted a small leather-bound journal. "Here's the poky thing."

"Poky thing?" Vann asked.

"In the academic world, we call those books," Lilah said.

Vann gave her an appreciative grin that made her flush for some reason, as if it were the rarest and most delightful of compliments.

"Right. I knew it was a big fancy vocabulary word, but I couldn't place it." Kaika handed the journal to Lilah. "I'll let you keep it for your bedtime reading, Professor."

Bedtime? Lilah flipped it open immediately. "If this was Captain Molisak's journal, I'm sure the family will appreciate having it returned." After she perused it thoroughly, of course. The officers might be enthused by finding a pile of power crystals, but who knew what treasures lay within this tome? It might hold the answer to the question of what had truly happened to the Referatu all those years ago. Was Sardelle's story, as relayed by Bosmont, correct? Or had there been a disease that only affected those with dragon blood?

"Anyone else feel a draft?" Vann asked.

"I thought I did," Kaika said. "From over there."

Lilah barely heard them. She had flipped to the last page of the journal with text on it. Even if the officer's body had been torn apart by some scavenger, the book was in remarkably good shape. She had no trouble reading the ink of the captain's neat hand, though the last few pages were more sloppily penned than the first. Hastily, she decided, skimming the words. A name jumped out at her and made her stomach lurch with unease.

I have learned that Major Therrik does not, as he claimed, have orders from high command for this assignment, an assignment that has filled me with trepidation from the beginning. I am a soldier, and it is my duty to follow my superiors without question, but as the king's man and as a loyal follower of Deago, the first God, I also feel it is my duty to act with honor. The words that I overheard the major speaking to the Referatu assistant president have confirmed my suspicions, but what do I do? Do I confront Therrik? The major is known for his temper, and I am but an engineer, not a warrior of great martial prowess.

Lilah swallowed, her heart racing as she read the words. Major *Therrik*? Known for his *temper*?

If the pages hadn't been so brittle, the ink so faded, she would have believed some soldier had been writing this about Colonel Therrik, perhaps before his last promotion. She hurried to read on, worrying that she would be caught learning this information, feeling as if she were intruding upon some terrible secret. Maybe she was.

It could be argued that the assistant president is to blame, and Therrik is simply obeying the wishes of someone with far greater rank in society than either he or I have, but she is not our commander, and she is certainly not our king. Though this mountain lies within Iskandian borders, the Referatu are a separate people, with a separate governing body. They cannot command our soldiers any more than we command their sorcerers. And what these two are planning is a betrayal to both societies. Worse, I am not certain Therrik is being honest with her—or with us. The explosives we carry have a great deal of power, more than would be needed for the small incursion we were told to plan for. I knew to be concerned when I was given the order to requisition them. Was that order even real? Or was it a forgery? Our party carries the power to blow up the entire capital. Or perhaps this entire mountain. Why would the assistant president target her own leader? And put her own people in jeopardy? I do not know, unless she plots against her president in the hope of earning the position. I am quite positive that she will not be within these tunnels when the bombs go off. But why risk killing so many? What is a king without subjects? Or does she have no idea of what Therrik plans? Is he acting on his own, turning a political skirmish into an opportunity for... much more?

"Lilah?" Vann asked.

She jumped, nearly dropping the book. Kaika was hanging from another light fixture, and the two soldiers who had caught up with them were working on a third. Vann pointed to a tunnel.

"Will you come with me to check out this draft?" he asked. "Your bodyguard is distracted."

Kaika cursed as she repeatedly jammed her dagger into the rock above the fixture, trying to dislodge it.

"Uh." Lilah looked from Vann to Kaika and back, suddenly uncertain about wandering off alone with Vann. Just because his ancestor might have been involved in something shady didn't mean that he knew anything about it, but what if she had stumbled onto some dark family secret that he wouldn't want shared? That he might protect, no matter what?

Seven gods, she had planned to write a *paper* about all of this. What if Captain Molisak had confronted Major Therrik, and Therrik had *shot* the man? What if the truth had never come out all of those years ago and she now held it in her hands? Could Therrik be punished for the actions of an ancestor three hundred years in the past? It had been a less sophisticated time back then, but murdering a fellow noble had been forbidden, the same as it was today. Could Vann's lands be revoked for a crime committed centuries earlier? His title? Even if he spoke indifferently about his noble ranking, it had to matter to him, or he wouldn't have brought it up at all.

"You can bring the book," Vann said, a furrow to his brow. Lilah gulped. She could only imagine what expression she wore. "Are you all right?" he added. "Anything interesting?"

She snapped it shut. "I haven't had time to determine the interest level."

She was proud of her voice for not coming out overly squeaky or distressed, but her mind whirled as she walked over to join Vann. She didn't want to lie to him, but she had no idea how he would react. Would he be ashamed of the actions of his ancestor? Or would he condone those actions, since it had been a plot against the Referatu? Perhaps the plot that had destroyed their civilization? The very witches that, for whatever reason, he utterly and completely loathed.

A howl sounded in the distance, and she almost dropped the book for the second time in two minutes.

Vann's head turned toward the tunnel opposite the one through which they had entered. Normally, the wails of a wolf or coyote out in the forest wouldn't distress Lilah, especially if she had her hunting rifle at hand, but she *didn't* have her rifle, and that howl hadn't come from the forest. What kind of wolves roamed about in mountain tunnels? And what would a wolf find to eat in here, anyway?

Her gaze drifted to the skull of the long-lost officer. No, whatever had feasted on his bones had done so centuries ago. There couldn't be anything left in here for a predator. She didn't think.

"Was that a wolf?" Kaika asked.

"No," Vann said.

"Coyote?"

He shook his head.

"Then what was it?" Kaika asked. "After all those tracking

and survival classes you taught, I assumed you could identify anything in these mountains."

"I should be able to, but that was more deeply pitched than a wolf's or coyote's howl." Vann shrugged. "It's possible I'm mistaken. The tunnels could be distorting the noise."

"Maybe it's the curse," one of the soldiers whispered. Lilah hadn't learned his name yet. She wished Boxcar had come along. He seemed steady.

"Curses don't howl," Vann growled. "Finish up with the crystals and take them out to Bosmont. Kaika, you come join us when you're done. We might need something else blown up."

"Like some wolves?"

"We'll see." Vann handed Lilah his rifle. "Here. I'll use the sword if I need it."

She accepted the weapon, though she was more worried about what lay in the book and about what he would think about it if she shared it. A hollow sense of unease swam in the pit of her stomach as she followed him.

CHAPTER 9

PROFESSOR LILAH ZIRKANDER WAS ACTING oddly. Vann studied her as they walked down one of the four passages that had exited from the chamber, intermittent ceiling lamps providing enough light for him to observe the worried glances she sent in his direction. She kept wiping her hands on her trousers, and she clenched that book as if it were a life preserver on a rough sea. He shouldn't have admitted he was relieved her husband was dead. At the least, that had been uncouth. Worse, it must have offended her. Or even worried her. What had she thought when he'd spoken of his family land? Why had he even brought it up? She probably thought he wanted to *marry* her. Who spoke of such things after three days? They hadn't even had sex. He had *thought* about it a great deal, but that was hardly the same.

The scent of pine trees and snow reached Vann's nose. Up ahead, next to a ceiling lamp that had fallen dark over the centuries, a hole gaped in the side of the tunnel. Debris littered the stone floor in front of it. Vann strode ahead and bent to pick up some shards of iron. They were thin, partially blackened by soot. He spotted some writing on the outside of one curved piece, but he couldn't guess at what the partial letters had said.

"Looks like shrapnel," he muttered.

"From black powder explosives," Lilah said. "That's what they would have had access to back then. Dynamite is relatively new, historically speaking."

"Yes." Vann tossed the metal shard aside and peered into the tunnel. It was even rougher and uglier than the one the thieves had drilled, and he wasn't sure if he could fit through it. He considered Lilah's smaller form, but rejected the idea of asking her to go in there alone, especially when some animal was roaming around the tunnels. Some *hungry* animal, likely. He couldn't imagine that the hunting was good.

"Want me to go first?" she asked.

"I was debating whether we should go at all." Vann sniffed the air. "I think this is where the draft is coming from. It's probably just another route to the outside. One that comes out above the one we opened up. We've been climbing slightly since we entered the witch tunnels."

"I'll just take a quick look." Lilah slid the rifle off her shoulder, keeping it in her hand, and headed into the rough passage, having to dip under low-hanging rock right away.

He frowned as she disappeared. He doubted she would run into any trouble in the fifty feet or so that he estimated the passage would be before coming out over the cliff, but he hated the idea of letting her out of his sight. He dropped to his knees. If the deceased Captain Molisak had come in this way, and if it hadn't changed over the years, maybe he could make it too. Of course, coming *out* again could be problematic.

"Vann?" Lilah asked, her voice soft and muffled. Also a touch concerned.

"Yes?"

"This may have been a bad idea."

"Are you stuck?"

"No, just a little... claustrophobic. I made the mistake of remembering that rockslide last night. It's dark and tight and—" She inhaled deeply, the sound of her breath audible from his spot. "I'm thinking about getting stuck."

"I recommend against it."

"Thanks," she said, a hint of dryness replacing some of the concern.

"Do you want me to join you?" Vann doubted that was logical. If she was likely to get stuck, he would be even more likely to get stuck.

Still, she answered with a tentative, "Yes, please."

Vann removed his sword, eyed all the knives, pistols, and ammo pouches on his waist, and wondered again at the odds of not getting stuck. He unclasped the utility belt and left it on the ground, in case that made a difference. Then he shimmied under the overhanging rock, keeping the sword scabbard in hand. His shoulders scraped the sides, and in the dim lighting, he bonked his head more than once. He worried less about claustrophobia and more that his ass was exposed if anyone came along behind them. It seemed unlikely—was some tunnel-loving wolf going to pick up his discarded pistols and shoot him?—but instincts honed over decades of risking his life in dangerous situations made him twitchy.

As he wriggled further, Lilah came into view, her outline just visible since she carried the lantern ahead of her. He sublimated an urge to catch up and pat—or squeeze—her butt to let her know he had arrived. That might alarm her more than the tightness of the passage.

"It's getting a little wider," she said, sounding relieved. "And I think I see some light."

"Daylight or creepy magical light?"

"Daylight, I think." She did not sound amused at what he had meant to be a joke, or at least irreverence.

He thought of those nervous glances she had been sending him. Was she angry because he hated magic? She *had* seemed surprised by his reaction when Bosmont had shared the history of the mountain. He couldn't understand why, since most people hated and feared magic. And he had more reason to detest it than most. Maybe he ought to share *that* story with her. He grimaced at the idea. Being a boy and losing a battle to his grown father was not reason for embarrassment, but being a grown man, freshly out of the academy and trained to be a supreme warrior, and losing to some witch with potions? *That* was embarrassing. What was even more embarrassing was that he'd been too much of a coward to ever go back and face the bitch. He—

"Definitely daylight," Lilah said. "Oh, Vann. Look at this view."

He looked at her butt. That was all that was visible, though he could see light seeping around her. "It is a nice one," he said.

"Oh, sorry, I'm corking it up, aren't I? Here, there's a ledge." She moved as she spoke, and the daylight she had promised came into view.

Vann scooted up next to her until he knelt at the mouth of their little tunnel. It looked out over the goat trail. He grunted when he spotted the place that had fallen away.

"Not sure I needed a view of that," he said.

"Not that. *That.*" She touched a finger to his chin and directed him to look outward, over the trees that had blocked the view from down on the trail. The sun was dipping toward the tops of the mountains across the way, glacier-laden peaks that gleamed orangish yellow under the late afternoon rays.

"It's all right," Vann said. "I was fond of my previous view."

She looked puzzled.

"Of—" Vann waved at her lower half. "Never mind."

"Oh." The sun provided enough light for him to see the pinkish hue that blossomed on her cheeks.

"So, this is how they originally came in three hundred years ago, eh?" Vann leaned out over the edge to gauge the distance down to the trail. He had no idea if that trail would have been there all those centuries ago. It hadn't been much when Bosmont had found it.

Lilah reached out and gripped his shoulder. "Careful. Some of it crumbled when I got close." She waved at the ledge beneath his hands.

"I'll be careful." He glanced at her arm. "But you can keep holding me if you like."

Her cheeks grew a brighter shade of pink, and she looked like she would let go of him, but instead, she moved her hand from gripping his shoulder to resting it on his back. Remembering that he had been looking for evidence that someone had climbed up, he returned his focus to the cliff that dropped away from the tunnel mouth. He definitely did not think about what it would feel like if she ran her hand from his shoulder down to cup his ass.

Looking down did not show him much, but when he turned his head, he spotted a rusty eyelet protruding from the rock.

"There's some evidence," he said. "Anchor for climbing. An old-style one."

"They came up from below, crawled through this passage, and blew their way into one of the Referatu tunnels," Lilah said.

"I agree with that. But what about the fossils?" He shifted his weight so that he could sit on his butt, since the rock was brutal on the knees. He was careful not to dislodge Lilah's hand.

"Given the way nature has reclaimed the area near the camp, it seems likely the fossils were placed three hundred years ago rather than a few weeks ago. I still don't know how or why." She shifted, too, and sat cross-legged beside him. She lowered her hand, alas, but her shoulder came to touch his as they sat together, so he did not mind.

"Three hundred years ago," Vann mused. "Suggesting this fossil plot was never about my mining outpost at all."

"Feeling insignificant?"

"Egotistical, perhaps." He massaged one of the fresh lumps on his head while he tried to figure out what the fossils could have accomplished back then. Some kind of distraction to allow a team of soldiers to sneak in?

"Vann?" Lilah said his name carefully while looking down at her lap. She gripped that book with both hands.

"Yes?"

"Is there a reason... I know everyone has been culturally indoctrinated to distrust magic, and that in less educated areas, it's deemed normal, if not acceptable, to persecute people based on whether or not they might have the ability to use it, but—"

"Lilah. I'm a dumb soldier, remember? Use small words, please."

"Vann, you said please." She beamed a smile at him, which warmed him as much as thoughts of ass cupping. Maybe even more. "Also, you're not dumb."

"Nevertheless, I'm a simple man. I like simple words. And direct women." He wriggled his eyebrows at her. That had seemed to fluster her in a good way, earlier.

"Oh." She opened her mouth, then closed it again, appearing derailed rather than pleasantly flustered. "Vann, are you and Kaika—"

"No."

"You didn't let me finish the question."

"It's hard not to jump out of the pot as soon as you know the water is boiling."

"But you said you like direct women and she... knows where all of your tattoos are."

"I'm positive she was too drunk during our one night together to remember where *all* of the tattoos are, but I'll gladly show them to you." He lowered his eyelids in a manner that women often found sexy. "In case you want to map them. For a research project."

She snorted. "What kind of research project would that be?"

"You're the scientist. You tell me." Vann rested his hand on her thigh, tempted to give her some non-verbal suggestions for research projects.

But she bit her lip, looking down instead of meeting his gaze, as he wished. It was hard to kiss a woman whose eyes were locked onto a book instead of him. He imagined he could distract her without too much effort and was debating on that when she took a determined breath and faced him again.

"Why do you have such a visceral reaction to the merest mention of magic or those with the ability to use it?"

Vann couldn't sublimate a scowl. He wanted to kiss her, not talk about the past. Hadn't they done enough of that? It had been all right in the dark, with the crackling of the flames making the moment private. Intimate. But there were things a man could speak of to a woman at night that he didn't want to admit—or *couldn't* admit—under the harsh light of the summer sun.

"Is that important now?" he asked. "I had other things on my mind." Before he could try his eyebrow waggle again, she frowned down at her new book.

He tamped down the urge to take it and throw it to the trail below. A tantrum wouldn't impress her, and he would instantly feel like an idiot.

"It might be important," she said softly. "If you tell me... No, sorry. It's not the kind of thing I should try to weasel out of you." She shifted her weight to her hands. "We should get back to the others."

He let her pull away from him, though a big part of him wanted to wrap an arm around her and keep her close.

"Thank you for following me in here," she said before heading into the tight passage. "I probably couldn't be an archaeologist, crawling around in ancient ruins. Tight spots, stale air, and darkness make me uncomfortable. I start to worry that the mountain or ruins or whatever's above me will collapse and crush me. Silly, I know, especially when I'm in a site that's been standing for millennia or more."

"Given what's been going on, it's not that silly." Vann looked in the direction of the camp, thinking of that tarp full of fossils. Had the trail been open, he might have gone back and ordered the men to drag them into the forest where he'd hung the first set, far enough away that whatever magic was about them couldn't affect his team.

As Vann and Lilah crawled back through the uneven tunnel, another howl came from somewhere inside the mountain. The fossils might be the least of their problems.

* * *

She'd almost told him.

When Vann had been looking at her through lowered eyelashes, his expression one of warmth and promise, so different from the stony facade he usually wore, she had almost divulged everything in the journal, but nothing had changed. If he'd told her why he hated magic, and if it had been something understandable, maybe she would have shared the text, but if he learned that Major Therrik had led the attack on the Referatu facility and ended up being *proud* of that, as he was for being descended from a dragon-slaying ancestor, what would she do?

She couldn't accept such heartlessness in a friend, much less in a lover. True, they hadn't even kissed yet, but she had sensed on a number of occasions that he wanted to. If *she* wanted that, she could have it—and more. And damn it, she wanted it. He was handsome, had that sexy growl, and had the kind of physique that she had only touched in dreams. Even in his gruff, flinty moments, she found herself drawn to him rather than repelled.

Maybe it was foolish, but she had the sense that if he had someone supportive in his life, he might mellow and find peace with himself. And he hadn't been gruff or flinty with *her*, not since that initial meeting with Ridge. He seemed normal, even friendly, when he was away from his men, his responsibilities.

Lilah and Vann returned to the chamber to find that Captain Kaika and the two soldiers had collected eight of the energy sources, leaving the area noticeably dimmer.

"This enough for now, sir?" Kaika asked. "Whatever's howling has been getting closer."

"Worried about fighting off some animal?" Vann asked.

"Not at all, but I wouldn't want to damage the crystals when I start hurling explosives at malevolent packs of predators."

"We could just shoot them."

"How would that be fun?" Kaika grinned and plopped the crystal she held onto a soldier's stack, his eyes barely visible over the top. "Go take those to Bosmont."

"Yes, ma'am," the other soldier, similarly loaded up, said. Their arms full, they headed toward the main entrance. The crystals did not appear heavy, but carrying so many was awkward.

"That's probably enough for one trip," Vann said. "We'll get the rest of the fossils cleared out, then put a team to work in here."

"You're not thinking of leaving, are you?" Lilah blurted, squeezing the journal in her hand.

"Why not?"

"We have a mystery here. Don't you want to know more about what happened? Why the king's soldiers, officers from the *nobility*, were part of the plot that destroyed a civilization?"

"A bunch of witches is hardly a civilization, and no, my orders are to extract crystals from the mountain, and that's it. Nothing about extracting mysteries."

"They had their own culture, customs, and government," Lilah said. "They were most certainly a civilization, by any definition of the word. And those soldiers wiped them out. I'd sure like to know why."

"They were *witches*," Vann said.

"They were human beings."

"They were part dragon. They used their power to *control* human beings."

Lilah glared at him, anger flushing her face and momentarily stealing her ability to form arguments. "Well, your ancestor used his power and influence to destroy *all* of them."

That was not the calm, rational argument she had wished to use, not at all, and she winced as soon as it came out. But what did it matter? He had already made his stance on "witches" clear.

Vann's eyebrows drew together in anger or maybe angry puzzlement. "What are you talking about?"

She tossed the journal at him. "Last entry."

Lilah took a deep breath, trying to calm herself, to still her anger. Her disappointment in him. She wouldn't be angry, she admitted, if some other soldier had made the same arguments, the same decisions. She just wanted him to be... *more*.

She met Kaika's eyes across the chamber. For once, the captain was staying out of the conversation, not interjecting any innuendos or jokes about blowing things up.

"Are you my bodyguard or his soldier, Captain?" Lilah asked. "I plan to remain here to continue my research, and I'd prefer that someone stay with me."

"Your mission is to analyze the dragon fossils," Vann said. He had turned to the last entry in the journal but hadn't started reading yet. "Not some witch maze."

"My mission as a scientist who studies the past is to foster a greater understanding of the present, of the evolutionary events that shaped the world we live in and the species we became." Lilah turned away from him, since he was scowling at her and not reading. Maybe he wouldn't bother reading at all.

"General Zirkander assigned me to you, ma'am," Kaika said, frowning over at Vann. "Happy to stay with you."

"Good. Let's check out that tunnel first." She pointed at the passage farthest from the one leading out, not because any evidence suggested she would find answers down there, but because it appeared most likely to lead into the heart of the mountain, perhaps the heart of the Referatu compound.

Unfortunately, it was also the tunnel from which the howling had originated. But she still had Vann's rifle—she wasn't going to hand it back to him, not if he was denying her his company and protection—and Kaika had a rifle, a pistol, and whatever explosives she carried on her person. Lilah doubted they would find any animals living down here that they couldn't handle. As far as she knew, the Ice Blades didn't possess anything more dangerous than bears, wolves, and mountain lions. Formidable creatures, but nothing she hadn't faced down on safaris.

"I'll lead, ma'am," Kaika said and headed into the tunnel.

Lilah strode after her, only glancing back once, hoping she might catch Vann reading or, even better, chasing after them. Instead, he turned his back and walked toward the exit.

Chapter 10

Lilah had been walking for less than a minute before she started to doubt her choice to storm off. She did not worry much about the intermittent howls, but she felt foolish because she had thrown the journal at Vann, and it was the biggest piece of evidence they had. What if he chucked it in the creek? All of the answers she sought might have been within its pages. What, if anything, did the dragon fossils have to do with that long-ago infiltration? Why had they been infused with magic? Why had someone high up in the Referatu government apparently plotted with Major Therrik, or someone who had commanded Major Therrik, to betray her own people?

Lilah halted, the image of Vann reading the journal—or not reading it—and throwing it into the creek flooding her mind. He wouldn't be so petty, would he? He wouldn't destroy history. He might if he read it, since, no matter what he thought of sorcerers, there would be some who would consider his ancestor's actions vile. What if the king felt that way? What if Ridge's Sardelle felt that way? Was she someone who would take revenge on him for hiding the past?

Kaika continued a few more steps before stopping and looking back. "We going the wrong way?"

"I'm afraid I made a mistake in giving Vann that journal, that he might do something to it. It's an important historical document."

"You want to go back?"

A howl drifted up from the depths of the mountain, sending a chill down her spine. Lilah checked the rifle for the third time, making sure it was, indeed, loaded.

"I don't know. Vann may need time to... forget that I snapped at him."

"Oh, just kiss him. He'll forget."

Lilah snorted. "So easily?"

"At least until after you have sex."

"Let's go a little farther," Lilah said. "I'm not sure I can have sex with someone so..." She shrugged, not wanting to badmouth him. Besides, Kaika had known him a lot longer than Lilah had. She might be more likely to take his side in a disagreement.

"He's a difficult man," Kaika said. "Come on. We'll explore a little more and go back this evening. He's not going to do anything to damage the book. You have more power over him than you think. All you have to do is complain to Angulus or Zirkander that he was inhospitable or destroyed something of scientific significance, and he'll get orders to stay out here, overseeing this outpost until he dies."

"Complain to Angulus? I've never even met the king."

"Doesn't matter. He'll still listen. And Therrik's not in the best position with him to start with, or he wouldn't be out here."

"How *did* he come to be stationed here?" Lilah picked up her pace to catch up with Kaika, who had long legs and a long stride, even when she ambled.

"Picked the wrong side when the king was kidnapped this winter."

"The wrong side?" Lilah thought of *Major* Therrik from the journal. "The side of the kidnappers?"

"The side of the queen. Who turned out to be the one in charge of the kidnappers. Was that in the newspapers? Or did Angulus keep it quiet? I didn't check to see."

"Why would Vann have sided with the queen? It's not as if queens have ever had legal power in the Iskandian monarchy."

"You'd have to take that up with his penis."

Lilah tripped, an impressive feat given the perfect flatness of the ground. "Pardon?"

"They were lovers a long time ago, before Nia was queen or even knew Angulus, I believe. From what I've heard, it didn't continue after the marriage, but when Nia needed someone to help take care of the witch problem infiltrating the capital—that being Sardelle, mostly—she turned to him. Maybe because they'd been lovers, or maybe just because she knew he had that magic-hating sword in his family's crypt. Probably some of both. She seemed to see him as someone who would do the dirty work for her. And maybe, when it comes to magic, he would. But he wouldn't help with the kidnapping of the king, even though Angulus is fairly certain she asked him to. Given that Therrik didn't come to Angulus with any of what was going on behind his back, Angulus wasn't—and still isn't—too happy with him. Turning your back on a crime is almost as bad as participating in it."

Lilah realized that this story must have come to Kaika through the king and not through Vann.

"So, Angulus personally signed the order to send Therrik up here," Kaika went on, slowing down as they drew close to another chamber. "Therrik helped out with killing a sorceress who was trying to assassinate Angulus this spring, and I thought Angulus might revoke the assignment. This place is truly horrible, especially in the winter, which is most of the year, but, ah, perhaps I should not have been the one to suggest it."

They stopped at the mouth of the tunnel, and Lilah looked curiously at Kaika.

"That was around the same time that Angulus found out that Therrik and I had spent a night wrestling in the sheets once, and even though it was years ago and meaningless, I don't think Angulus is ready to accept me as Therrik's defender. He wouldn't bat an eye at me sleeping with a dragon, mind you, but it's a bit of a stab to the heart that both his wife and I had already been with *him* before Angulus came onto the stage."

"That would be off-putting, I suppose. What are the odds? I mean, surely Vann doesn't sleep with every woman in the capital."

"Nah, I don't think so, but not for lack of offers." Kaika grinned. "You've seen him with his shirt off."

"I've also seen him yelling and growling," Lilah said dryly, looking out upon a chamber similar to the first one they had entered, except this one had a solid octagonal pedestal that rose up in the center.

"He used to do less of that. Command has made him cranky. And that sword makes him extra cranky when magic is around. Sardelle says it has the ability to influence him. It certainly influenced... someone else we know. That's a different story."

Lilah pressed a hand against the cool wall. She knew almost nothing about the sword or what powers a magical weapon could possess, but that was an interesting notion, that his crabbiness about magic might not be all his own. Maybe Vann just needed to go somewhere far from magic and far from the headaches of command.

"But my point," Kaika said, "in sharing all of that is that I don't think he's going to risk crossing his special guest, not when she arrived with orders signed by Angulus himself. He doesn't want to be stuck up here for the rest of his life, I'm sure."

"I wouldn't..." Well, *would* she have? Made an unflattering report about him if he'd destroyed the journal? Maybe, maybe not. Not now that she had this extra knowledge. "I don't want to cause him trouble."

"Good. Now, are you going to tell me what's in that book about his ancestor?"

"I'm not sure that's my secret to share, but if he lets you, you can read the journal for yourself." Lilah walked into the chamber, noting that one of the tunnels that exited from the area had collapsed. Broken chunks of gray rock littered the floor, too, and one lay right on the pedestal, half covering symbols carved into the top.

"Ugh," Kaika said, frowning down at a dark, dehydrated pile of animal scat on the floor.

More interested in the pedestal, Lilah pushed the rock to the side, so she could see more of the symbols. They lit up with a yellowish glow, and she jumped back. A dark circle in the center of the pedestal also lit up, projecting a cone of swirling light into the air. Shapes and colors came to life, including words and a maze of dark gray lines that twisted about like noodles. Red lines ran through many of the gray lines.

"A map?" Kaika asked.

"So it is," Lilah said as she sorted out what she was looking at, a three-dimensional display of the corridors and chambers within the mountain. Maybe the red lines showed which ones had collapsed and were no longer accessible? If so, it was over ninety percent of the compound. She wondered why this part of it had survived mostly intact.

"Hm." Kaika frowned up at the ceiling, then hopped onto the pedestal, the lights shining oddly on her clothing.

"What are you doing?"

Without answering, Kaika stood on her tiptoes and reached toward a dark ceramic sphere nestled up against a light fixture. She hesitated before touching it, though her fingers twitched, as if she ached to.

"That explains why this room is still standing." She moved around, eyeing the sphere from different angles.

Lilah remembered the shrapnel she and Vann had found near the other entrance tunnel. "Is that—"

"A TE-18. One of the earliest bombs. They made these when our people were still running around with flintlocks." Kaika lifted her knife, and a soft scraping sounded as she carefully pried away some three-hundred-year-old glue—or whatever had been used to affix the bomb. "The fuse burned down, but obviously, it didn't explode."

Kaika hopped down, and Lilah skittered back. Just because it hadn't exploded in the past didn't mean it couldn't do so now.

After examining it for a moment, Kaika shrugged and set it in the center of the pedestal. "I'd keep it to throw at a wolf, but it's useless without a fuse."

"Technically, that's a historical artifact."

"So it shouldn't be thrown at wolves?"

"Probably not." Lilah wouldn't necessarily advocate putting unexploded ordnance in a museum, but some historical weapons aficionado might enjoy studying it.

"Think that's us?" Kaika asked.

Lilah lifted her gaze from the bomb to the display still hovering over the pedestal. Kaika pointed at two tiny blue dots inside a square—a chamber—near the outer edge of the map.

"If so, that's, uhm." Creepy was the word that came to mind, but a professor should use something more scientific. Or at least more erudite. "Disconcerting," she decided on.

"Because it knows we're here and where we are?"

"Because I don't know what *it* is."

"Magic." Kaika shrugged as if this was a comprehensive answer.

Lilah wondered if there was a way to make parts of the map larger. The writing was too small to read. Since Kaika had stood in the midst of it, she supposed nothing bad would happen if she tried.

Careful not to disturb the bomb, Lilah prodded a finger into the space where the two dots hovered. Her finger went through the boundary of the map, and the light shone on her skin, turning it a mottled blue and gray. When she wriggled her hand around, the display enlarged in the area around it. The writing came into view, mostly Iskandian, with a couple of labels that were presumably Referatu. From what Lilah had read, the sorcerers had spoken and written in the same language as the rest of the continent, but they'd had a lot of their own terminology for discussing magical things. "It says the western exit is closed off for the time being, due to the discovery of a potential dragon burial site that should not be disturbed."

"Uh, does that mean now, or three hundred years ago?" Kaika asked.

"Three hundred years ago, I assume. But maybe I shouldn't assume that, if those two dots represent us in the here and now. And, ah, what do those other dots represent?" She pointed at a knot of at least eight in a corridor that would eventually join up with the chamber they were in. The dots were moving.

Kaika eyed the dried scat near the base of the pedestal. "Nothing friendly, I'm betting."

* * *

Vann crouched with his back to the wall, the light of a ceiling fixture illuminating the words in the journal. He could hear Kaika and Lilah up ahead. They'd stopped moving and were discussing something. He had followed them after quickly telling his men where he was going, but he had stayed far enough back so they wouldn't see him, since he had the feeling Lilah didn't want anything to do with him and might not appreciate his company. If there hadn't been unknown dangers around, he would have let them explore on their own. He had no doubt that they were both capable, but to twiddle his thumbs in camp while they potentially risked themselves would not have been acceptable.

Now, he waited while they discussed whatever they had found. He had been tempted to inch closer earlier when he'd heard his name come up, but Kaika wasn't an adventuring neophyte, and she would have detected him if he'd drawn too close. Even though he hadn't made any noise, she might already know he was back here.

Turning the pages silently, Vann flipped to the front of the journal. He had already perused the entry Lilah had mentioned and had been quite stunned to find his family name mentioned. Even more alarming was the insinuation that his ancestor might have been the one to shoot the officer who had penned the journal. Captain Molisak. Vann had met a Molisak in the service, even boxed with the man when they'd lived in the same barracks as lieutenants. To think that Vann's ancestor might have killed Molisak's ancestor was disturbing. True, he didn't know what had happened and couldn't, unless Lilah found some further evidence. The long-dead Captain Molisak might have tried to stop Major Therrik from completing his mission. They could have fought for their lives. The gunshot might have been an act of desperation or a defensive measure. Except...

Vann grimaced, remembering the skull, the location of the bullet hole. Captain Molisak had been shot in the back of the head. No, it hadn't been self-defense. It had been murder.

The words on the page grew fuzzy, and Vann realized he wasn't seeing them. He closed the journal and rested his chin against the binding. This wasn't proof. Oh, Molisak had been shot; there was no denying that. And it had been an army-issue musket ball, but there was no way to know if Major Therrik had done it. Still, Vann's stomach knotted at the idea that his ancestor might have shot a fellow officer. Over a disagreement on a mission, a mission that may or may not have been authorized. What had Major Therrik been thinking? Had he hated witches so much that he would go on an unauthorized mission to kill them? What bothered Vann was that he could almost see himself doing the same thing. What if he had lived back then, surrounded by witches—cowards who hid behind their magic while thinking themselves better than everyone else? And what if he had been given the opportunity to get rid of them? With the assistance of one of their own people? Might he have jumped at the chance? Maybe he would have told himself that it was for the good of the country and that the king and his superiors would forgive him later, if he was successful. Maybe they would have even given him awards.

Except that hadn't happened, had it? Vann had read through his family history when he'd developed his interest in military history in general, and he couldn't put a finger on who this ancestor might have been. There had been army officers in every generation of Therriks back through the centuries, and only those with distinguished records had been flagged, their stories shared in the family records. Vann had read about the dragon slayer and dozens of ancestors who had been honored for their victories in battle and their selfless sacrifices for the crown. He remembered nothing about a Therrik who had killed witches three hundred years ago. That meant the man either hadn't been honored and remembered for his actions, or he had been killed before his history had been recorded. Had he died somewhere within this mountain when the explosives had gone off? Forgotten by the gods and his family? And history? And had he taken his soldiers to their deaths with him?

Vann rolled the musket ball between his fingers, the musket ball that had killed Captain Molisak. He didn't know what he would have done in Major Therrik's place. And that disturbed him.

"Stay back," came Kaika's voice from up the tunnel, much louder than the murmurs she and Lilah had been sharing.

Vann jumped to his feet, stuffing the musket ball and the

journal into his pocket. He yanked Kasandral from its scabbard as he ran up the passage. The blade glowed a pale green.

A shot fired. Vann sprinted around a bend, cursing himself for dithering with his thoughts instead of staying closer to the women. A chamber with a stone pedestal came into view. He didn't see Lilah or Kaika. He pumped his legs harder, almost leaping from the mouth of the tunnel and into the room.

A blur of black scales shot past in front of him. He reacted before having any idea what he faced, slashing at the four-legged figure sailing through the air.

Another shot fired from right beside him. A bullet slammed into the creature at the same time as his sword cut into it. It had the head and shape of a wolf, but was twice the size, with a huge barrel chest, and was covered in snake-like scales instead of fur. His blade cut into sleek and powerful muscles that armored it as effectively as chainmail. Fortunately, Kasandral had been designed to cut through metal as well as magical defenses, and even though the blade did not bite in as deeply as he wished, it was enough to derail the scaled creature. The strange wolf yowled and tumbled into the pedestal.

Lilah was the one who had shot it, and she was already spinning toward a second wolf, one running toward her from another tunnel. Kaika knelt, preparing some explosive to throw. Four more wolves were racing down an open tunnel and toward the chamber, claws clacking on the stone floor.

Vann pushed Lilah's rifle aside, having already seen that they were dealing with magical creatures, and that bullets would be useless. He stepped in front of her, meeting the charging wolf. Even before it sprang, its head was even with his shoulders. Then it leaped into the air, rising above him, jaws like bear traps opening up.

He whipped the sword toward its chest. The wolf tried to twist to avoid it, but couldn't maneuver much while airborne. Kasandral sank into the side of its neck. Once again, the tough scales and muscles partially deflected the blow, but the creature howled with pain and was knocked several feet to the side.

A resounding boom came from the other side of the chamber—Kaika had thrown a grenade at the mouth of the tunnel from which the four remaining wolves had been about to exit. They halted, their bodies disappearing behind smoke and fire. Bangs and crashes sounded as rock fell from the ceiling in the tunnel. Yelps sounded.

Lilah fired again, aiming for one of the two already in the chamber. Neither was running from the noise or their injuries. They stood shoulder to shoulder, snarling at Vann and Lilah. Her bullet hit one square between the eyes and bounced off. The creature shook its head, but didn't even cry out. It snarled, only enraged, and it crouched to spring while its companion leaped onto the pedestal. Vann was tempted to rush forward and meet one of the attacks, but he didn't want to leave Lilah exposed. Instead, he backed up, waving for her to stay behind him, with her back protected by the wall.

As rocks continued to tumble down and fill the mouth of the tunnel, Kaika turned her attention on the two wolves. She fired at the one on the pedestal as it crouched, readying to spring. Her bullet bounced off.

"What *are* these?" she demanded.

Vann didn't take the time to answer, not when the creatures were coordinating an attack. It would take all of his focus to—

They leaped as one, the creature on the floor charging for Vann's leg at the same time as its comrade sprang from the pedestal. He chose the one in the air as the greater threat and slashed at it first, but he also kicked out with his boot, hoping to keep the other from sinking its fangs into him or from getting around him to attack Lilah.

He connected with both targets. His boot slammed into the lower wolf's jaw as Kasandral smashed into the head of the airborne one, the blade coming down above its eyes. The animal on the ground whipped its neck too quickly for him to follow, and fangs sank into his calf even as the other wolf collided with him. He'd struck a powerful blow, but its momentum and weight took it into Vann since he'd been unwilling to dodge, unwilling to leave Lilah exposed.

Pain erupted in his leg, and he tried to yank it away from the fangs sinking in, but he had to focus on the one that was close to his neck. Even though the wolf seemed stunned, its jaws still snapped reflexively, trying to grasp him even as he knocked it away.

Kaika raced behind the wolves toward the one with its jaws wrapped around his leg. She must have seen that the bullets were useless, because she had a grenade in hand. Lilah slid out from behind Vann as the airborne wolf landed and he pounced on it, slamming his sword down onto its spine. Using the butt of her rifle, Lilah tried a similar move. But her weapon did not have the power or bite of Kasandral. Vann hacked at the wolf again and again, hurrying to finish it off so he could help with the other one. It had released his leg, but now it snapped at Kaika. She clubbed it with her rifle, jamming the butt into its mouth, intentionally it seemed, because she tried to shove the grenade down its gullet while the other weapon held the jaws apart.

"Get back," she yelled. "Other side of the room. Go, go!"

Vann landed a final blow on the wolf in front of him, and its legs slid out from under it. Lilah was already moving, diving behind the pedestal. Vann risked staying long enough to take a cut at the remaining wolf. He wouldn't have resorted to grenades and doubted it had been needed, but it was too late to put the pin back in now. After chopping into the creature's leg, hoping that would keep it from running, he leaped onto the pedestal and then rolled to the other side.

The grenade clanked as it fell from the wolf's mouth—had Kaika truly thought she could get it lodged in the creature's gullet?—and blew as Vann came down on the ground. Kaika and Lilah were already there, covering their heads. He put his arms around them and tried to further protect them as the explosion ripped through the air, hammering the walls of the chamber like mallets on a drum.

More rocks crashed to the ground, one giant boulder landing on the wolf. Its cry was just audible over the noise of stone tumbling down. Vann resisted the urge to look up, lest a rock fall on his face.

Kaika wriggled out of his grasp. "Got it, sir." She gripped the pedestal and peered over the top. "That was the last one. Oh, yes. Flattened him."

"You almost flattened *us*, Captain." Vann winced, his leg throbbing. Saliva stuck to the tears in his trouser leg, and he could feel blood dripping down to his sock.

"Nah, it was just a little grenade. I'm surprised any rocks came down at all. This area must be unstable."

"Unstable, in a mountain that people have been blowing up for centuries. Imagine." Vann touched Lilah's back as she lifted her head. She still gripped his rifle and appeared ready to shoot more wolves if the rest of the pack found a way around.

"The minor, well-placed explosion didn't even bother the pedestal." Kaika flicked her hand toward a ceramic sphere resting on the flat surface.

Vann frowned at it. "Is that an old—"

Rock shifted in the mouth of the tunnel that Kaika had collapsed, and he paused. A plaintive howl came from the other side of the rubble pile, muffled but audible. It reminded Vann of the howls he had heard in the woods, and he wondered if the strange wolves had been patrolling out there the night before. Were there other ways into and out of the tunnel system? It wouldn't be surprising.

He gripped his sword and stood, eyeing the blocked tunnel. How many wolves remained alive in it? Was there another way for them to get to the chamber? He considered the three-dimensional map hovering in the air above the pedestal. It would take time to decipher it.

"Captain Kaika?" came a distant yell. Captain Bosmont. "Colonel Therrik?"

"Back here," Kaika returned the call. After another glance at the wolf, which had indeed been flattened by rubble, she headed for the passage leading back to the camp. "He might not know which tunnel we went down. I'll get him." She jogged for the exit.

Vann did not know if having more people back here would be a good idea if the tunnels were unstable. Also, if explosives and his sword were the only weapons that could hurt the creatures, having more men back here armed only with rifles wouldn't add anything useful.

"Any chance you've explored enough and that we can go for

now?" Vann asked Lilah, leaning on the pedestal with one hand to support his leg and lowering his other to help her up.

A clack and an angry hiss came from within the pedestal itself. It spat like a cat, and he stumbled back. More snaps and cracks sounded, along with a hum that seemed to fill the air with electricity. The hairs on his arms stood up, and he forgot the pain in his leg.

His gaze locked onto the sphere sitting on top of the pedestal, a centuries-old bomb. Smoke wreathed it as sparks flew up around it. Vann thought about grabbing it, lest it be ignited by whatever electrical or magical short that had clutched the pedestal, but no, better to get away from it.

Lilah bumped into him. She was already moving away from the pedestal. The map disappeared in a brilliant flash of white light that hammered Vann's eyes with the intensity of the sun. He grabbed Lilah, not wanting to lose her. He couldn't see a thing, though he sensed the light fading. He blinked, trying to clear his vision, even as he continued backing away. His shoulders bumped against a wall, and he could go no farther.

"The tunnel," Lilah said. "We might want to—"

The pedestal sputtered angrily, then seemed to explode. It didn't boom, not like one of Kaika's grenades, but the wave of power it unleashed slammed into Vann like a shockwave. The back of his head cracked against the wall. He took a step in the direction of the exit tunnel, but a massive upheaval threw him off his feet. The floor bucked and writhed like a horse trying to throw its rider. And then a second explosion came, this one far more familiar, the igniting of a bomb.

Flames surged from the center of the chamber, and the floor heaved again. Vann lost his hold on Lilah as he was hurled to the ground.

"Vann," she protested, falling away from him.

Rocks snapped and cracked. He wanted to lunge for the exit, but not without Lilah. Hells, he was so disoriented now that he wasn't even sure where the exit *was*.

"Lilah? Over here. Where are you?" The sound of breaking rock drowned out his words. A crash sounded, and he had the sense of the pedestal falling through the floor, but he couldn't tell for certain. He couldn't see *anything*.

"Colonel Therrik?" Kaika called from somewhere in the distance.

Then the rest of the floor vanished.

Chapter 11

Lilah tumbled for what seemed like ages but was probably seconds, then landed hard on her butt. Rocks slammed down all around her. Fighting back whimpers of fear, she rolled into a ball and tried to protect her head and neck. Something hard was to her left. A wall? No, a boulder. She curled against it, hoping it would deflect some of the rockfall away from her.

Rubble hammered the ground all around her. Something that sounded like it was the size of a wagon crashed down a few feet away. That pedestal? Shards of metal or rock, she wasn't sure what, struck her side. She stayed in her ball and tried to focus on controlling her growing panic.

Eventually, the rockfall dwindled, but she did not feel safe. Not at all. Though she could not see anything, she had the sense of the walls looming close, trapping her. She peered upward, knowing she had fallen, but not sure if she had tumbled straight down. She had bumped against walls a couple of times, almost like laundry sliding down an angled chute.

The darkness was absolute, and she could see nothing, not even her hand in front of her face. The rock walls weren't pressing in on her, forcing her to keep her head to the ground, as they had in that tunnel she had crawled through, but she had no idea where she was, how she would get out, or what was waiting down here with her. She could hear her own rapid breaths, as if she stood somewhere outside of her body. Though she repeatedly told herself to calm down, she couldn't manage to slow her breathing. When she tried to inhale more slowly and more deeply, she got too much air and started to feel lightheaded. She was panicking, and she couldn't stop it, damn it.

Something stirred in the darkness nearby. What if it was one of those wolves? She patted the ground around her. Somewhere in the fall, she had lost the rifle. Not that it did any good against those creatures.

Lilah climbed to her feet, having a notion that one shouldn't face danger from one's knees. Her body ached from the fall, fresh scrapes and bruises stinging.

"Lilah?" Vann said from several feet away.

Not a wolf. Good. But she still couldn't calm her nerves.

"Lilah," he said again, closer this time. His hand bumped her back. He patted his way up to her shoulder and gripped it. "We're fine."

"Uh huh," was all she could get out. Logically, she knew nothing was happening, at least not right now, but she couldn't stop thinking about the ceiling collapsing or their air running out.

"Lilah," Vann said again, stepping close, brushing her back with his chest. "What would help?"

"Daylight," she croaked.

She closed her eyes, trying to get ahold of herself. Being this afraid of some dark cave was stupid, and she knew it. Further, having a witness to her panic embarrassed her. She blamed the fear she'd felt during the wolf fight for starting this. Her heart was still pounding. One of those cursed beasts had almost gotten Vann. It *had* gotten his leg. He must be in pain right now, and here she was, worrying about herself.

"I'm sorry," she managed to say. "I'm fine. How bad is your leg? Does it hurt?"

"Yes." He slid an arm around her from behind, bending his neck so he could rest his chin on her shoulder. A soft clank came from beside him—he must still have that sword in his other hand. "I can walk on it, though," he said. "It'll be all right. *We'll* be all right. I can distract you if you like."

She leaned back against him, relieved that he didn't seem too badly injured and also relieved that she wasn't down here alone. Perhaps it was silly—she was a grown woman and shouldn't need to be cuddled by a man to find her equanimity—but her breathing slowed and some of the tension seeped out of her muscles as she leaned against him. Minutes passed without any more rocks falling, and she began to believe that they would not be crushed, that Vann would lead her out of this mess.

"I would guess we fell the equivalent of three or four stories," he said. "I can't imagine why there was hollow space underneath that chamber, but the walls here are rough, not smooth like the witch tunnels. Maybe there was a cavern system or at least some pockets of air that existed before they built here."

"That bomb went off, didn't it?" Lilah asked.

"Yes."

"Kaika found it attached to the ceiling. We assumed it was placed there by the invaders, that it was supposed to go off three hundred years ago."

"It likely was." He stopped speaking, his chin turning on her shoulder, and she had the sense that he was tilting his head to listen above them. "The ceiling gave way as well as the floor, and I wouldn't be surprised if the tunnel Kaika ran down collapsed too. It may be some time before they can dig their way into what remains of the chamber and lower a rope to us."

He didn't say that Kaika herself might have been crushed if the tunnel collapsed, but Lilah had no trouble envisioning the scenario. She shuddered. "So, we're trapped."

What if they ran out of air? What if there was nobody left up there to look for them? Or what if more of the ceiling gave way, and rocks buried them forever?

"Perhaps not. We haven't explored. We will." Vann held her loosely, his short hair brushing her temple, his relaxed body exuding calmness.

She wished she hadn't snapped at him earlier. Even if she had been disappointed in him, that wasn't a reason to behave poorly. Especially to someone who was going out of his way to comfort her now. She leaned her head back against his shoulder, appreciating his warmth and his closeness.

"What kind of distraction?" Lilah whispered.

"Hm?" Vann stirred, his jaw brushing her ear, and she shivered at the roughness of his stubble, unshaven since the previous morning. It prompted delightful sensations within her. So did the hardness of his chest against her back, the heat of his forearm across her stomach, the tickle of his breath on her neck.

"You offered to distract me."

"Did I?" He seemed to consider this for a moment, then kissed her on the neck, his lips warm and pleasant. "Unfortunately, it's not a good time for both of us to be distracted."

No, and she reminded herself that she still didn't know how he felt about his ancestor, about the idea of killing an entire society of people. It wouldn't be wise for her to settle back further into his embrace and ask for more kisses.

"Talk to me, then," she whispered. "Please. For a few minutes. Then I'll help you search for a way out." After she grew convinced that more of the ceiling wouldn't fall and crush them. "I know it's silly, but I can't help thinking about... I feel powerless in situations like this."

He sighed softly, his breath tickling her skin. "I get feeling powerless. It's vile."

"But it's not something you deal with often, I'm sure," Lilah said, then reconsidered the comment. Maybe he referred to being an officer who always had superiors to deal with, men giving orders that he had no choice but to follow.

"Often enough to hate the feeling. It's why I loathe magic."

"Oh?"

Perhaps his comment had nothing to do with his rank and the military, after all. Lilah waited, hoping he would continue, that he would give her something to focus on rather than the blackness around them and the weight of the mountain atop them.

He rested his face against the back of her head for a moment, then lowered his arm. "I better hunt down a lantern and see if there's a way back up to the others."

"Wait." She clasped his arm to keep it close—to keep *him* close. "Tell me? Please."

He didn't ask to what she referred. "Because you still need to be distracted? Or because you're nosy?"

"Both of those things, and because I'm trying to decide if you're someone..." Lilah stopped herself before saying, *I can be friends with*. It seemed a silly thing to say when she was leaning against him, and he was letting her use him for support. Anything else that came to mind, such as that she wanted him to be a good man, would come out sounding condescending. Maybe it was best to drop it, at least for now. "I forgot to thank you. For coming to help Kaika and me. Your rescue was quite timely. You must have been nearby?"

"I was following you," he admitted. "I should have gotten there quicker, but I was reading that journal."

"Ah." She didn't know if she should encourage him to discuss what he had read or not.

"I haven't heard of that Therrik, so maybe he got killed down here, forgotten before much could be recorded about him in the family history."

Maybe he *wanted* to discuss it? "Do you think he was the one to shoot Captain Molisak?"

"It seems likely that he or someone on his team did. Someone following his orders, maybe."

"How do you feel about that?"

"Feel?" he asked, as if she had used some strange, foreign word.

"Yes, feel. A feeling is defined as an emotional state or a reaction."

He grunted. "Thanks."

Lilah waited, hoping he would answer her question, but again, not wanting to push him to discuss it. They could talk more when they had escaped the mountain and there were fewer threats around.

"I wondered if I would have done the same thing," Vann said quietly, "if presented with the opportunity to lead a team to assassinate the witch leader. From what I gathered from the entries, that was the original assignment until Major Therrik decided to take the opportunity he was given, free access to this compound, to rid the world of all of these people."

Was that what had happened? He must have read more of the journal and pieced more together. Lilah hoped the book had survived their tumble down here and that she would have the chance to read the rest.

"Do you... approve of what he did?" she asked, careful to keep the judgment out of her tone. She thought about turning to face him, but this seemed less confrontational, less direct.

"Of giving himself his own mission and then shooting an officer who objected? No."

"What if the mission had been sanctioned? Would it have then been acceptable to..." She stopped, knowing she wouldn't be able to keep the judgment out of her voice. Why ask? She was fairly certain how he felt. She would only be disappointed in his answer. In him. She laid her head back against his shoulder. She didn't *want* to be disappointed in him. She wanted him to be someone whom she could trust to be honorable.

"I don't know, Lilah. I hate magic, and I hate those who..." He sighed and rested his face against her hair in silence for a moment. "I told you about how I ended up in the army, first two years as a soldier, then four years in the academy, and finally another two years of training for the elite forces. Those eight years, which were quite intense, shaped me, turned me from a street thug to a soldier. That's what the army is designed to do, after all. It's not usually necessary for boys from noble families, but I was more like a wild animal at that point in my life. I needed it."

Lilah made a murmur of encouragement, not sure where this story would lead, but wanting to hear it.

"By the time I graduated from the academy and had passed a few of the early tests in my career training, I'd started to believe I was going to be able to serve my king and country like someone... heroic. I met a woman about this time, and we started spending time together." He spoke slowly. Editing his words before they came out of his mouth? It wasn't as if she would judge him for past relationships. "She seemed to think I was heroic too. She didn't know about my past, or if she did, she didn't care. She loved me, and I guess I felt the same, though I'm not sure I ever managed to say it."

She was tempted to ask him if this had been Nia, the woman who had become Angulus's wife and the queen. If so, it was a foregone conclusion that the story wouldn't have a happy ending. That seemed to be a theme for Vann, stories without happy endings. Had he ever known enduring contentment in his life?

"She took me to meet her parents. The family had a big estate overlooking the sea down south. They were of noble blood, which I hadn't realized, since she never spoke of it, but I was, too, technically, so I didn't think much of it. I thought we were a good fit. Her parents were reserved but polite enough. Nothing much came of that dinner until months later, they called me back to their house. Alone. I'd proposed to her, so I expected a man-to-man conversation with the father, a promise to treat her well, that sort of thing. As it turned out, he'd been doing some research into me, and he'd dug up everything, that I'd lived on the streets, defended my life by taking other lives. A wild animal, not a nobleman and an officer, or not always one."

A soft clink sounded as he shifted his grip on the sword, and it bumped against rock.

"The mother greeted me, her manner the same as before, reserved but polite. I didn't feel like I was in danger, not from some woman in her forties." His tone grew dry briefly when he added, "That was old to me then."

"I think the definition of old is always at least twenty years out from where you are."

He made an agreeable noise, but his humor faded as soon as he continued the story. "She gave me cookies and tea, both of which seemed perfectly normal. Then she took me down to a basement room that was full of—I don't know what you'd call the equipment. Alchemy stuff, I thought, though I had a hard time imagining her as a home scientist. Then she locked the door behind me. From across the room. I distinctly remember her waving her hand and the lock thunking. I had never run into anyone who could use magic before, but I'd grown up hearing stories of witches, like most kids do."

Lilah thought he might ask if she'd grown up listening to similar stories, and she would have to say that her mother had simply supplied books on all manner of topics, often contradictory topics, so she'd learn that there were always at least two sides to every story. She probably had her mother to thank for her indifference to magic. She'd also never run into anyone who had done anything magical—and scary—to her. It sounded like Vann couldn't say the same.

"She said I wasn't good enough for her daughter, that I was an animal who'd been taught to dress like a man. And besides, she had been planning Nia's marriage for a long time. She had someone else in mind and wasn't going to let me get in the way. If I did, she said she'd kill me. I scoffed, of course, and told her that Nia and I *would* marry. What could a little woman do to someone like me, who'd been trained to kill by the best men in the infantry? But she'd already drugged me with the tea, or the cookies. I don't know. I'd had no reason not to eat them. I'd just assumed that my fiancée's mother would be a *normal* person." The word normal came out as a growl. He seemed more emotional about this story than he had been about the horrible death of his mother.

"I tried to get out," he continued, "but the door might as well have been made from steel. It was thick and stout, the hinges fresh and new. I couldn't budge it, not with all of my strength." His shoulders flexed behind her, as if in memory of pulling on that door. "She came up to me, and for some reason, I thought she was going to let me out. There was definitely an idea in my head that I couldn't—shouldn't—attack her. I later learned that witches are telepathic and can control you."

Another growl.

"She laid her hand on my arm, and I saw her lifting a syringe with the other hand, but I was powerless to move away or to knock it away. She stabbed me with it. I don't know if it was a sedative or some magical potion, but my legs went numb. I dropped to the floor. Then her husband came out of a side room. He reiterated that I wasn't good enough for their daughter. He told me to break it off with Nia, or he'd have me killed. I couldn't move most of my body, but I could still speak. I was too proud for my own good, and I told him to fuck himself. He proceeded to beat me until I was almost unconscious. His wife sat back and watched, smiling as if she was enjoying a good sporting event. I think she was even getting aroused. I wanted to club her in the head, but thanks to her damned magic, I couldn't touch her. Eventually, the father chained me up, got some servant to help throw me in a wagon, and drove me to a cliff overlooking the ocean. The potion was starting to wear off by then, but I was careful not to show it. I was still pretty numb, so I doubted I could have overpowered them. The mother was there the whole time, watching, pleased. She said nothing as the men shoved me off the cliff."

"Seven gods, Vann," Lilah whispered, her voice almost a croak. She'd listened in growing horror, hardly able to believe him, and she shifted to face him now, to rest her hand on his chest.

"If I had hit one of the rocks down there, I would have been dead," he went on, his tone dead now. Unemotional. "I landed in the water and immediately sank. I nearly twisted myself inside out—and I did dislocate a shoulder—trying to get out of the chains. Had that potion not mostly worn off by then, I never could have escaped, but through sheer desperation, I wriggled my way out. I made it to a beach, and it took me all night to walk the ten miles back to the city. I collapsed in front of the gates to the army fort and woke up in the infirmary two days later. I was there for a couple of weeks before I could return to active duty. My C.O. wanted to know what had happened. I told him everything. He scoffed. Witches? There's no such thing as magic, and there certainly weren't witches among the nobility. He ended up reporting that some of my father's old mafia enemies had come after me. As if I couldn't have fought off mere *men*," he snarled, bitterness returning.

"What did Nia say? Did she know about any of it?"

"When she came to visit, my C.O. told her the mafia story. I was debating whether to tell her the truth, that her mother was a witch and an evil bitch at that, but she came in with tears in her eyes, took my hand, and said she couldn't marry me. Her mother had arranged another marriage for her, and it was her duty as the eldest daughter to marry for status if she could. As it turned out, Angulus had lost his first wife and was willing to accept Nia as his next. Or rather, his father, who was king at the time, was willing to accept Nia for his son. I was too hurt to think straight, and only later did I realize that the mother had probably been setting things up for a long time, and that she might very well have been controlling Nia, at least in that moment. She acted strangely, not like the woman I'd come to know."

"Did you ever try to... You must have wanted revenge," Lilah said.

"By the time I got out of the infirmary, Nia was already married to Angulus. The capital was abuzz with how quickly everything had come about, but who would have suspected witchcraft?" His shoulders flexed again, with irritation and old anger. "Revenge, yes, I thought about that a great deal. I thought about sneaking out there and killing them both. If I'd been able to the day after it happened, I might have tried to do it. But by the time I recovered, knowing Nia was already married—and that no woman was going to divorce the future king—deflated me a lot. I still cared about her, too, and as I said, I don't think she had any inkling of what her parents were capable of. If I'd killed her mother and father, she never would have forgiven me, and it would have been the end of my career, most likely the end of my life. You don't just kill noblemen."

Lilah thought about pointing out that the laws had evolved and killing *anyone* wasn't allowed these days, at least when it came to Iskandian subjects. But it didn't matter. He hadn't done it. She felt relieved, though it horrified her that the parents had nearly killed him and were presumably still walking the capital's streets, having never been punished for the crime.

"I was afraid too," Vann whispered so softly that she wasn't sure she had heard him correctly. "Of the mother. The witch. For a long time, I worried that she would come after me and finish what she and her husband had started. But after Nia was married, I guess they figured it didn't matter that I had survived. They must not have seen me as a further threat. And they were right," he said, his voice a growl again. "All my fighting skills, all my strength, and I was powerless against that woman."

No wonder he hated magic. It not only evened the odds in a battle, but it tipped the scales, emasculating him, making all of his training mean nothing.

"Sardelle reminds me of her," Vann said glumly.

Lilah blinked in surprise. "Ridge's Sardelle?"

She couldn't imagine her cousin falling in love with some woman with demonic tendencies, beauty or not. What was Vann implying? That Ridge didn't know what she truly was? That she was controlling him?

"Just the way she looks. Dark hair, freckles, *polite*. And reserved. Like you never quite know what she's thinking."

"Do you think... I haven't met her. Is it just their *looks* that are similar?"

"Yeah. Been hard to see that, to accept that she's not evil. She even saved my life once. I had to go on a tracking mission with her a couple of months ago when Zirkander was presumed dead but was only missing—guess you heard about that."

"After the fact, yes." Her aunt Fern had sent a letter to her mother, but by the time it had arrived, the newspapers had already announced Ridge's glorious return. The requests for autographed undergarments had tripled that week.

"It was just me and her out there. And her sword and dragon." Vann snorted. "I kept having to remind myself that she'd saved my life and that I should feel grateful to her. Hells, sometimes I did, and I wanted to—well, she's also a pretty woman. But more of the time, I was having to repeat to myself that she wasn't Nia's mother. But it was hard. Didn't help that I had Kasandral, and the sword wanted me to kill her, because it hates all things magic."

"But you didn't kill her," Lilah said.

"No. She had a dragon protecting her. And her sword warned me it could melt my balls off."

Lilah's mouth gaped open at the idea of someone possessing such allies and even further at the notion of a sword that could think and talk, but she kept focused on what was important, what seemed to be haunting Vann.

"*Would* you have killed her if they hadn't been there?" she asked. "If you thought you could overpower her and get away with it?"

He chewed on that question before answering it, and Lilah held her breath.

"No," he finally said. "Like I said, she saved my life. That's not a debt you ignore."

"Good." Lilah kept the word simple, not letting her relief seep into it. He probably sensed it, regardless. "You wondered if you would have accepted the assignment that your ancestor accepted—or took on for himself. I don't believe you would have. You wouldn't have shot a fellow officer in the back, and you wouldn't have agreed to kill a mountain full of people that hadn't proven themselves your enemies. And the Referatu weren't enemies, were they? There were a few sorcerers who used their power for evil, as Nia's mother did, but many more helped our nation stay free from the Cofah over the centuries. If you can find the books that survived the burnings, that's in there. You wouldn't have done it, Vann. You're an honorable man." She lifted her hand to the side of his face—he was standing very still as he listened to her, and she hoped her words mattered, maybe even helped. "You're definitely not an animal."

"No?" he murmured, sliding his hand up her back. "Not at all?"

"Well, I haven't gotten to know you in all situations, yet."

"Hm." Even in the darkness, he had no trouble finding her lips with his.

Earlier, she had shivered when he had kissed her on the neck, but this was much better. She melted into him, some of her doubts about him fading, and her fears over their surroundings fading further—she'd forgotten about their predicament while he'd been telling his story.

His kiss was gentler than she would have expected, and she sensed that he appreciated her being here with him, listening to him talk. It warmed her soul—and other parts as well. Long neglected desire awoke within her, and she slid her arms over his shoulders, wanting to mold herself to him, to keep him close as she enjoyed the attention of his mouth, his tongue. She had been attracted to him from the beginning, even when he had been scowling and yelling, and his touch did not disappoint. Some of the gentleness disappeared, replaced by hunger and need as his arm tightened around her back. She imagined him dropping his sword, forgetting everything except her, sweeping her up in both arms, and pressing her against the closest boulder to—

Vann broke the kiss, his chest rising against hers as he took a deep, steadying breath. Disappointment surged through her, and her first instinct was to hold him tighter, to keep him from escaping. She could feel the tension in his body and knew he wanted to continue, that he might have boulders in mind too.

But he cleared his throat and stepped back, lowering his arm.

"We need to find Kaika and the others," he said, "and there may be more of those wolves down here."

"Duty first?" she murmured, reluctantly releasing his shoulders.

She wished they could have more time together, preferably time outside of this mountain, but time all the same. What would happen when she had to return to her work back home, and he remained here, hundreds of miles away? She resolved to get more than a kiss from him before that happened.

"*Survival* first," Vann said. "Right now, duty can suck a—"

"Toe?"

He snorted and rubbed her back. "Exactly."

Chapter 12

Vann picked his way carefully up the nearly vertical wall, the cold rock jagged underneath his hands. Aware of the drop below him, he made himself focus on the climb and definitely not on the kiss he had shared with Lilah. Nor on the delightful feel of her breasts squeezed against his chest, her body warm and eager in his hands. Nor did his mind linger on the sympathetic way she had listened to his story, a story that he hated sharing since it revealed his weakness. But she hadn't cared that he had been defeated by some witch woman. She'd kissed him back enthusiastically, wanting his touch as much as he had wanted hers.

His hand slipped, and jagged rock scraped his knuckles as his weight shifted to compensate. He growled at the poor lighting—and his easily distracted mind—and continued upward. He wished there were some magic about so that Kasandral would glow. He'd found his lantern, but it hung from his belt since he needed both hands, and the warm glass was in danger of burning him through his clothing and leaving a new scar. He didn't know how long he would have light, since a puncture in the cache was dribbling kerosene. The flame did not illuminate much, anyway. Too bad his rope was dangling from a tree along a destroyed goat trail.

"Any luck?" Lilah called up, her voice echoing from the darkness below.

The utter darkness. Since they had only been able to locate one dented lantern amid the rubble, she was down there without any light. He hoped she wasn't worrying. Fortunately, her voice had calmed down and lacked that panicked edge now. Probably because she now believed he was some noble hero who would keep her safe. He would love to be her noble hero, and her faith did please him, but he wasn't nearly as confident as she seemed that he wouldn't have made some of the same choices as Major Therrik had, if he had been given his opportunity. Oh, he wouldn't have shot the captain, but the witches? He was less certain about that. He'd meant it when he said he wouldn't have hurt Sardelle, but she was different. He owed her a debt.

"It looks like I'm almost to the chamber—where the chamber *was*," he called back, continuing his climb.

He squinted into the gloom above. This was definitely a natural cavern, nothing the witches had hollowed out. Higher up, however, the remains of a couple of those flat gray walls were visible, gray patches left behind over darker and rougher rock. In the shadows, he could make out the shapes of two tunnels, the mouths of both filled in with rubble. One was the one Kaika had collapsed to stop the wolves. The other was the one through which Vann had entered the chamber. They wouldn't be getting out either way, not unless someone could blow the rubble clear. If Kaika or Bosmont applied explosives, Vann realized that it would be deadly for him and Lilah to be standing down below when that happened.

"Captain Kaika?" Vann called as loudly as he could. "Bosmont? Can anyone hear me?"

He leaned his forehead against the cool stone, listening for a response. Nothing but silence greeted his ears.

He was surprised Kaika and Bosmont hadn't found a way to communicate with them yet, if only by banging on a distant rock. Maybe that tunnel had collapsed all the way back to the exit. Or maybe something was keeping them busy out there? More wolves? The cursed fossils?

Shaking his head, Vann started back down. The wall turned from vertical into a rough slope and back to vertical again before he reached the ground. They had been lucky with the contours in the terrain, or they might have been hurt much more in the fall. They had dropped a good thirty feet. Vann's leg ached where the wolf fangs had punctured it, but he hadn't suffered any other major injuries.

"We'll have to find another way around," he said when the weak light of his lantern shone upon Lilah.

He thought she might be standing with her arms wrapped around herself, alarmed by the darkness, but he found her making a charcoal rubbing of something on a panel on that pedestal. Its surface was mangled and blackened, the symbols now indecipherable, but she must have found something scientifically interesting. She waved the paper.

"Mind if I put this in your pack? I didn't think to bring one into the tunnels."

"Go ahead." Vann turned so she could stick it in a pouch.

Dirt smudged her face, dust caked her hair, and scrapes covered her hands and one cheek, but he would happily go back to kissing if he weren't worried that Kaika would plant explosives above them.

The determined expression on her face did not suggest she had kisses in mind anymore. She must have been able to put her earlier fear behind her, as she grew accustomed to their situation.

Once she had put away the paper, she picked up his rifle. She must have found it under the rubble while he had been climbing. Good.

"Do you think there *will* be another way?" Lilah looked toward the lone tunnel that opened up from the rubble-filled chamber into which they had been deposited.

The mouth was half-filled with boulders. He had no idea whether it went up or down or how much of these passages remained accessible.

"At the least, we won't want to be sitting here, under this hole—" Vann waved toward the former chamber above them, "—when the others start blowing things up. We'll investigate the tunnel. Maybe we'll get lucky, and it will connect to the one where the infiltration team blew their way in. If we can get to it, we can climb out that way."

He bumped a boulder when he started through the dim cavern, grimacing when the fang punctures in his calf throbbed in protest. He had been happy to ignore the injury when he had been holding Lilah, but if he was going to walk on it, he ought to bandage it. He did have a first-aid kit with him.

Lilah touched his arm. "I'm sorry. I forgot about your leg. Can I clean it for you?"

"Yes, but let's get out of this area first." Vann waved toward the tunnel. "That smaller space will be more defensible, too, if magical wolves find us."

"You're sure they were magic?" Lilah asked, staying close as they picked their way through rubble and toward the tunnel. Vann had no intention of limping or leaning on her for support, but he appreciated her presence. "That attack happened so quickly that I didn't get a good look at them."

"My sword glowed. It does that when magic is around. Or people with dragon blood."

"It's glowing now."

Vann halted and pulled Kasandral from its scabbard. He cursed. She was right. It hadn't been before—he'd had it out and at the ready when he had been comforting Lilah.

"We may have company coming, then," he said grimly, glancing toward the open chamber above them and also toward the tunnel they had been about to clamber into.

Soft clacks reached his ears. Claws on stone. Kasandral flared a brighter green.

"We'll fight out here." Vann moved away from the tunnel mouth and to a curving wall where the ground was mostly clear from rubble. It wasn't quite a corner, but at least he would have some stone at his back, and he should be able to fight without tripping over anything. He set his lantern on a boulder, though with the sword glowing, they did not need its light now.

Vann waved for Lilah to stay behind him. She did so, but she also lifted the rifle to her shoulder, aiming it toward the mouth of the tunnel. He could tell she hated having to hide behind anyone. But he knew the firearm would be useless, and he needed her safe and out of the way. He couldn't understand where these wolves had come from, but he had no doubt that they were magical.

Two black forms shot over the rubble and out of the tunnel. The rifle cracked, echoing loudly in the enclosed cavern. The bullet struck the closest creature in the side. As had happened with the other scaled wolves, the projectile bounced off, doing no damage.

Vann lowered into a crouch with Kasandral raised. Anger

and hunger flowed through his veins, along with the usual surge of blood that came when he anticipated battle.

The creatures spun toward their corner. Their eyes glowed yellow. Vann hadn't noticed that before, but it was unmistakable in the darkness.

They did not charge right away. They padded toward him, those claw clacks filling his ears. One emitted a deep growl.

Had Vann been alone, he might have charged them, trying to disrupt their hunting style, because he recalled the uncanny way the ones up above had timed their jumps, with two of them springing at him at once. But he would not leave Lilah unprotected. He would just have to be fast enough to strike at both animals before they could get through.

The wolves stalked into Kasandral's pale green light, as large, scaled, and powerful as the ones up above had been. Vann's leg throbbed at the memory of that encounter. His sword remembered too. Kasandral thrummed in his hand, filling him with the urge to kill these filthy magical creations. He forgot the pain in his leg, his mind emptying of all thought, his muscles relaxing, ready to strike with the speed of a cracking whip.

The predators parted, one going left around a pile of boulders, the other going right. Vann backed up a couple of steps, as far as he could without running into Lilah. He couldn't let them flank him.

They slowed, crouching low, their tails swishing. So similar were their actions that it was as if one brain controlled them.

Without warning, they sprang. One leaped toward his right side, the other toward his left. He couldn't dodge, or they would reach Lilah. He braced himself, timing his first strike. He lashed toward the one on the left, cutting into scale, then whipping the sword across to hit the other one. His first blow knocked his target aside, but the other wolf made it farther, jaws snapping for his face. He ducked, and its paws struck his shoulder, its head twisting and fangs snapping, trying to sink into his neck. He shifted his stance just enough to avoid that fate while thrusting upward with the sword. Its green glow washed over the beast's black-scaled stomach as Vann plunged the blade into its flesh.

The creature cried out in pain, the noise jarring so close to Vann's ears. He shoved it away with his free arm, even as gravity combined with the wolf's weight to drop it further onto the sword. The other animal had landed and recovered. It lunged for Vann's unguarded side. With his sword busy eviscerating one wolf, he couldn't bring it to bear quickly enough. Lilah leaped out from behind him and slammed the butt of her rifle into the creature's head.

The blow barely fazed the creature, but it paused for an instant. An instant was all Vann needed. As it lunged toward Lilah, he hurled the other wolf away from him and smashed the sword down before this one could reach her. Rage burned in his veins—it *dared* threaten her—and he hacked into it again and again, the sword slicing through those scales and tearing into flesh and muscle.

A snarl from his side warned him that the other one wasn't ready to give up. He slammed his sword into his magical foe one more time, then kicked it into the boulder pile as he spun back to meet the second one. He had wounded it badly, and it staggered toward him instead of springing. Half of its entrails dragged on the floor. He couldn't believe it wasn't running, but he met the weak charge, smashing the sword into the top of its head.

The glow left the wolf's eyes, and it slumped to the ground, its scaled legs crumpling. Vann turned toward the other one, but it had also toppled. Lilah stood with the rifle pointed at its head.

Kasandral's green glow dimmed, but did not go out entirely. Vann waited, eyeing the beasts, half-expecting one to rise again, that whatever magic powered them would come into play. The animals did not move.

"If those are the same ones that were blocked by Kaika's rockfall up above, it should mean that this tunnel links back up with the upper ones." Lilah nodded toward the passage they had been about to explore. Her voice was calm, her hand steady, the hunt apparently not scaring her nearly as much as being squished into dark spaces by rocks.

Vann lowered Kasandral and wrapped his free arm around her shoulders, glad for her steadiness. He would gladly hold her hand during cave-ins if it meant she was ready to stand beside him in battles against magic.

Lilah quirked her dusty eyebrows at him. "Is that a sign that you agree with me?"

"It's a sign that I'm having appreciative and amorous feelings toward you."

"Feelings? You?" She smiled and leaned into his chest.

"*Amorous* feelings."

"Are those hard to have when your shirt is spattered with wolf blood and there are entrails at your feet?"

"Not at all." Vann released her, in case that was a hint that she didn't want wolf blood smeared onto her clothes, but she was smirking at him, so he found that heartening.

"You *are* a ghoul."

"Yes. Do you mind?"

"Not when you're carrying my finds."

Lilah picked up something from the ground behind the boulder pile. It looked like a piece of trash, but he supposed it might be some interesting Referatu artifact. She waved for him to turn around, so she could stick it in his pack. He wondered how many doodads he would be carrying by the time they found their way out. She patted him on the shoulder when she had finished.

"Is this the kind of work the soldier in your books does for the heroine?" Vann asked. "Carrying things?"

"No, they have a corporal for that. Commander Asylon helps her with solving puzzles. He also drives off evil Cofah invaders for her."

"As any man should." Vann nodded toward the tunnel. "Shall we see if we can find our way out now?"

"Yes, but Vann?"

"Yes?"

"I want you to know that even though my life is in ruins—" Lilah waved toward the battered pedestal, "—I'm having a good time with you."

It took him a moment to recognize the pun for what it was. "Ruins, huh?"

She nodded solemnly, not quite squelching the gleam in her eyes. "That was one of my husband's jokes. He was an archaeologist."

The lantern chose that moment to wink out, the last of the kerosene leaking out. Maybe the gods did not appreciate science jokes.

"Good thing we still have your sword." Lilah pointed at the blade's glow.

"Yes, but I think it will go out as soon as we move away from the wolves."

"What if we cut off one of the tails and take it with us?"

Vann snorted at the idea of such a lurid trophy dangling from his belt, but would it work? Or would Kasandral's glow dim as soon as the blood of its enemies cooled? "Are you sure *I'm* the ghoul?"

She grinned. "Positive."

He snorted again, then bent to do the deed. They could try.

While he worked, Lilah poked around the chamber and found a few more historically significant doodads to collect. He stole a few glances in her direction as she bent over and crawled between two boulders. He wondered what she would think if he offered to distract her again soon, perhaps with more than words. He smiled wolfishly at the thought of taking her off to his room to visit his weapons collection, this time with the door shut and no distractions.

"Are you enjoying cutting off that tail or are you thinking of something else?" Lilah asked, noticing his smile as she strolled back and picked up the rifle.

Vann clasped her hand and kissed her. Even though he hadn't minded comforting her when she had been scared, he preferred the adventurous gleam that rode in her eyes now.

"You didn't answer my question," she murmured when he broke the kiss.

"I was thinking that it's rare that you find a woman that will accept a kiss from you when you have a wolf tail hanging from your belt. You find someone like that, you better keep her."

"Wise words," Lilah murmured, squeezing his hand. "And I

wouldn't mind being kept, but you know I can't stay here, right? I have to go back to the university, to my work, my career."

Vann knew that, of course, but the words made his shoulders slump. Once her research was done, she would return to civilization, and he would be stuck here for another nine months. And after that? He was a soldier; he could be sent anywhere. Unless she wanted to give up everything to follow him around, this couldn't be anything more than a brief affair. He couldn't imagine her walking away from her career, not when she was so proud of those papers she was publishing.

"Maybe you could retire and join me," Lilah offered, eyebrows rising with hope. That heartened him, made him think that she wanted more, something long-term. But he couldn't give up everything to follow her around, either. The job frustrated him, but what other work was he qualified for?

"I'm too young to retire, Lilah," he said softly. "And pummeling people—and magical wolves—is all I know how to do. I doubt your university would give me a job as your bodyguard."

"Sadly, I don't usually need a bodyguard in the lab or the classroom. I'm sorry my life isn't as exciting as the heroine's in the *Time Trek* novels."

"You wouldn't have much time for research if it was."

"I suppose not."

* * *

Lilah followed Vann across boulders and through a mix of natural passages as well as old Referatu ones, sometimes crawling, sometimes walking, and once, squirming through a narrow gap on her belly. That was the hardest, with her claustrophobia threatening to return in full force. Vann was fearless, though, and stopped to wait for her, clasping her hand or her shoulder reassuringly. He even smiled when she made a few more jokes to distract herself. Those smiles had been nonexistent when he'd been around his troops. It was too bad he hadn't been interested in the idea of retiring or switching jobs. But as he had said, she did not know what other employment she could imagine for him. Bodyguard? Security specialist? Professional assassin? She shuddered at the last. At least working for the king and the army was working for the good of Iskandia.

An hour turned into two and then three, and they did not encounter any more wolves. Desiccated droppings *did* promise that some creatures visited the tunnels from time to time. Lilah thought she and Vann were gradually moving upward, but it was hard to tell. Not that they had any choice insofar as options. They had come across other tunnels, but they had all been blocked. Fortunately, Vann's sword continued to glow, activated—or perhaps irritated—by the presence of the magical wolf tail.

"Some bones up ahead," Vann said, crawling down a rubble pile and into an open section of tunnel, this one lined with smooth gray walls. A power crystal had survived the destruction and shone down from the ceiling. Twenty feet farther on, more rubble had fallen, another pile that they would have to climb past.

Lilah skidded off the rocks and came to her feet beside Vann. She caught him stifling a yawn and wondered if night had fallen outside. He handed her his canteen and nodded toward a partial human skeleton up ahead, the lower half stuck under the rubble pile. Even allowing for that, it seemed too small to belong to an adult.

Lilah took a drink before heading forward. Fossils might be her passion, but the deaths of these people were too recent, too disturbing. Further, the link to Vann's family made the horrible fate the Referatu had suffered more personal than she would have liked.

Vann walked forward with her, holding his sword aloft so it would shed light on the passageway.

Lilah bumped something with her foot. She thought it a rock, but it rolled away, bouncing off a wall before slowing to a stop. A ball?

She picked it up, and it hummed in her hand, then flashed with blue and red light. Startled, she almost dropped it. After having that pedestal all but explode, she felt gun-shy around artifacts that glowed.

The hums shifted in tone, then discernible notes came from the device.

"It's playing a song," Lilah realized.

Vann stopped at her side, his knuckles tight around his sword hilt as he eyed the device. The blade glowed a stronger green.

"I think it's a child's toy," she said.

"You don't think weapons can play songs before blowing up?" he asked, apparently also thinking of explosions.

Lilah bounced it on the ground, and the song changed, a *dong* ringing out in the middle when it hit and again when she caught it. The tune continued happily, inviting her to play with the ball. She looked sadly toward the skeleton, having a hunch as to why it appeared small.

She walked slowly toward the bones and knelt beside them. It was definitely a child's skull, perhaps that of an eight- or ten-year-old. A boy, she guessed, from the dusty trousers and button-down shirt, the clothing still largely intact. The scavengers hadn't been as savage as with the soldiers. Maybe they had known this had been a resident instead of an invader.

She snorted to herself. Probably not.

A shadow fell across her shoulder. Vann.

He picked up something that lay a few feet from what would have been the boy's hand. A slingshot. The band had grown brittle and snapped, but the ends still dangled from the Y-shaped wood. Lilah wondered if the mother's or father's bones were under the rubble, or if the child had been trying to escape on his own.

"My nephews have one of these," Vann said, his voice hard to read. "I had one as a boy too."

"A childhood staple throughout the ages."

"Yeah." He looked to the skull and back to the toy. "I didn't really think—I mean, I guess it's obvious—but I didn't imagine that the witches—that there would be children here. When it happened."

"I hadn't considered it, either."

Vann turned the slingshot over in his hand a few times, then laid it back on the rock where he had found it. "I'll check the next stretch of the tunnel."

He headed into the gloom, not waiting for a response.

Lilah decided to add the ball to the small collection of artifacts she had taken to study further, this one for practical reasons if nothing else, since it lit the way whenever she bounced or shook it. The cheerful song also seemed to fight against the oppressive darkness, the feeling that they were walking through catacombs.

They traveled another hour or so, Vann speaking little. He started to limp, and she remembered that he had never taken her up on the offer to bandage his leg. When she spotted an alcove mostly empty of rubble, she spoke up.

"Can we take a break?" Lilah decided he would not want to appear weak in front of her, and would deny the leg bothered him if she pointed it out. "I'm getting tired and hungry."

He had already seen her panicking, so she felt no need to pretend toughness.

Vann looked down at his sword—he had been carrying it and using it as a light instead of sheathing it. "We can rest for a while. I'll stand guard. I don't want to relax too much since the sword might not warn me about approaching magic right now, not while it's being fooled by a wolf's tail."

"Ah." Lilah headed into the alcove. "Does that mean we can't have sex?"

She'd meant it as a joke, but his head swung around like a pointer catching sight of a pheasant in the bushes. That weary expression completely disappeared.

"I can have sex without relaxing," he said.

"Oh? I don't think you're doing it right then."

"I'm open to instruction."

"Are you? I thought you might be mature enough to be set in your ways."

He lowered his sword tip to the ground and raised an eyebrow at her. "I'm fairly certain you just called me old, but I'm still willing to have sex with you."

"I bet your troops have no idea you're so magnanimous."

"That's because I'm not willing to have sex with them."

"No wonder you're lonely." Lilah waved him toward the alcove. "Come let me clean your leg, will you?"

Perhaps a testament to how much it was bothering him, he did not object. He limped toward the alcove, which was little more than a side tunnel that had collapsed part way in. It felt a little like a room, even if it did not possess anything so cozy as furnishings. Vann paused at the entrance, considered the sword again, then said something to it in a different language.

It flared brighter for a moment, before returning to a steady glow. He propped it against the wall, then removed his pack and sat down beside it, his back to the same wall. He stuck his legs out straight.

"What did that do?" Lilah asked.

"Maybe nothing, but it came with a few commands in some old dead language. That's supposed to be the one to tell it to stand down but to remain on guard."

"Should I be concerned that your sword is as smart as a dog?"

"You should be concerned if it's not smarter than a magical wolf." Vann closed his eyes, leaning his head back.

Lilah had seen the first-aid kit earlier, when she had been slipping rubbings into his pack, and she pulled it out now. He did not open his eyes as she untied his boot and rolled up his mangled trouser leg. The punctures were red and swollen and should have been cleaned hours ago, but she could understand why he had prioritized getting out from under the potential blast path of any explosives Kaika might set. Of course, no explosions had come, at least none that they had heard. He had to be worried about the rest of his people. Had Kaika and the others been caught in that same cave-in?

"How do you think such strange wolves came to be?" Lilah asked.

"Witch guard dogs."

She dribbled water from the canteen and did her best to wash the wounds without waste. Even though they had been reserved with their sipping so far, the one canteen was all they had.

"They're very old guard dogs then. And what's left for them to guard?"

"Maybe they've been sleeping for three hundred years and just woke up to terrorize my leg."

Lilah dug an antiseptic tincture out of the first-aid kit. "You must have a very special leg."

"You don't agree now that you've seen it?" He opened his eyes as she dabbed the abrasive liquid on, not flinching, though it must sting. "That's disappointing."

"Well, it's slightly macerated at the moment. Perhaps it will be more impressive after it heals."

"Hm." He watched her work through half-closed eyes.

As she wrapped a bandage around his leg, she wondered if he was thinking bedroom thoughts. The gods knew, they were flitting through *her* mind. He seemed so mellow compared to his usual gruff soldier self, almost playful as he traded banter with her. This wouldn't be the ideal place for bedroom activities, but what if they didn't have many more chances? What if this tunnel never led to a way out? What if they ran out of food and water and—

"Lilah?" Vann asked, his gaze locked onto her face.

She swallowed. Had her concerns been visible? "Yes?"

"I didn't expect witch children to have normal toys."

"No?" She tucked in the end of the bandage and pulled his shredded trouser leg down.

"I figured they ran around throwing fireballs at innocent people from birth."

Lilah scooted up to sit against the wall beside him. "They are—*were*—just humans, Vann. And from what I've seen of the archaeological evidence of multiple cultures on multiple continents, balls for toys are almost universal."

"I was thinking of the slingshot," he said, gazing thoughtfully down at his feet. She hadn't put the boot she had removed back on, since his shin was swollen.

After a time, he stirred and offered her his arm. "Do me a favor, Lilah?"

"Yes," she said, her heart speeding up as she considered what favor he might want. She leaned close, accepting the arm around her shoulders, then looked into his eyes, aware of the ridged muscles of his torso through his shirt.

"If I take a short nap, don't wander off to look for artifacts."

Oh. That wasn't *quite* what she'd had in mind.

"You seem like someone who might let curiosity override caution," he added, an eyebrow twitching.

She couldn't muster any indignation. It was true.

"You should probably ensure I'm too tired to wander off then," she said.

His eyelids drooped, and he gazed at her through his lashes. "Any suggestions as to how that might be done? You seem perky."

"I—"

The ground shuddered, dust trickling down onto them. Had that been a boom in the distance? She gripped Vann's leg. If Kaika and the others were setting off bombs, trying to clear that passage near the entrance, would Lilah and Vann be in danger all the way down here? Not that they had truly gone that far. With all the climbing, they might have only covered a mile or two, and the tunnel had been winding. What if they weren't all that far from—

"Lilah," Vann said.

She forced herself to focus on him, not to think of the whispers of dirt shifting, of pebbles bouncing down old rubble piles. "Yes?"

"You're breathing heavily, and I don't think it's because you're imagining me naked."

She closed her eyes and made herself take a couple of deep breaths before meeting his gaze again. She had done enough panicking. She wasn't going to allow herself to need comforting again, not over a little trickle of dust falling.

"As a matter of fact, I *am* imagining you naked. You said something about a tattoo on your ass, and I've been wondering what it is."

"Really," he said dryly. Skeptically.

"Absolutely. For instance, is it fierce and manly? Like a lion or a tiger? Or is it a butterfly or flower? Maybe a heart? Scientific minds are brimming with curiosity, you know."

Another distant boom sounded, and she couldn't hold back a grimace. More dust trickled down, and she looked upward. That wasn't a crack in the ceiling, was it? If so, had it been there for centuries? Or was it new?

Vann lifted a hand to the side of her face, brushing his knuckles along her cheeks. She lowered her gaze to his, aware of the dust trickling out in the main tunnel but also aware of him, of the way their faces were only a few inches apart. The touch of his fingers made her nerves come alive, delighting in the sensation. It had been a long time since those nerves had had a reason to live.

He shifted his fingers from her face to her hair, stroking it, rousing more nerves, making her scalp tingle with pleasure. She leaned more of her body against his, her breasts pressing against his chest. The logical part of her mind knew she wouldn't be any safer from cave-ins while in his arms, but she wanted an excuse to slide into his lap, to let her hands explore, just as his were doing. Having his fingers in her hair, rubbing and stroking, felt wonderful. He shifted his other arm from her shoulders to her waist, his hand slipping under her shirt, warm calloused flesh sliding along the smooth skin of her back. Yes, she was definitely tempted to crawl into his lap, to give him easier access to all of her, and to feel his muscular form beneath her. Just because they couldn't have a future together didn't mean they couldn't enjoy the now, right?

He paused long enough to unfasten his belt—and that garish wolf tail. She grinned impishly as he tossed it toward his sword. The blade pulsed once, as if to say it was on guard. Or maybe that was disdain for having a tail thrown at it.

Lilah lifted her hand to his face, tracing his strong jaw, fingernails scraping along the days' beard stubble. Though it was rough against her palm, she enjoyed the sensation. She bit her lip as she rubbed her thumb along his mouth. They had already shared a kiss, but she felt tentative. He was tired, injured. Did he truly want—

"Kiss me, Lilah," Vann said. It came out as a command rather than a request, his dark eyes intense.

That obstinate part of her thought to object, but did she truly want to? When she had been contemplating that very thing? And when he was stroking her hair and rubbing her back, driving every worry from her mind while kindling heat throughout her body...

He could have leaned away from the wall and kissed her first, but he waited for her to raise her mouth to his, to brush his lips with hers. After letting her explore and taste him for a moment, his arm shifted and he pulled her astride his lap, his body tight and hard beneath her. Outwardly, he may have appeared patient, even drowsy, but she could feel the tension in him now as he returned her kiss, his mouth hungry and demanding. A stronger desire sparked deep within her, and her own tentativeness faded as she found her own need building, pushing her to match his passion. Her hands roamed, no longer hesitating. She tugged open buttons, eager to slide her hands over his warm bare chest, rubbing sleek, contoured flesh.

"Lilah," he said, his mouth still against hers.

She managed a muffled, "Yes?" wondering if he would give her some other order. A tingle of anticipation went through her as she imagined what it might be, and she pushed his shirt further back, wanting to look at and feel all of him. Perhaps to taste all of him.

"If your university *did* have a job for someone like me," he said, "I would work for you."

She leaned back enough to meet his eyes, her hands stilling on his shoulders. She remembered the conversation he was referencing, the discussion of how Commander Asylon worked for Sashi on their expeditions.

"To help capture a Cofah time wizard and solve the mysteries of eternity?" she teased.

"To keep you alive on whatever crazy research mission you went on."

"I wish my university could hire you, because I would appreciate that," she whispered, more emotion than she would have expected tumbling through her, tightening her throat and making her want him for reasons that went beyond the powerful body underneath her.

He nodded, seeming to acknowledge her appreciation and also that there was no job for him in her world. That didn't stop him from moving her from his lap to the ground, his arm cradling her head as he shifted atop her. They didn't speak again, words lost in kisses, thoughts lost to pleasure.

Chapter 13

NEXT TIME, A BED, LILAH thought as she dozed in Vann's lap, some of her clothes on, some strewn nearby. She hadn't wanted to leave his embrace to gather them. She enjoyed the feel of his arms around her again—still—and her own arms wrapped around his broad shoulders, her face buried in his neck as she inhaled the masculine scent of him. The sword continued to glow softly from the tunnel entrance where Vann had tossed his belt—and the wolf tail. Fortunately, no new creatures had come to disturb them. If there had been any explosions while they had been enjoying each other's company, she had been too distracted to notice them. She smiled against his neck. Perhaps that had been his plan.

His head was turned toward the exit as he listened for trouble, and she feared he wasn't resting, that he was on guard once again even as he cradled her in his arms. Maybe someday, she could take him somewhere that he wouldn't have to be the soldier, where he could relax fully. She kissed his neck, imagining him walking along the beach back home, barefoot and shirtless, flicking sand dollars over with his toes.

"Careful," Vann murmured. "You get me excited, and I'll start thinking of more ways I can work for you."

She flushed at the memory of how much she had enjoyed his attention. "Won't your soldiers miss us if we linger too long?"

She pushed her fingers through his short hair, knocking out dust and crinkling her nose. Her hair was probably coated with the fine particles too. So sexy. She would hope for a bed *and* a bath next time.

"They might miss *you*." He stroked the back of her head, fingers threading through her hair, the hand that been demanding earlier, now tender.

"I just realized something. I forgot to look at your tattoo." She glanced down.

Vann had not donned his shirt yet, but he was wearing his trousers. Apparently, one didn't perform guard duty with naked legs.

"That's unfortunate."

"You won't give me a peek?" She slipped a finger into his waistband and offered her best mischievous smile.

"You'll just have to have sex with me again."

"Now?"

"I thought you were tired, and that's why we stopped here," Vann said. "I'm beginning to think you only wanted to seduce me."

"You didn't seem to mind being seduced."

"No."

He kissed her, not a quick, chaste kiss, but one that left her slightly breathless and seemed to promise that she would, indeed, get another chance to see his bare cheeks. His hands started exploring, and she thought she could get his trousers off him again right there, but he broke away and took a deep breath. She smiled, seeing his reluctance to leave her and pleased by it.

"We should get going if you're not going to sleep," he said. "We don't have unlimited food and water."

"There's nothing like reminders of possible starvation to excite a woman." Alas, she *was* hungry. She knew that Vann had a couple of ration tins in his pack, but did not want to ask for one yet, since she didn't know how much longer they would be wandering.

"I want to make sure you survive your mission more than I want to excite you."

"Is that why you're still fondling my breast?" She looked down at his hand, though she didn't particularly want him to stop.

He gave her a wolfish grin, not at all ashamed by his roaming hands. "That's for *my* excitement." He followed that with another kiss, then sighed and shifted her to the side, though not before his gaze raked her, taking in her half-clad state in the soft glow of the sword.

Lilah took her time getting to her feet, giving him a bit of a show. Unfortunately, he remembered his duty and picked up the sword and walked to the mouth of the tunnel. He looked left and right. Had he heard something? She was *not* in the mood for another battle with wolves.

In case that was inevitable, she hurried to collect her clothing, buttoning her shirt quickly. How had that shoe ended up halfway up that rubble pile?

"Almost ready?" Vann asked softly, donning his shirt and boots quickly, then returning to the tunnel mouth, where he once again looked like the consummate soldier. "Kasandral has grown brighter."

"Almost. I can't find my panties."

"Did you look on the floor in your barracks room?" he teased.

"I put that pair away. I was disappointed that you didn't ogle it."

"A trained warrior scans the battlefield in an instant, seeing all, remembering it for analysis later."

She poked through the rubble pile, which lay mostly in the shadows since he had picked up the sword and moved away. Ah, there they were. "Did you just admit to saving the memory of my panties for later analysis?"

He grinned back at her. "Do you know that you're sexy when your hair is a mess and your buttons are mismatched?"

"Do you know that you avoided answering my question?"

"Yes." He stepped out into the tunnel, leaving the alcove even dimmer.

Lilah finished dressing, picked up the rifle, and joined him. He was squinting into the gloom in the direction they had been heading. Would he want to continue in that direction or go back and see if Kaika and Bosmont had managed to clear the way to the destroyed chamber?

"Did you find your panties?" He glanced back at her.

"I did. Someone had flung them on top of a rubble pile. So thoughtless."

"Someone? Me?"

"*I* would certainly never do such a thing."

Vann wrapped an arm around her. He looked like he wanted to get going, but he took a moment to stand there, resting his face against her hair and inhaling her scent. "Promise me you'll give me another chance to fling them before you leave," he murmured before releasing her.

"That's an easy promise to keep. I absolutely must see that tattoo." She swatted him on the butt.

"Good." He stepped away and frowned into the darkness ahead again. "Stay close. Something's out there."

Lilah followed him, having no problem with staying close. Whatever was out there, she doubted it was the bathtub and dinner that she desired.

* * *

Wolves.

Vann caught the distant clacking of claws on stone, so he was certain more of the same predators waited for them. Yet, these did not attack. Kasandral hummed in his hand, eager to destroy more magical creatures, but the wolves stayed out of sight. As he and Lilah continued to climb over rock piles and squeeze through narrow openings, he tried to guess how many were out there. He'd handled two and was confident in his ability to do so again, but what if the ones out there were waiting for backup? If an entire pack attacked, even Kasandral wouldn't be enough to destroy them. His leg throbbed as a reminder.

He and Lilah came to an intersection, this one in as much disarray as all of the others. The green glow of his sword highlighted a dusty plaque affixed to one corner, and she rushed past him to take a look. He stayed close, raising the blade so the light would help her see. He'd belted that disgusting wolf tail back on to keep it glowing. Maybe wearing the trophy was what kept the other creatures away. He could hope anyway.

"Exit, directory, and this is an old term that's essentially the equivalent of what we call laboratories now, isn't it?" Lilah asked, rubbing the dust away and squinting.

"Was that question for me?"

"Those are the words I can read that are in Iskandian. There are some other words, Referatu terms, I assume." She patted her clothes, delving into pockets until she came up with another sheet of paper for making a rubbing.

Vann had no insight into witch terms, so he simply held the sword, watching her cover the plaque with the paper as he listened for the wolves. Laboratories? Maybe that was where they had come from. Some crazy witch scientist running experiments on forest creatures and turning them into monsters. To what end, he couldn't guess. Guard dogs? Maybe one of those witches had possessed an inkling about how the outside world felt about them. By habit, he almost added the thought, *rightfully so*. But he felt too tired to feel his usual irritation toward all things sorcerous.

Or maybe it was more than weariness. He thought of that slingshot, of the boy's bones. When he had first read the captain's journal and envisioned a mission to destroy this mountain, he'd envisioned a stronghold of malevolent witches, a military-like place. It hadn't occurred to him that children might be here. Families. Maybe Lilah had been right. Maybe he wouldn't have made the choice that his ancestor had made. Had Major Therrik known about the children? Or had he just assumed he was infiltrating an enemy stronghold, as Vann might have?

"The arrow pointing to the exit is pointing that way," Lilah said quietly. She pointed toward a tunnel completely blocked by rubble.

"How about the directory?" Vann guessed that was the map-thing that had been hovering in the air when he'd first charged into the chamber with the pedestal.

"Also that way."

"And that way?" He pointed in the direction they had been heading, the only way that lay clear.

"Laboratories."

"Great." That was the direction the clacking claw sounds were coming from too.

"Maybe the labs link up to the corridor with the tunnel that we were in earlier." Lilah finished her rubbing, folded it, and returned the implements to her pocket. "I'm curious about what the Referatu did in laboratories."

"I'm not," Vann grumbled.

Lilah looked at him, her lips turning downward.

He thought about pointing out that there were wolves up there and that his leg ached, but he couldn't bring himself to admit a weakness to her. No, it was more than that. For whatever reason, she seemed to believe he was a better man than he was. He did not want to disappoint her.

"But I'll hold the light for you while you look at them," he amended, twirling Kasandral once and leaving green streaks in the air.

Her lips curved upward. "Thank you."

He remembered that smile from earlier, as she'd lain under him, her arms wrapped around his back, gazing up at him as if he was something special, not some army brute. He wasn't sure what he had done to earn that look, but he hoped to see it again. He also hoped to spend much more time pressed together, with her breasts squished delightfully to his chest.

"I'm not sure how to interpret that smile you're wearing," she said.

Vann straightened his face. "I was having lascivious thoughts."

"Ah, that was going to be my guess. Either that or that you were looking forward to battling more wolves."

"No," he sighed. "I'm tired of wolves."

It would be better to deal with them sooner rather than later, and to get out of this dark hole. He saluted her with the sword and strode down the tunnel again, toward the laboratory.

After all the crawling, climbing, and walking they had done, he expected another hour before they reached anything, but the way soon grew clear. Surprisingly so. For the first time, they walked through a tunnel without rubble on the ground and without cracks in the walls and ceiling. Soon, they rounded a bend, where a door came into sight, standing ajar. A lamp crystal, the first working one they had seen in hours, illuminated the hallway ahead of it.

Something dark darted through the open doorway before Vann had a good look at it. Suspecting one of those wolves, he tightened his grip on the sword and lifted a hand to make sure Lilah stayed behind him. Another plaque hung on the wall near the door, and he imagined he could already hear her digging into her pocket for rubbing paper.

Listening for clacking claws, Vann crept forward. Light escaped from the room beyond the door. At least he wouldn't be fighting in the dark again.

The familiar soft scrapes came from behind the door. The way it stood, he couldn't see into the room. Or chamber. Or laboratory. Whatever hell awaited them.

He stopped outside and eased the door fully open with the sword tip. A large room lay inside, the walls smooth and gray, the ceiling lit with two of the energy crystals. Tables and desks filled the space, and Lilah made an excited noise when she saw cabinets and shelves full of books, dusty jars, and canisters. Some of the jars still held liquids, and Vann shuddered to think what terrible potions they represented. Something that would turn him into a frog or a rodent, no doubt.

If there had been other options, he would have chosen another tunnel over entering the lab. He didn't even know if it was worth going inside. Was there another exit somewhere on the other side? Or was this a dead end?

A shadow darted through Vann's line of sight. A large black shadow.

Kasandral hummed hungrily into his mind, and the blade flared brighter. An urge to leap inside and start swinging filled him.

Vann took a deep breath, asserting his will over that of the sword. He debated on closing the door and walking back the way they had come. There had been those explosions earlier. Maybe Kaika and the others were even now looking for him in the room he and Lilah had originally dropped into.

He looked over his shoulder at her, tempted to suggest turning around. But her eyes gleamed brightly as she peered around his shoulder and into the room. She met his gaze and bit her lip, looking like she wanted to grip his arm and share her excitement over this find with him. She was probably delighted at the prospect of poking into jars of witch potions.

Vann sighed softly to himself. He wouldn't let her down.

Besides, Kasandral wanted him to advance too. Energy coursed from the hilt and into his hands, thrumming through his body. Its familiar hunger surged through him, demanding that he stride inside and destroy all things magical.

"Wait here," Vann whispered. "I'll deal with the wolves."

"Be careful. I haven't seen that tattoo yet."

He thought about pointing out that she could easily take a look at it when he was dead, but that seemed a gruesome response, so he nodded instead and stepped inside.

Vann spotted the two wolves right away. They stood like statues in front of an alcove on the far side of the room, their heads lowered, as their yellow eyes stared into his soul. The first threat, however, came from beside the door.

Something huge, gray, and on two legs rotated toward him, big blocky arms rising, an axe as tall as Vann gripped in its human-like hands. A square jaw opened, revealing two rows of flat stone teeth. The squarish face also contained yellow eyes, *glowing* yellow eyes. The jaw moved again, and words came out, words like the grinding of rock on rock.

"Access forbidden without an invitation," the creature spoke, walking toward Vann on those blocky legs, the axe upraised.

"Where do we get an invitation?" Vann asked, not truly expecting an answer.

He stepped away from the door, giving himself room to maneuver while putting his back to a sturdy-looking cabinet. From there, he could see the creature—the guardian?— approaching him, and he could also watch the wolves out of the corner of his eye. He couldn't tell what they were doing—also guarding something—but a curtain partially covered an alcove behind them. He hoped some further enemy wasn't waiting in there to jump out at him.

"Assistant President Mistress Jyalla," the towering guardian said in its rock-grinding voice.

"Happy to talk to her," Vann said, lowering into a crouch. "Where is she?"

The creature paused, its head turning toward the alcove. Hells, there wasn't a three-hundred-year-old witch back there waiting for him, was there?

"Leave, intruder," the guardian said, shaking the axe slightly.

The ceiling was just high enough to give it clearance.

Vann might have left, if only because there seemed little to gain from engaging in this fight, but he had spotted a second door on the other side of the room, behind tables and work stations. Another way out. Perhaps the way that would take them out of the mountain.

The axe swung down, aiming for his skull.

Ready for the attack, Vann leaped to the side. He expected the axe to slam into the cabinets behind him, the lumbering guardian unable to react quickly to his move. Instead, the weapon halted in mid-air, turning from a swing into a swipe. The axe whizzed toward Vann's chest.

He leaped back again, this time whipping Kasandral up to meet the attack. The blades slammed into each other, and sparks flew. Even with all his strength and all his training, the power of the blow nearly drove him to his knees.

He sprang away, not wanting to deflect many more of those magically enhanced attacks. When next he jumped in, he aimed for the axe haft instead of at the blade. It appeared to be wood, so he hoped to cut it in half.

Kasandral flared brightly as it dove for the haft. It bit into the wood, but only slightly. Yellow sparks sprang from the axe where his sword hit. Whatever that weapon was, it was as enhanced as the guardian.

Vann continued on the offensive, launching a barrage of blows at his foe, attacking from several angles. The guardian did not bother to defend itself. It accepted the strikes, none of which did more than chip tiny flecks away from its stone body, and focused on hitting Vann instead. That axe swung for his head again.

"Behind you," Lilah yelled at the same time as she fired her rifle from the doorway.

Vann blocked the axe before it came close to his head, his joints protesting the abuse, then skittered sideways again, putting his back to the wall. The wolves had given up their guard post and were charging across the room at him.

He might have run back into the hallway, in the hope that

all three adversaries would not follow, but he glimpsed Lilah slipping into the room.

"Lilah," he protested, but he didn't have time to say more.

The guardian's axe swung toward him at the same time as the two wolves leaped for his throat.

Vann ducked the axe and jumped sideways, finding a corner to back into as he swung at the closest wolf. Kasandral's green glow gleamed off black scales as the creature flew toward him. He bashed it in the side of the neck before those jaws could latch onto him. Almost before the blow landed, he was jerking the blade away to deflect the snapping maw of the other creature.

He alternated his attacks, targeting one wolf and then the other, settling into a moment of utter focus as he watched both, trying to do damage at the same time as he parried their attacks. He needed to dispatch them quickly, since the guardian strode toward him again, the axe raised over its head once more.

A crash of glass sounded as something struck the guardian in the back. Vann couldn't take his attention from the wolves to pay much attention. One came in low, diving for his shin. Vann shifted his grip and drove the point of his sword toward that head, determined not to suffer an injury to his other leg. His aim was precise, and Kasandral's tip pierced the creature's skull.

Its momentum carried it forward, and Vann had to jump into the air to avoid being pinned against the wall. The creature howled in pain as it crashed into the spot where he had been standing. Vann yanked the sword free as the other one leaped for his chest.

More glass shattered, and an acrid smell stung his nostrils. He glimpsed smoke coming from behind the guardian's back, and it stopped its advance. Vann didn't know what Lilah was doing, but he welcomed the distraction of one of his opponents.

He slashed at the wolf's face, determined to finish the beasts as quickly as he could. The one that had struck the wall had dropped to its belly, but it was trying to get up. Vann launched a series of quick thrusts and slashes at the one still attacking him. Blade met scale, biting into flesh over and over. The creature howled in pain and fury, and gathered itself for one last leap. It sprang for his head.

Vann dropped, rolling away from the wall before springing to his feet. The wolf sailed past, trying to twist in the air to snap at him as he rose, but he was quick enough to meet its fangs with his blade. Then, as it landed, he slammed Kasandral down onto its spine. The creature yowled, its tail going rigid. Vann hacked at it several more times, then drove the point of the sword into the back of its neck, severing its spine.

Fearing the other one might be rising, he spun back toward it. The wolf had only managed to get its front legs under it. Vann rushed in and finished it with several quick, efficient blows.

When he turned toward the guardian, he found it standing still, its stony flesh smoking from a dozen spots. The axe remained over its head, but the glow in the yellow eyes had dimmed.

He strode forward, intending to attack while it was dazed, but it toppled over backward before he reached it. It landed on the gray floor, broken glass all around it. The axe skidded free from its grip.

"Careful," Lilah warned from across the room in front of a bookcase full of glass bottles and jars. "Don't get close. That stuff will burn right through your boots."

Vann halted. Smoke wafted not only from the fallen guardian but also from spots on the floor.

"What is it?" he asked, curious if she knew or if she had grabbed random jars off the shelves and gotten lucky.

"If I read the formula correctly, perchloric acid, and the label said it had been enhanced. I thought that sounded promising."

After making sure the wolves were truly dead, Vann skirted the smoking guardian and crossed the room to give Lilah a hug. He decided not to take offense that she peered all about as she distractedly returned the hug.

"I can't believe this room is completely intact," she said, touching a dusty shelf. "So many amazing artifacts."

"Amazing. Hm." Vann eyed the remains of the guardian, then walked toward the alcove.

"I wonder if some magical reinforcement protected the lab," Lilah said.

Kasandral's glow softened, though it still burned brightly, as if offended by all the magic around. At least it no longer hummed with an eagerness to slay things. Still, Vann kept it in hand as he approached the curtain, not sure what else he might find in here.

"Well, isn't *this* interesting?" Lilah asked, her voice muffled. Her head was stuck in a box under a desk filled with tools.

Vann paused in front of the curtain. "What?"

Lilah pulled out a sizable scapula, the bone far darker and more stone-like than the skeletons they had found in the tunnels.

"A dragon fossil?" Vann asked.

"A dragon fossil, indeed. There are several in here." Lilah rubbed her fingers and set it on the desk.

"Are you tingling?"

"Yes."

"Is it caused by something more than the proximity of my magnetic sexual aura?"

"Possibly." Lilah pulled a few crinkled and yellowed pieces of paper out of the box. "Hm, I was hoping this might be a diary describing someone's diabolical plans for magicking up the fossils."

"What is it?"

"Looks like a shopping list. This one might be a menu from the cafeteria."

"Maybe a museum will pay handsomely to know what witches ate."

Vann turned back toward the curtain. He already believed those bones had been placed in the mountain to spook the residents so that the entrance wouldn't be used and nobody would be around when the military team infiltrated the mountain.

Using the tip of the blade, he nudged the curtain aside. He wasn't sure what he expected behind it, but what he found was someone's bedroom.

Enough light came from behind him to illuminate the bed, the blankets still rumpled. If not for the skeleton lying atop the bed and the cobwebs stretching across the alcove, he might have believed it had been abandoned weeks ago instead of centuries ago. No, *abandoned* wasn't the right word. The occupant hadn't left, after all.

When Lilah came over to look, Vann backed away, giving her room to poke around. She eased straight into the alcove, far less daunted by dead people than by claustrophobic situations. Vann's gaze fell upon the floor in front of the curtain. Hollows had been worn into the stone in the exact spots where the wolves had been waiting. He crouched and slid his fingers over them, finding the stone oily. A few dried black scales dotted the floor. He looked across the room to where the dead wolves lay.

"Is it possible those creatures are—were—three hundred years old?" Vann asked. "And that they were standing guard all of this time? Protecting this room?"

"Or protecting this woman." Lilah leaned over the skeleton's skull. The bones did not appear to have been disturbed—unlike some of the ones in the tunnels, they hadn't been pulled apart and gnawed on by rodents or other scavengers.

"They never figured out she was dead and didn't need protecting anymore?"

"Maybe they were given the same command that you gave your sword. Guard." After a pause, Lilah asked, "Vann?" Her voice had an odd note to it.

He stood and stepped into the alcove. In addition to the bed, there was a table and an armoire. A faded note lay folded in half on the table, and he almost reached for it, but Lilah had stuck her hand into the skull. For the first time, Vann noticed a crack and a hole in the side of it. A familiar feeling of unease came over him. Captain Molisak's broken skull came to mind even before she fished out the musket ball.

Lilah laid it in his hand. "It seems the guard wolves failed."

Vann stared down at the army-issue musket ball. It was identical to the other one they had found.

"How could she have been shot?" he asked. "I've seen Sardelle deflect bullets with her mind. You can't just shoot a witch."

"If she was asleep..."

Vann chewed on that. Yes, he supposed Sardelle would have to be awake to raise a magical shield. That soulblade of hers never seemed to sleep, but he didn't think all witches had those.

"Still," he said, "what about the wolves? If they were always around and protecting her, how did they let an enemy soldier get by?"

"Maybe she didn't consider him an enemy." She spread her hand toward the bed.

"Him," Vann said hollowly.

The uneasy feeling in his gut intensified. The musket ball could have belonged to anyone who came on that infiltration mission, and yet, he did not miss the significance of the look Lilah gave him when she stepped toward the table and picked up the note.

"I do not believe you will need as much of the energy amplification powder as you implied," Lilah read, "but I've made the requested number of vials. Be extremely careful with them, Major. You could bury yourself and your own men as well as our target. It would upset me to lose you."

Lilah set the note down.

"That's all it says?" Vann asked.

"Yes."

"I guess that explains how they brought the mountain down. I'd wondered, especially when I saw the TE-18. Explosives were primitive back then. It was hard to believe…" Vann stopped, since Lilah was frowning fiercely at the note. "What is it?"

"This isn't proof," she said, "not exactly. It just insinuates."

"That Major Therrik talked her into making something that would let his explosives take down the whole mountain instead of just the room or chamber she must have intended? That he used it—used *her*—to destroy a civilization?" Vann didn't bother to hide the distaste in his voice. He had already been displeased with this distant relative of his for shooting a fellow officer. The idea of him sleeping with a woman and then shooting her made Vann like him even less. Even if she had been a witch. An enemy should be battled honorably, not through trickery and assassination. He clenched his hand around the musket ball.

"Possibly." Lilah met his eyes and laid a hand on his forearm. "He's not you."

"No, but I prefer to think of myself as descended from heroes rather than villains."

"We don't all get the ancestors we wish." She snorted softly. "And it doesn't have a damned thing to do with who you become."

Reminded of the father she had told him about, Vann nodded. Yes, she understood what it was like to be disappointed in one's family. Hells, she was stuck with that flying glory hound, Zirkander. Vann was relieved that she was nothing like him.

He laid his hand on hers. "Mind if we get out of here, for now? You can come back to explore later, assuming there aren't more three-hundred-year-old wolves lurking in the tunnels."

Lilah gazed wistfully around the laboratory, but she nodded. "I'm with you."

"Good," he said, wishing it was forever.

"At least until I see that tattoo."

He snorted. "Maybe I'll come up with creative ways to keep it hidden then."

She slid her arm around his waist as they walked out of the alcove. "I'm rather crafty when I want to be."

He glanced at the smoking guardian. "I believe that."

Chapter 14

As soon as they left the protection of the laboratory, they returned to unlit, rubble-filled passages. Lilah followed Vann over a pile that stretched to the ceiling, though she kept glancing over her shoulder. A big part of her had wanted to object when he'd suggested that they continue on, but he had been so polite. It hadn't even been an order. And he'd been right. Even though her stomach kept growling and they had limited supplies, she wanted to sift through every inch of that lab, to learn everything she could about the people who once lived in this mountain. To find so many artifacts in such pristine condition in the middle of these demolished tunnels was amazing.

"We're getting close to something," Vann said.

"The way out?"

"Doubtful." He hefted his sword, which continued to glow a faint green as they walked. That glow had increased again. "More wolves, probably. Unless there's something else magical down here."

Lilah fought the urge to slump back against the rubble pile. Even if Vann had been the one dealing with the wolves, she felt weary at the thought of battling more of them. It was so pointless, since they were fighting to protect someone who had died three hundred years ago.

Their tunnel curved, then widened into a cavern, but she could not see far. Piles of rubble littered the ground ahead. She listened for the clack of claws on stone as they wound through the piles.

Vann stopped abruptly as they rounded one in the middle of the cavern. Lilah almost bumped into his back. Bones lay scattered around the base of the rocks. Bones and a dusty army boot.

Vann held his sword over the remains and looked around. Lilah spotted a scrap of dark fabric on the side of the rubble pile. She walked over and picked it up. It was part of a uniform jacket that had been ripped and torn. By an irate wolf? She brought it back to the light and turned it over to the front. A couple of buttons remained, as well as the nametag.

THERRIK.

She looked at Vann's face, checking to see if he was reading it. Yes, his gaze locked onto the nametag, and grimness took over his face.

"Looks like he didn't make it out." Vann walked a few steps and nudged something at the base of the rocks, an old flintlock musket.

"Was he crushed in the rocks that fell in the wake of their explosions?" Lilah wondered. "Or did the residents find out what he had done and send someone after him?"

"Whatever happened, he deserved his fate. I hope the rest of his team made it out."

"Maybe he stayed behind to guard the way, so they could escape," Lilah said, finding herself wanting to suggest a possibility that would make his ancestor seem like less of an ass, though after what the man had done, that seemed impossible.

Vann grumbled something unflattering and turned toward the far end of the cavern. Kasandral pulsed, its glow intense and hungry.

Thumps and scrapes came from the darkness ahead of him. Lilah fingered the trigger of her rifle. What would they face next?

"Wolves?" she whispered. Maybe the sword gave him a hint as to what magic he would face.

Vann sighed, his shoulders slumped, and his blade drooped. She stepped up next to him, trying to interpret his reaction. He had never shown any sign of defeat.

More thumps followed, then clanks and clunks. It sounded like rocks being hurled against walls, but there weren't any explosions to suggest that Kaika might be at work.

Greetings, humans! a male voice spoke into Lilah's head, almost startling her into falling over.

She glanced back in the direction of the lab, thinking some magical creature might remain alive, some creature that was now talking to them. She'd heard that the Referatu possessed telepathic powers, but she'd never had anyone speak into her mind.

Vann groaned, his sword lowering further, the tip touching the floor. The blade flared an angry green, the brightest that Lilah had seen it, but he did not react as if an enemy headed toward them.

"I know that voice," Vann said.

"Who is it?" Lilah asked.

I am the god, Bhrava Saruth, the voice spoke into her mind again. She had no idea if she should be terrified or amused. It was an oddly perky voice and did not sound that threatening. *If you are in need of my healing powers, I will reach you shortly.* A thud sounded, another rock—or giant boulder?—being hurled against a wall. *After I heal you and bless you, you may worship me!*

"Goodie," Vann said.

"Who is it?" Lilah asked again.

"Sardelle's dragon."

"Sardelle's dragon is a god?"

"He *thinks* he's a god."

"So we're being rescued?" Lilah asked.

"We didn't need to be rescued," he snapped. "We could have made it out on our own." He waved in the direction of the noise. "I don't think we're far from that tunnel that the soldiers used to get in."

Amazing how much grumpier Vann could sound when others were around. Others who possessed magic, Lilah supposed, eyeing the sword and its angry green glow. Wondering if he was fighting a compulsion to rush forward and confront the dragon, Lilah eased closer to him.

She clasped his free hand and smiled at him. "Of course we could have made it out on our own, especially with you distracting me from the dark. But if the dragon is friendly, perhaps he can make the journey easier. Will Sardelle be with him?"

"Likely," Vann said.

He still sounded a touch grumpy, but he returned her handclasp. He also sheathed the sword in its scabbard. Some of the green glow escaped around the hilt, and Lilah swore she sensed a feeling of indignation radiating from it.

"Does sticking it in there make it try to influence you less?" she asked.

"No."

"Ah."

"Putting it in its box does. Somewhat. It's still managed to get me to do foolish things, even when it's locked inside of that."

"Foolish things?"

"I tried to kill Sardelle."

"Ah," Lilah said again, perhaps getting a gist for why there was tension between Ridge and Vann, aside from the different career paths they had chosen. "Was that before she saved your life?"

"Yes."

More thuds sounded, then the soft murmur of voices. Some kind of bluish-white light came into view, limning a rubble pile.

"If you manage to remain polite and cordial with our rescuers, I will—" Aware of others drawing closer, Lilah rose onto her tiptoes to whisper the rest in his ear. Considering the implicit naughtiness, a whisper seemed appropriate.

Vann's eyelids drooped, and he gave her a sexy look that heated her from the inside out. "*How* cordial?"

"Well, definitely don't kill anyone. If that's an easy request, maybe you could invite them to a nice dinner at the outpost."

Vann's jaw sagged open. "The dragon too?"

"I know that Captain Kaika, for one, would like to sit next to him." Lilah turned toward the approaching light, the voices growing easier to pick out now. She recognized Ridge's irreverent tone, as he said something about spending entirely too much time in caves this year. Lilah craned her neck, eager to get a look at this dragon, especially after having only dealt in dragon fossils for most of her life.

"As a soldier loyal to the king, I'm not sure I should act as a procurer for his woman's dragon infatuation. But, I will attempt to be hospitable, if you add in—" This time, Vann bent to whisper a suggestion in *her* ear.

She wasn't sure whether to grin or flush with embarrassment and ended up doing both.

Vann released her hand as the first of the approaching group walked into view, Ridge. Lilah almost grabbed his hand back. She didn't want him to feel that they had anything to hide. She had no intention of skulking around and keeping the world from knowing that she cared about Vann, and she certainly hoped he found nothing shameful about his new relationship with her.

From the way Vann crossed his arms and stared defiantly at Ridge, maybe his withdrawn hand had more to do with feeling the need to put up a strong front for his superior officer. Or his enemy, as he seemed to consider Ridge.

Lilah wondered what had brought Ridge back out here so soon. She hadn't expected to see him again for weeks.

A black-haired woman with blue eyes walked at his side. Sardelle? She had elegant features and carried herself with a quiet dignity that seemed an odd match for Ridge's restless energy. He waved effusively at them. As always, he looked like he longed to be in the air, flying around and shooting holes into enemy airships. Indeed, he wore his flight jacket, cap, and scarf, as if he'd just flown in. Sardelle wore typical travel clothes, but the sword in her hand, the sword responsible for the bluish glow, was anything but typical. Perhaps Lilah should feel inadequate since *she* did not have a sword to carry about?

Kaika and Bosmont came behind Ridge and Sardelle, their faces stained with soot and Kaika's sleeve ripped from cuff to shoulder. They must have had another run-in or two with the wolves. A fifth person ambled to the side of the group, a handsome young man with mussy blond hair that fell into his eyes. He looked like one of Lilah's beach-loving students who might stroll into class with sand stuck between his sandaled toes and no sign of his books or even a pencil. Had he not glanced at her with the most startlingly vibrant green eyes, she wouldn't have guessed that he was anything other than what he appeared.

"Lilah?" Ridge asked, looking her up and down. "Are you all

right? I was worried about the reception you might be receiving up here and decided to come back early and bring Sardelle out to meet you. When Kaika explained that you'd been trapped down here with—" His gaze flicked toward Vann, but he didn't finish the sentence. "That you'd been trapped down here since yesterday, I was afraid I'd come too late."

"I'm fine. I've had Vann to protect me." Lilah pointed at his leg, though he was too proud to favor it if it was bothering him. "He was chewed on by a magical wolf on my behalf."

"Vann?" Ridge mouthed.

Sardelle looked from Lilah to Vann and smiled. It was a knowing smile, which seemed odd, since Lilah had never met the woman before. She couldn't possibly know about the evening Lilah and Vann had spent together, could she?

"Yes, we've had an eventful day. Or night." Lilah shrugged. "I'm afraid I've lost track down here. There's a laboratory back there, and we've been piecing together what happened here three hundred years ago."

"Have you?" Sardelle breathed, her eyes holding a mix of emotions. Interest, certainly, but something else as well. Pain? Fear? If Bosmont's story was true, and Sardelle had been here three hundred years ago, she must have known the people who were now nothing but buried skeletons.

"It's a... tragic story." Lilah looked toward Vann.

"Yes." Sardelle closed her eyes for a long moment, and Ridge silently clasped her hand. Finally, she focused on Vann, waving at his bandaged leg. "Colonel, if you like, I can take a look at that injury."

"Not necessary," Vann said shortly.

Lilah nudged him with her elbow.

He glanced at her, inhaled deeply, then faced Sardelle again. "Yes, I would appreciate that, and I wish to invite you all to dinner at the outpost." He spoke rapidly, as if he'd been rehearsing and wanted to get the loathsome words out as quickly as possible.

Lilah grinned, pleased at the attempt.

Ridge tripped over a rock and nearly fell over.

Sardelle's eyebrows rose, though only for a second before she recovered and said, "We would like that very much."

The young blond man—the *dragon* in human form—ambled between them and peered in the direction of the laboratory. "I sense a great deal of magic back in that direction, high priestess."

"That's where the lab is," Lilah said as she tried to figure out with whom the dragon was speaking. High priestess? "It's mostly intact. I believe that's where she—the assistant president—put the curse on the dragon bones. I'm not sure if curse is the appropriate term. But I think she was the one who stole them from a museum and brought them up here as part of a ruse, to keep people from using this entrance to the mountain, so nobody would be around to notice that soldiers were infiltrating it."

Sardelle frowned as the explanation continued. "We don't—didn't—put curses on things, at least not in the Iskandian sense of the word, but that's actually the term that came to mind when I first sensed the fossils. The field they're emitting is subtle and almost seems natural to me. It was Bhrava Saruth who sensed that someone had tampered with them, giving them a... *herashi malish*. A field of chaotic energy. He said it would be capable of causing the erratic incidents that Captain Bosmont was describing to me."

"I believe he called those incidents crazy witch craziness," Kaika said.

"Yes, it was a short but pithy description," Sardelle said dryly.

"Engineers like pith, ma'am," Bosmont said.

Vann grunted, managing to make the inarticulate syllable sound both sarcastic and derisive.

Sardelle walked over to join the blond man, murmuring a question to him. What had his name been? Bhrava Sur-something?

Bhrava Saruth, the god, the voice spoke into her mind again, and he smiled over his shoulder at Lilah. *Are you in need of a deity to worship? I am pleased to bless my human followers.*

I... ah, I'm an atheist actually. What would a blessing from a dragon be?

Then you are in need of a deity. His smile broadened. *We will discuss it later, yes? I am a most excellent god.*

"Are you *sure* you're all right?" Ridge asked quietly, coming up to Lilah's side, the side opposite from Vann, as Sardelle and Bhrava Saruth continued to talk. "You look dazed."

"Because that young man is trying to recruit me as a worshipper," Lilah said, pointing.

"He does that to everyone. He doesn't seem to mind if you say no, as long as you're willing to rub his belly." Ridge lowered his voice. "I'm sorry I sent you out here without more resources. I had no idea magic would be involved. I should have put more stock in Bosmont's report of curses."

"I wouldn't have," Lilah said.

Bosmont sniffed. "That's disappointing. I thought civilians were more open-minded and less crusty than generals."

"Crusty?" Ridge's eyebrows rose.

"You're not as crusty as most, sir, but you're definitely not a colonel anymore," Bosmont said glumly.

Ridge did not seem to know how to respond to that comment, so he turned back to Lilah.

"I'm relieved you don't seem to be hurt," he said, still sounding apologetic as he looked her over.

"Thank you, and there's nothing to be sorry for," Lilah said. "I've been honored to be a part of this exploration, to see things that haven't been touched in centuries."

She brushed her pocket, where the child's ball made a bulge, and thought about giving it to Sardelle. She had planned to take her finds back to the outpost to examine, but she was starting to wonder if the army truly had the right to excavate this place. That might be an argument for the future.

"I hope Sardelle doesn't mind our intrusion," Lilah added quietly.

"I doubt she does," Ridge said. "She has long wondered what truly happened to her people. Did you hear her story? Oh, I neglected introductions, didn't I? Sardelle, are you done communing with your god?"

"We were discussing the feasibility of lodging ancient dragon fossils into solid rock and how it might have been done," Sardelle said.

"That's a yes, or...?" He wriggled his eyebrows at her.

Sardelle walked over to join him, actually to swat him.

Vann stood quietly, watching everyone, especially Bhrava Saruth, his arms still folded across his chest. He seemed tense. Just because he didn't care for these people? Or because the sword made him tense in the presence of a sorceress and a dragon? Lilah was tempted to hold his hand.

"I remember when the fossils were discovered," Sardelle told Lilah. "Word was sent to the university in the capital, since my people didn't have any experts in archaeology at the time." She smiled. "I don't think paleontology was even a separate science back then. We actually believed that a dragon burial ground had been found and that it might be haunted. You see, there were some strange things happening even back then to travelers who passed near them. Since we were worried about that and also about the ramifications of walking in and out through a potential burial site, this exit to the complex was completely closed down. I've recently learned—" Sardelle waved toward Bhrava Saruth, "—that dragons don't bury their dead or have anything like human burial grounds."

"Not that we've ever discovered," Lilah said.

"You said you gained some insight into what happened here?" Sardelle asked. "I know that there were soldiers with explosives, but there wasn't time to figure out how they got in or how to stop them before the mountain started crashing down around us."

"Vann," Lilah said, "do you still have that journal?"

"Yes." He made no move to reach for his pocket or pack or wherever he had stashed it.

"Would you like to share it? Cordially?"

Vann gave her a flat look. Lilah could see why he wouldn't want his family history shared, especially when Major Therrik's role had been unflattering, but if Sardelle was truly an heir to the Referatu society, then she would want a look. She would *deserve* a look.

"That thing you mentioned," Vann said, tapping his ear. "How many times?"

Ridge tilted his head, a perplexed expression on his face.

"No less than three, I should think," Lilah said, smiling at Vann.

It was amusing to see a big, strong army colonel heave a dramatic sigh worthy of a teenager, but after he did so, he removed his pack and handed Sardelle the journal. She opened it, and Ridge stood next to her, reading over her shoulder. Vann's jaw tightened. He was probably even less enthused at the idea of Ridge learning about his family's past. Lilah eased closer to him, her arm brushing his, as if she could lend him some of her calmness. Nobody should blame him for what had happened in the past.

"Your assistant president seems to have been instrumental in the fall," Lilah said, "even if what happened wasn't quite what she wished to happen. I assume that is her lab back there?"

Sardelle lifted her gaze from the book, her eyes grave. "It is. She was a scientist and an animal speaker."

"Animal speaker?" Vann grunted. "That what it's called when you make creepy, scaly wolves that live for centuries and kill intruders?"

"The *sashpur*, magical guard dogs essentially, were more a result of her science interests. I'm not sure what species were originally crossed, but my people didn't let them out of the mountain, and they aren't fertile. I hadn't realized they were so long-lived." Sardelle rubbed her head, fiddling with one of the clips that held her hair back. "Why would Mistress Jyalla have been instrumental in the fall?"

"You'd have to ask her. Her skeleton is that way." Vann pointed his thumb over his shoulder.

"We believe she instigated an assassination plot against your president," Lilah said. "Would that have been likely?"

"I had no idea Mistress Jyalla had such aspirations," Sardelle said, "but I was aware that she disagreed with Tiyarda on some matters. And our leadership positions were long-term, ten years, so almost like a monarchy. It wasn't easy to remove a president from office once instated."

"So she invited some soldiers in to help her with her problem," Vann said, "maybe wanting to keep her hands clean of blood."

His lip twitched, and Lilah wondered if he was thinking of the way Nia had asked him to help kidnap the king.

"And then, she was taken advantage of, I suppose," Lilah murmured.

"By the soldiers who came into the mountain with explosives?" Sardelle asked.

"By a Major Therrik, it looks like." Ridge had kept reading over her shoulder, and he stabbed his finger at the page, then arched his eyebrows at Vann.

Vann clenched his jaw again.

"It's hard to know exactly what happened with Major Therrik," Lilah said, though those musket balls hadn't left much doubt in her mind, "since that journal was written by one of his men, but we found its owner's skull. With a bullet hole in the back of it. It's possible Major Therrik turned on Captain Molisak when the officer questioned him about the mission. He also seemed to have turned on your assistant president. Once he had what he needed." Lilah was making suppositions left and right and resolved to stop. There would be more time in the future to use evidence to piece together all that had happened back then.

"I have often wondered how our people came to be caught so unaware by the soldiers with their explosives," Sardelle murmured, a haunted expression in her eyes as she turned them toward the page again. "And also how the soldiers knew to pick a day when almost all of us were here in the mountain, celebrating the president's birthday."

"Whatever Major Therrik's plan was," Vann said, "it must not have worked out completely, because he died here. If anyone else made it out, they didn't speak of it to the Therriks, because this officer and this deed aren't mentioned in the family history."

"This deed." Ridge shuddered. "Seven gods, do you think they'd have been proud of him over it?"

Vann did not speak or even move, but Lilah had the impression of a pot about to boil over.

"Many people feared the Referatu back then," Sardelle said, resting a hand on Ridge's forearm, a suggestion for him to stop glowering at Vann, Lilah hoped. "I do wonder how she allowed it to go from an assassination mission to genocide. I'm sure Mistress Jyalla would not have helped bring that about."

Several sets of eyes turned toward Vann, even Bosmont and Kaika seeming to think that he had the answer, or maybe that he should stand accountable for his ancestor's actions. Most of the looks were curious rather than accusing, Sardelle's in particular, but Lilah stuck close to Vann's side, worried he would feel that he was under attack.

"Someone must have taken it into his own hands to upgrade the mission," Ridge said.

"We may never know if Major Therrik acted on his own or was under the orders of a superior," Sardelle said. "From Captain Molisak's entries, it sounds like he didn't know of a superior, but that's not evidence to the contrary. It does sound like Major Therrik was known for his hatred of sorcerers. If you can imagine such a thing." Surprisingly, Sardelle smiled at Vann. It wasn't exactly a friendly smile, rather being one that spoke of irony and a less-than-pleasant shared past.

Sardelle handed the journal back to Vann. He seemed surprised by that and stared down at her hand before accepting the book. "I would like to read the rest before we return home," she said, "but perhaps you could see that the journal makes it back to the captain's family?"

Vann continued to stare down at it. That was a hard thing to imagine him having to do, delivering it to the ancestors of the man his ancestor had shot. Lilah almost suggested that she could undertake the task, perhaps copying the tome for the university records on the way, but Vann nodded and spoke first.

"I will see to it."

"Is the way to the lab clear?" Sardelle asked.

"I can help open it if necessary," Kaika said, patting her utility belt.

"Haven't you blown up enough today?" Bosmont asked her.

"Hardly. It's been *hours* since I got to blow up anything. Bhrava Saruth has simply been waving his hands and melting huge piles of rocks. I've felt largely decorative on this rescue mission. I'm afraid we've disappointed Colonel Therrik by taking so long to get to him."

"He's probably too busy being disappointed that his ancestor killed everybody in this mountain," Bosmont whispered, his voice loud enough that everyone heard.

"Not sure he's disappointed by that," Ridge muttered.

Vann glared at him, glared at Bosmont, clenched his fist, then stalked away, disappearing into the darkness that the others had walked out of earlier.

"You're exceedingly good at offending that man," Sardelle told Ridge.

"Who isn't? He's an unstable bastard."

Lilah scowled at him. "He is not. He's brave, honorable, and he's protected me ever since we entered these tunnels."

"Are you sure you would have needed protecting if he hadn't charged in recklessly? How did you end up in this mountain to start with? Weren't you just supposed to study those fossils?"

"I was curious. What kind of historian would I be if I didn't take an opportunity to explore an archaeological site when it was discovered?"

"Archeological site," Sardelle murmured, sounding dazed as she looked around.

"He shouldn't have brought you in here until our engineer deemed it safe," Ridge said.

Lilah clenched her jaw, annoyed that he immediately thought the worst of Vann.

"You know you never would have succeeded at keeping *me* out while you deemed something safe," Sardelle chided him gently.

"Yes, but you're special," Ridge said.

"And your cousin isn't?"

"Not in the I-have-a-glowing-sword-with-an-attitude-and-we-chew-up-shamans-like-dog-bones way."

Sardelle waved away the argument and nodded toward Lilah. "I'm still confused about much, but at least this is more than I knew before. It illuminates what's been a mystery to me since I woke up. I thank you for working on this puzzle."

"You're welcome."

Ridge looked a little chagrined by Sardelle's maturity—and

the lack of his own—but not enough that he would go after Vann to apologize.

"I'm going to look at this lab now," Sardelle said, frowning as she walked past Major Therrik's bones and headed into the darkness.

"Do you wish me to accompany you, high priestess?" Bhrava Saruth called after her.

"Maybe in a while," she said without looking back. The slump to her shoulders said she might not be as delighted to find that lab, and the mysteries explained within, as Lilah had been.

"Did someone mention that dinner would be served soon?" Kaika asked. "Because blowing up wolves is hard work, and I haven't had a decent meal since I got here."

"Nor have I," Bosmont said dryly.

Ridge walked over and patted the engineer on the shoulder. "We need to get you reassigned somewhere tropical and nice, Bos."

"If you have the power to make that happen, sir, I'll kiss your toes. Maybe other things too."

"It's been too long since you were with a woman, Bos."

"Oh, I know it, sir. Not everyone who works up here gets to have a sorceress wander out of the tunnels and fall into his arms."

Ridge smiled in the direction Sardelle had disappeared. "She didn't fall into my arms right away. That didn't come until she attempted to use snowshoes."

"The grumpy human did not allow me to heal his leg," Bhrava Saruth said, his gaze toward the tunnel Vann had stalked up. He seemed oddly distressed.

"Let's hope those guard dogs didn't have rabies," Ridge said. "We don't need Therrik biting anyone in the outpost."

"No more than usual, anyway," Bosmont said.

"He usually only bites the people who deserve it," Kaika said.

"Unless they're sorcerers. Or pilots." Ridge rubbed the back of one shoulder. Remembering a physical confrontation with Vann? He couldn't have come out on top in that.

"Pilots deserve it," Kaika said. "They're uppity."

"Really."

Lilah wanted to defend Vann, but she was barely listening to the conversation, thinking instead of Bosmont's comment that Ridge might have the sway to affect someone's assignment. Was that true? Or wishful thinking from the captain? Maybe Lilah could talk Ridge into getting Vann assigned to a more appealing post. He had worked in the capital before. Perhaps it could happen again. And perhaps she could also apply for a position in the capital. There were two universities there with archaeology departments.

"Ridge?" Lilah said, rubbing her chin thoughtfully. "Can I talk to you for a moment? Before we head out?"

"Head out? Are you in a rush to leave this delightful graveyard? Have you seen all the skeletons yet? We passed three on the way down."

Lilah waved for him to join her a few steps away from Kaika, Bosmont, and Bhrava Saruth. By the time he stopped beside her, a concerned expression had replaced his usual irreverence.

"What is it?" he asked quietly. "Are you truly all right? You look... rumpled. Therrik didn't do anything, did he? I know he's an ass, but I thought—"

Lilah stopped him with a raised hand. "He's not an ass."

Skeptical eyebrows rose. "No?"

"As I said, he protected me from a bunch of magical wolves, wolves that were impervious to my bullets." Lilah looked down at her rifle, remembering that it wasn't even hers. Vann had given it to her, keeping only the sword for himself. "I'd be dead if not for him."

"*Lilah*," Ridge said, "are you telling me I'm going to have to be nice to him?" His exasperation did not sound very convincing, not with his eyes crinkling at the corners.

"Not necessarily. I think he likes having you as an enemy. But I was wondering if you had the sway to get him reassigned. Perhaps to the capital. This duty station doesn't suit him."

"The capital? Where I'd have to see him and interact with him?" His exasperation was less feigned this time.

"Yes, I'm thinking of applying for a position at the university there."

"That's wonderful. We'd love to have you close by, but what does that have to do with Therrik?"

"It would be easier for me to have sex with him if we're in the same city."

"I—*what?*" The word came out squeaky and loud, and Kaika, Bosmont, and Bhrava Saruth all looked over. Ridge reached out a groping hand toward a boulder, the image of a man who needed support. He almost missed the boulder when he collapsed against it.

Perhaps Lilah should have been more subtle with her revelation, but she didn't know how much time she had left up here with Vann. What if Ridge and Sardelle had come to pick her up and take her back? She'd barely gotten started with the fossils. She'd barely gotten started with *Vann*.

"Ridge?" Lilah shook his shoulder, feeling a touch impatient. "The sway? Do you have it?"

"I'm swaying all right." He rubbed his hand down his face. "You should make friends with Sardelle and ask her. The king likes her more than he likes me. Hells, why don't you ask Kaika? The king likes her a *lot* more than he likes me."

"Kaika?" Lilah peered over at the tall woman, who was busy chatting with Bhrava Saruth. Judging by her expansive gestures, she was describing an explosion. Or perhaps some interesting move that could be performed in bed.

"Kaika," Ridge said firmly.

"I don't think I can ask her to intercede on Vann's behalf. Perhaps I'll write a letter to the king myself." A letter or a paper, listing the reasons why another duty assignment would be better for Vann. She could include footnotes with references to recent psychological papers that might apply to him, making a persuasive argument.

"Good. Do that," Ridge said, still sounding dazed. He pushed away from the boulder and walked in the direction Sardelle had gone, his legs a touch wobbly. He did not seem to notice that he didn't have a light.

"He'll get over it," Lilah said, shouldering her rifle and heading off to find Vann.

* * *

Vann sat with his legs dangling from the ledge as he looked over the trees and the trail below. Kasandral rested in its scabbard on the rocks beside him, the damning journal atop it. He planned to take that journal to the Molisak family when Sardelle was done with it, because it was the honorable thing to do, but he wouldn't mind if it spontaneously burst into flame before he could deliver it.

Soft scrapes and thumps came from the narrow tunnel behind him.

"I didn't think you would squeeze back through here again," Vann said quietly, not looking back. He knew who it was. Nobody else would bother to come find him.

"It *is* claustrophobic, but I assumed you were here, and you've proven apt at distracting me from my fear of close, dark places."

"How did you know I would be here?" Vann offered Lilah a hand and moved the sword so she could sit beside him.

"Kaika and Bosmont went back to camp, and Ridge and Sardelle went to the laboratory, and I think the dragon went with them. I figured you'd want to be alone." It was dark, so he couldn't see her face, but he sensed her looking over at him, silently asking if he would prefer to be entirely alone. "Do you?" she asked.

He rested his hand on her thigh, glad she had come looking for him, though he couldn't fathom why she bothered.

"I've been alone for most of my life. It's lost the allure."

"Good." Lilah laid her hand on his and threaded her fingers between his. "How do you feel?"

"Feel?"

"You didn't already forget the definition of that word, did you?"

Vann looked out on the night, remembering sitting beside the fire with her and talking of his past. Had that been a day ago?

Two days ago? He had lost track of time in the tunnels.

"I'm used to being hard, Lilah."

"Hard? Is this going to be a different kind of conversation than I was imagining? Because I was hoping for a bed for the next time we discussed that."

He snorted. "I don't know how to be anything else. When you kill people for a living, it's not smart to get introspective. But when someone shows you a mirror, and it reflects back an image different from what you always thought was there, it's hard not to look."

"Major Therrik isn't your twin across time or your reflection in the mirror. What he did doesn't have anything to do with the man you are today."

"No? We seemed to have shared a lot of the same..."

"Prejudices?"

"Outlooks."

"Maybe he also had a run-in with a sorcerer at some point in his life that left him scarred."

"I'm not scarred."

"Please, Vann. You're a giant, swollen, angry knot of scar tissue."

"Do you say such things to all of your lovers?" he asked.

"I haven't had any lovers lately."

"Odd."

She shoved him. He deserved it.

"The point is that you are not him," Lilah said, "and you didn't make the mistakes he made. You've chosen not to let your *outlooks* dictate your actions. You would never betray someone who trusted you."

"You seem rather certain after only knowing me for three days."

"Because *I* trust you, and you never betrayed me during those three days."

Vann tried to swallow, but a lump had formed in his throat. He didn't know what to say. He wasn't used to people having faith in him, or caring enough to come find him and try to make him feel better.

"Perhaps, in time, you could let go of some of your anger and learn to relax more often." Lilah recaptured his hand. "Especially if you have someone whispering loving thoughts in your ear and giving you a massage now and then."

"A *massage* is not what you promised me in exchange for my cordiality," he said, sliding an arm around her waist and pulling her into his lap. Despite his teasing and what she had promised, he felt more inclined to give *her* favors now. He wondered if the application of such favors would be audible down in the camp. He smiled, remembering that she had been less reserved than he expected when they'd been enjoying each other's company in that alcove.

"Vann, are you going to be a *greedy* lover?" she teased, sliding her hand up his chest to his shoulder.

"*Extremely* greedy. What else would you expect from a hard man?"

"Terrible double entendres, among other things."

"You started it."

"Did not."

He kissed her before the conversation could devolve into further silliness. Encouraged by her roaming hands, he let his drift upward, stroking her through her shirt, finding delightful curves to cup. He decided he did not care if they made noise that would be audible in the camp.

Greetings, humans! a perky voice spoke into his head.

Vann groaned. Lilah gasped and pulled back, looking around.

"I doubt he's anywhere nearby." He rested his hand on the back of her head, trying to guide her lips back to his. But before he made progress in this endeavor, his sword flared to life, the green glow visible even with it in the scabbard.

"What—"

Flaps sounded, and a breeze stirred Vann's hair.

Bhrava Saruth, now in his massive, golden-scaled form, rose into view. His talons latched onto a protruding rock beside the ledge, and it took all of Vann's manliness to keep from squawking and crawling back into the tunnel. Rationally, he knew the dragon was on friendly terms with him—or at least had no plans to incinerate him—but the great beast still had a presence that could make a man lose control of his bodily functions.

Fortunately, that did not happen. It would have been difficult to explain, especially with Lilah in his lap. Not that she would have noticed. She was gaping over her shoulder at Bhrava Saruth while holding onto Vann much more tightly than she had been before. He slid his arms around her protectively.

"What do you want, dragon?" he asked, half-expecting Sardelle to be astride his back. But Bhrava Saruth had come up alone. Or perhaps he had been *sent* up alone.

I believe you mentioned a dinner, Bhrava Saruth said into his mind.

"We're not *it*, are we?" Lilah asked.

"I don't think so," Vann said.

My high priestess has suggested that dinner might happen sooner if I give you two a ride back to the fortress. Will there be sheep at the meal? And mango tarts? I adore tarts.

"Who doesn't?" Lilah murmured.

"Unless your buddy, the general, brought tarts, you won't find them in the cupboards of the mess hall. There may be a box of dehydrated sheep bits somewhere."

"Ew, Vann."

"The supply ship doesn't exactly spoil us."

Vann sighed and lifted Lilah from his lap. He couldn't be too grouchy, considering the dragon was offering them a ride, and they had no way across that gap in the trail without one. Still, he lamented that he would have to wait many hours to resume what he had started with Lilah. Whose idea had this dinner been, anyway? He frowned down at her.

She laid her hands on either side of his face and kissed him.

Dehydrated bits sound unpalatable, Bhrava Saruth said. *Perhaps I will go hunting for a fresh sheep. Climb onto my back. I will allow you to join me on the quest for proper meat.*

"Should we be alarmed or honored?" Lilah asked, inching closer to the dragon.

"More one than the other, I'm sure."

"The heroes in *Time Trek* get to ride dragons. I'm going to find it an honor."

Vann decided not to mention his tendency to get airsick.

Epilogue

A KNOCK SOUNDED AT THE DOOR, and Vann sighed. He'd been about to head out for some exercise before twilight came to the mountains, but now he would likely get stuck dealing with some new emergency for the next three hours.

"What?" he asked.

Lieutenant Kraden poked his head through the door, hesitating before committing any more of his body. "We finished sorting through the supplies from the ship, sir."

"And?" Vann braced himself, expecting another shortage or some lesser disaster.

"You have mail, sir."

"Mail?"

"Yes, sir. It smells nice." Kraden leaned further in and held up a box wrapped in brown paper and tied with a bright purple ribbon.

"You smelled my mail?" Vann asked, more perplexed than annoyed.

The sight of the box—the ribbon—filled him with anticipation. Was that from Lilah? Who else would send him a package? It had been more than three weeks since she left to return to her university, and he missed her company. A lot.

During the two weeks she had spent cataloging the dragon fossils and researching the Referatu artifacts, they'd had more time to get to know each other—intimately and otherwise. He had gotten better at interpreting her paleontologist jokes and had been rewarded with beaming smiles every time he said something witty in reply. He planned to find some books on the subject so he could more reliably be witty. She seemed to think he had a brain. He didn't want to disabuse her of the notion. The last few weeks had been lonely without her company; it would be worth putting in some effort to ensure she wanted to see him again when he escaped this loathsome duty station.

"Not on purpose, sir." Kraden risked scurrying inside to deposit the box on the desk. "It's aromatic. Maybe someone sent you flowers."

"Enclosed in a lightless box, yes, I'm sure." Vann waved for the lieutenant to depart. He didn't want a witness when he opened his mail. "Go home, Kraden."

"Home, sir? To my room? It's still a half hour until the end of the workday."

"Yes, I'm letting you go early. Sing about my magnanimity to the other soldiers, will you?"

Judging by the perplexed expression on the lieutenant's face, there would not be songs in the mess hall tonight. Kraden did manage a head bob and a, "Thank you, sir," before disappearing.

As soon as the door closed, Vann lifted the box, giving it a curious sniff before untying the ribbon. Lavender. It didn't grow up here at this frigid altitude, and he felt a nostalgic twinge, thinking of the capital. Had Lilah put in that request for a transfer to a university down there? She had said she would, but who knew what she had decided once she returned to her normal world. Maybe she had realized she had been crazy to think about changing her life for some soldier who had no idea where the future would take him.

"One way to find out," he muttered, untying the ribbon.

As he unwrapped the package, he tried to remember the last time someone had mailed him something. A few years ago, his brother's wife had sent him jars of jam made from blueberries produced on the family land. He had given the cloying stuff to a lieutenant with a sweet tooth.

Vann poked into the box, hoping for something more interesting than jam. He pulled out a tin that seemed to be the source of the lavender scent. A tea strainer and a note dangled from it, tied on with more ribbon. After eyeing the tin suspiciously, he opened the note.

Vann, I had lunch with Sardelle and mentioned I was putting together a care package for you. She insisted on sending you some kind of relaxation tea. I'm told it's been blessed by a dragon and will soothe your tense muscles. It's possible Sardelle and her dragon just want to drug you, but she seemed sincere in desiring to make your life more pleasant. I won't, however, be offended if you stuff it in a desk drawer. We both know the best way to soothe your muscles.

Indeed. He grinned wickedly at the memory of shared massages that had led to other things, and set the tea aside.

He poked further into the box and found a tin of butter crackers, a wheel of cheese, salt-cured bacon, and a trio of exotic meat jerkies. Three books lay nestled into the bottom, the first three novels in the *Time Trek* series. There was another note stuck inside the first one. He felt ridiculously pleased at this hunt for goodies and messages. It was like being a boy again, receiving birthday gifts.

Vann, I will be slightly more offended if you stuff these into a desk drawer without trying them. At least take a peek at the first one and let me know what you think of the story. The characters are enjoyable, but I would love to discuss the historical and scientific inaccuracies with you. You'll find several errors in regard to Before Dominion crossbows! In case the novels ultimately aren't to your taste, I've included a couple of recent publications that you may find more appealing.

He slid two magazines out of the bottom of the box, the most recent issues of *Tactical Bow and Blade* and *Military History Explored*. Ah yes, he would enjoy catching up. It didn't even matter that they smelled of lavender. He would give the books a try, if only to meet this Commander Asylon she had occasionally compared him to. And her promise of inaccuracies sounded like a challenge to him. He would make a list.

Vann spotted two envelopes under some crinkled paper stuffing and slid out a card with a photograph of Lilah in it. She sat in a chair with her legs crossed, wearing a shy—maybe embarrassed—smile, perhaps because her skirt was arranged in such a way that it displayed a lot of leg, and her blouse dipped low enough to similarly fuel his imagination. He swallowed, noticing right away that she wasn't wearing the promise necklace that had once led him to assume she was still married. He blinked a few times, surprising himself with emotion at how much that unspoken signal meant.

A longer message waited for him inside of the card.

Vann, I felt extremely silly—and chilly—posing for this, but a... relative... promised that a man gets lonely up there and would want a memento of his lady.

His lady. Yes, she was. He felt his chest swell with satisfaction. She hadn't decided to return to her regular life and forget about him, after all.

I won't ask you not to stuff it into a desk drawer.

Hardly. He would sleep with the photo under his pillow.

I do hope you will enjoy these small items, but the main reason I am writing is to inform you that I will be moving to the capital next month, to prepare for my new research position at the small but highly respected Erenhurst Science and Mathematics College near the harbor. I also wanted to send you this time-sensitive application for employment. I haven't had much luck in talking your superiors into reassigning you, but I have learned that King Angulus does think you're a competent soldier. That may help, if you find yourself interested. This application is for a position that is opening soon and which you might enjoy as an alternative to commanding an entire outpost—or teaching young upstarts at your military academy.

An application for employment? Vann stared at the words, reading them again to make sure he hadn't misunderstood. He looked at the second envelope. Did she think he would retire from his career to manage some ice cream parlor in the capital? He did wish to join her down there, but he couldn't imagine leaving the military unless it was to accept some nobler employment. What could possibly be better suited for him?

King Angulus is seeking a new captain of his personal guard, someone with the background necessary to train his existing men to be even more capable of protecting him and those he cares about. It sounds like many people will be applying, but with your experience, I thought you might be a more suitable candidate than most. I understand that the guard exists outside of the military, so you would no longer be obligated to salute any overly witty generals you encountered. You could also frisk those generals when they visit the palace. I thought this position might appeal to you, since it would allow you to live in the capital and work closely with the king, but please disregard if it doesn't.

I miss you and hope to hear back from you soon.

Love, Lilah.

Love? They had talked of a possible future together, but they hadn't used such charged words. He didn't even know if he was capable of speaking in terms of love. But to imagine the word coming from her lips... it warmed his heart. As did the rest of the package. Even the suspicious tea. It was nice to have someone care.

"Captain of the guard?" Vann thoughtfully pulled the application form out of the second envelope.

He'd never considered leaving the military and applying for a private security job, since that seemed a step down from being an officer, but working for the king would be as prestigious as being a soldier. It would also keep him in the capital where he could see Lilah all the time. He might even have a steady schedule and regular hours. A novel idea. Working in the castle might not be as exciting as going on missions to enemy nations, but since Iskandia and Cofahre weren't technically at war right now, there might not be any more missions on the horizon. Besides, how often did colonels get sent on covert missions? If he requested a return to the capital as a soldier, he would probably end up back at the academy teaching.

After checking to make sure he hadn't missed any more photographs of Lilah, Vann slid into the chair at his desk and withdrew a couple of sheets of paper. He propped Lilah's picture against the box, so she could observe while he filled out the application. Maybe she could keep him from saying something that would offend the king.

THE END

AFTERWORD

Thank you for picking up *Shattered Past* and coming along on this adventure. If this was your first experience with this world, and you would like to read more, I recommend starting with *Balanced on the Blade's Edge,* where we first meet Ridge and Sardelle. If you've already read the whole series, feel free to stop by my website (http://www.lindsayburoker.com) to let me know what you want to see next.

Lastly, if you have time, please consider leaving a review for *Shattered Past* wherever you picked up the novel. Reviews do a lot to help authors sell books, so we definitely appreciate them. Thank you!

Printed in Poland
by Amazon Fulfillment
Poland Sp. z o.o., Wrocław